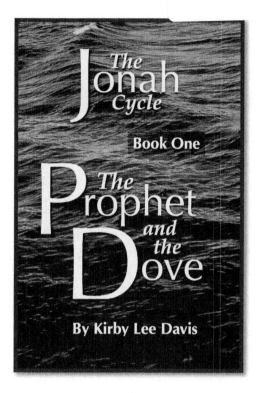

"I grew up hearing the story of Jonah from the Bible, but it had never come to life for me as it does in this fictional tale. Through the eyes of the young narrator Benjamin, we grow to understand much about the possible details of Jonah's thoughts and actions concerning God's leadings and expectations for obedience. We also learn about the Israel and Assyria of that time. In the process, Benjamin grows from having no faith to a faith that is seemingly stronger than Jonah's. Quite a good read!"

"This book will help you see the story of Jonah in new and fresh ways. The vivid characters stir the imagination. A very enjoyable book."

Read more at www.kirbyleedavis.com!

The **J**onah *Cycle*

Book Two

Lions *of* **J**udah

By Kirby Lee Davis

Book design, covers, maps, and graphics
by Kirby Lee Davis.

Published in the United States and overseas
for Fashan Books, Tulsa, OK.

ISBN Number (paperback): 9798366264006

First Printing 2023

A word to new readers

Lions of Judah is the second novel
in The Jonah Cycle, an action/adventure series
set in a turbulent Old Testament era.
While it is not necessary to read Book One
before tackling *Lions of Judah*,
new readers adverse to mystery may find
helpful background information
in this novel's Afterward and Glossary.

This book is dedicated

to Pat, Becky, Nancy, and Janet,
friends and proofreaders
who supported me through many early trials,
and Darla, Dana, Katie, Rob, and Sonnia,
who encouraged me through later ones.

The books of Kirby Lee Davis

The Spawn of Fashan
(a roleplaying game rulebook)

The *God's Furry Angels* series:
God's Furry Angels
A Year in the Lives of God's Furry Angels

The Road to Renewal

The Jonah Cycle:
The Prophet and the Dove
Lions of Judah
Faith
(in production)

The Spawn of Fashan 40th Anniversary Edition

Learn more at www.kirbyleedavis.com

Table of Contents

Maps

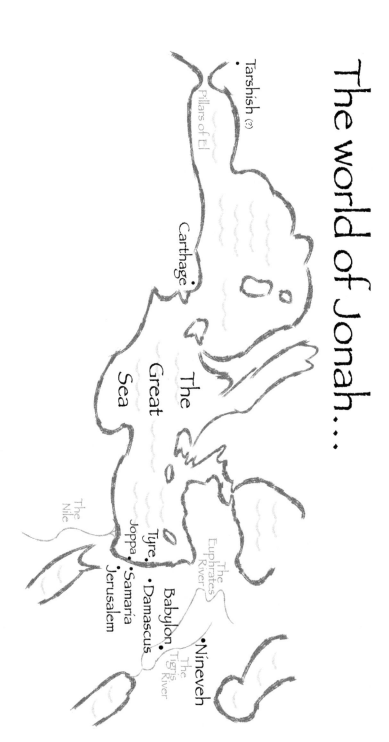

The world of Jonah...

Tarshish (?)

Pillars of El

Carthage

The
Great
Sea

The
Nile

Joppa
Tyre

Samaria
Jerusalem
Damascus
Babylon

The
Euphrates
River

Nineveh
The
Tigris
River

Damascus

ARAM

Mount
Hermon

Dan

PHOENICIA

Tyre

Hazor

Acco

Sea
of Chinnereth

Aphek

The

Great

Sea

Mount
Carmel

Mount
Tabor

Megiddo

Taanach

Jordan
River

ISRAEL

Tirzah

Samaria

Shechem

Mount
Gerizim

Aphek

Joppa

Bethel

PHILISTIA

Mount
Pisgah

Jerusalem

JUDAH

Salt
Sea

Chapter 1
Deathmatch

It served as both a warning and summons to doom. Such was the scream of Seth, my son – the self-proclaimed king of Gerizim in the mountains of Ephraim. I smiled as his tearing roar pierced the night, knowing my skilled offspring used its chilling echoes far more as a lure than a wall of foreboding. But then I heard the human's steady footsteps, smelled his calm patience, and realized this equally young man-cub was not one to cower. When his path continued with care toward Seth's weak side, away from the trap my son prepared, I knew this was no mere human, just as my son was no mere lion.

It was then, I think, that love for this man-cub took root in my heart, as difficult as that is to imagine, considering what nuisances humans can be. But as these two titans maneuvered against each other, I sensed the Maker held great plans for both – should either survive this encounter.

Curious, I slipped into their battle zones and watched, confident their destinies hinged on what would soon follow. Little did I realize that, by following this path, I sealed my own fate.

Ah, few alive have witnessed such a spectacle! In his own feeble way, this fourteen-year-old man proved as fine a specimen as my Seth. Long, balanced limbs graced this human, all knitted and jointed well, with hands and feet that adapted to just about any terrain. Believe this, for he scurried barefoot up the steep, rocky incline as if born to it. And he must have gained his vision from a hawk! At the slightest hint of a sign, this fellow – called

Simon, I soon learned – could kick into motion like a desert hare!
A fluid drive propelled his swift feet across the most demanding
paths, and he lost not one step, whether skipping over tree roots
or sliding under low branches. Not once did his toes slip in loose
earth.

You laugh, but I tell you this: few humans display such precise
agility, for it requires the perceptions and coordination only a
rascal squirrel or wise falcon possesses. You may pull your claws
in on that bet – your prey would not escape.

That's not to say my son could not dispose of this Simon.
Seth, after all, stood out as the best of my brood. Four cubs rose
from my union with old Elessa, including one prince senior to our
monarch, but Seth soon chased the others off. Which was right,
after all. A pride may have but one king. The others could run
rogue for a time… it would do them good. But Seth did not need
such training. In time, he might even have chased me away had I
presented a challenge, but events intervened. His women sought
meals from a flock of loud, appealing sheep, not knowing or
caring that their targets took shelter under Simon's crook. That
youthful shepherd sent each conniving lioness away hungry – an
affront Seth could not ignore.

These limestone peaks offer wonderful settings for blood
duels, their wind-scoured heights providing many cuts and vales
adorned with winding ledges, rapid waters, plunging walls, fields
of tall grass and grain, and terraced hills sporting prickly brush
and gnarled trees. All held choice options for surprising and
slaughtering one's foes.

Seeing his first trap unhinged, Seth charged down the opposite
slope to a narrow chasm pitted with dark caves. Perfect for an
ambush. But this human, who hid his flesh under what his type
call a tunic – that's a covering of sheep's wool or other spun
stuff, entwined, fitted, and bound to their fragile bodies as a sort
of a removable skin – anyway, this man-cub did not approach the
ridge my son just left. Acting as if he could sense Seth's silent
retreat, Simon continued around the stone knob, the wind at his
face, and with his rod as an anchor, he climbed the ridge topping
my son's dry cove. There Simon girded his cloth about his waist

2

with a strip of woven goat hair –

Yes, the hair of goats! These humans harvest such things! And take note now, for humans do this binding ritual when they prepare for battle or running or many other aggressive acts, so watch for it. Such girding tells of their mind and intent.

Now pay attention as I return to our tale. Simon girded his loins but did not get the chance to do more, for Seth had already left. Having heard the low rumble of dislodged sand, my king guessed the human's countermove and crept further down the slope.

So went this hunt, sometimes by moonlight atop ragged crests, sometimes within the black shadows of upturned limestone teeth. Our peaks echoed with fierce roars as Seth led his adversary on, once switching back to threaten the penned sheep, only to retreat before the human's crook and baying dogs. My king's trail hinted at some intricate design employed with lazy confidence, as if Seth enjoyed pretending to be prey rather than the hunter. From my central perch, I twice saw my son discard prime vantage points for ending his game. Both times he retreated with the arrogance of a champion taking pleasure in the chase, seemingly determined to extend this contest rather than face its final challenge. But that suggestion ignored his worthy adversary – and the laws of our Maker.

My son's fifth trap looked almost perfect. Wheeling about the slopes to get between the shepherd and his flock, Seth found a gift from the Maker: a narrow ravine leading straight to the sheepfold. It offered ideal security, with sides so cluttered by brush and barbed vines that a human could not hope to penetrate them without entangling himself. Charging within, happy to lose telltale hairs to the thorns, my son discovered an eroded hole overlooking all possible passages, its cold walls shielded from the moon's light. There Seth waited, silent, almost breathless. The sweat slicking his fur surely chilled within that still tomb, yet I doubt he felt it. This opportunity was worth its cost.

I crept forward, my head swelling with pride in anticipation of my son's sweet victory. The human proceeded with caution into that dark gorge, probing the brush with the base of his rod while the upper knob pushed aside branches and vines. Ever nearer he drew to the kill zone, his prudence betraying him here, even as I crept in silence against the grain of the slope, keeping my silhouette still within the moonlight.

Then I made my first mistake.

Padding close with light steps, a bit distracted by the drama below, my left paw sent tumbling a small wave of sand.

The night froze. Simon stood as one with the limestone, his body still, his ears open, his eyes ever vigilant. Tense, feeling the fool, I clung to the earth, listening to the tiny rocks bouncing into the deep darkness. I had no wish to betray my child and king! But the human did not look my way or abandon his course. Bending behind a leafy tree trunk, the man-cub used the worn tip of his rod to probe markings in the clay and rock piles below Seth's perch. Only then did I realize the human had heard my steps and ignored them, concentrating on the trail left by my son.

Betrayed by his paw prints to an opponent shielded by thick, thorny branches, Seth slipped away to find a new defense. That trek led my offspring to the southern sheepfold and three alarmed hounds. At most times such a ruckus would not trouble my son; he had feasted before after similar troubles, on both lamb and dog. But a shadowy figure followed the barks, and young Simon came on oh so quick, the briars failing to delay him. Seth howled from angry stings to his left foreleg and flank, both caused by stones cast from the human's sling. Such blows spurred my son back into the craigs, a deadly plot on his mind.

I crept to a new position. Watching Seth maneuver, I recognized a cunning trick my son once used on me. With deliberate strides the king loped against a sharp breeze and savage slope. By all appearances he ran to escape the last call of those hounds, who did not give chase, restrained by some human commands. But the man-cub followed Seth with swift steps, even as my son disappeared into moonlight shadows.

I sank low to the earth. Simon had every reason to pursue the fleeing lion, his scent sharp in the breeze. But if the lad had known the lay of this land, as I did, he would not have charged like a shrieking wind into the Maker's Tongue, a bitter slide that ended with a steep plunge of death.

When Seth had so baited me into this snare, I survived only by the slimmest of margins – leaping across a chasm four times my outstretched length. That effort both exhilarated me and left my flesh numb to my bones, but Seth must have admired it, or so I assume. Perhaps that explains why he allowed me to stay among his women… not that it matters now. Still, knowing this, I watched the lad with rising trepidation, for no human could match my feat. Especially as the surrounding walls shielded the drop from the moon, leaving the pit almost invisible at night.

Reaching the limits of our faint light, Simon slowed his pace but stayed on the scent. On he traveled, following the trail across a dark rock spine, through a scrub brush line, then around a second ridge. Reaching the entrance to the Tongue, he stopped. His body actually froze in place, helping his ears sift for clues. Surprised, for my son's scent remained active, I crept closer to see what Simon meant to do. That's when the human went in.

Even with his sure feet bare to the earth, the sandy slope overwhelmed the man-cub. He slid against the grain, his staff little good as a brake. I heard his heart and breathing surge. Caught by sudden fear, Simon dropped his bottom and back to the ground, stretching out his limbs to collect the sand and grasp the rock walls. His speed increased. His fingers dug at the slope, to no avail. A harsh curve shoved him against a stone wall. He bounced off and tumbled downward.

I felt swelling anxiety, which surprised me. Perhaps at this, the place of my last great challenge, I hated to see one suffer who had performed so well. I sank my claws into the earth, frightened that this cub would indeed fall to his death, even though such a turn could provide a satisfying meal. When the lad managed to straighten his back, then lurch up to a running stance, I knew his fate was sealed. His last steps propelled Simon with blind recklessness into the chasm.

Watching this, I prayed to the Maker for this human to meet a gracious end. His skills deserved that much. Imagine my wonder when, at the very lip of the crevasse, Simon planted the tip of his staff and leaped forward! The rod itself provided a boost, bending

and swaying with such force that it helped propel the fleet cub
over the chasm. Where I, in my challenge, had landed with two
feet in the gorge, the others rooted to the rim, this Simon fell
upright upon that far lip of rock and soil, secure on both feet, his
limbs balanced, the rod still in his tight grip, his mind ready for
battle.

My heart almost stilled at that sight, both in admiration and
fear. After all, I had prayed for this one – and yet, while I
respected his skills, I did not want the Maker to deliver this cub
over my son.

Ah, but while Simon's feat may have stunned me into
inaction, Seth acted on an opportunity. Poised among the rocks
above the human, my king threw himself forward with his claws
primed to kill. Simon dove to the sand, rolling to escape. Seth
caught up with him just as the man-cub settled into a crouch on
his toes, his rod perched against his left shoulder.

That – not my prayers – saved him.

Hurdling through the darkness, Seth could not spin from the
hard knob of that upraised staff. The impact forced the lad to
tumble away, even as my son drew his four paws against the
shepherd's tunic. My king's hind legs missed Simon's flank by
the width of a limb, but Seth's left foreclaws latched into the
cub's muddy cloth and tore it from his shoulders.

Though I saw nothing, I smelled blood.

Simon jumped up, striking first with the sharpened tip of his
rod, then with its gnarled head. While skillful, the manner of
blows revealed the human's near blindness in the dark. With
superior eyesight in such shadows, Seth dodged the sweeping
attack as he maneuvered left. Then he lunged, but Simon, having
found nothing but rock within the radius of his rod, changed his
stepping pattern. Seth saw this at the last moment and reared
back, just missing the human's exposed side. Frustrated, my son
released a brief, angry snarl. Simon struck at the sound, a blow
my king avoided with more luck than skill. He tried to dart in
while the man's stomach lay exposed, but Simon spun his staff
about and warded my son off.

In this way they strove against each other, taking turns

striking, countering, dodging, evading. They circled like the winds of a dust devil, growing ever nearer, challenging each other with their power, avoiding strikes through their grace. Seth twice tried to maneuver Simon into the abyss, but the human had enough presence of mind to recall the danger and escape destruction. The cub also worked to corner my son against the rock wall, only to find Seth's reflexes too quick to counter in such gripping blackness.

I settled behind a limestone crest, sheltered from the wind, and waited for one to tire or err. Through the slow passage of the moon, this human, while hot with sweat, showed few signs of strain. Neither did Seth, though he began to pause in his circular stalking to issue deep, grinding roars that rumbled through the canyons. Undeterred, at the fourth tearing scream Simon drew a smooth stone from a girdle pouch and, with a flick of his wrist, sent it sailing into my son's open maw. I could not help chuckling, though Seth responded with unbridled fury. Charging, he flew over Simon's empty footsteps and felt the darting human's rod strike his skull. Undaunted, Seth pounced again, once more suffering a hard blow from the knobby wood. But he did not slow, throwing himself backward from the wall – which tripped his foe.

Together they rolled ever nearer the great fall. Simon managed to crawl away as Seth came to rest on his stomach. The human struggled in loose sand, dazed by billowing dust. My son pivoted with slow, determined force, crouching in his hatred to make his final attack.

Into this tense moment sprang a sliver of man's light.

On the crest opposite mine, atop a ledge far above the Tongue, emerged a second shepherd upholding a burning chunk of wood. Its fearful flames lit the deep rock drifts with shifting hues of yellow, brown, and gray. Seth's damp fur sparkled of gold. And Simon? Well, but for what remained of his torn tunic, the blond human looked surprisingly attractive. A somewhat tasty one, if you preferred strong bones and muscle under lean, glistening skin – and you dared face the imposing challenge it took to chew upon such youthful flesh.

At that point, confronted by clear views of their adversaries, both titans hesitated. But Seth's fury consumed too much of his mind for this revelation to daunt him now, and so he charged, forgetting his greatest advantage all along had been the black night. Simon, though weary, pivoted on nimble toes to what I guess must be his favored side. Driven by his thirst to slay, my son could not adjust his aim in time. As Seth passed by, Simon planted the narrow point of his rod between my king's shoulders. Seth landed with poise against the sod and thrust himself back, but the human prepared for this, having seen my son reverse course that way before. Pressing forward, the shepherd rammed the pointed tip of his rod against Seth's spine. Aided by my king's efforts to pursue, the wood punched deep into my child's flesh, piercing his heart and lung.

With one choked scream, Seth's writhing spirit left for the Maker. I almost wept at that, knowing my son would have wished to make one final call to honor his conqueror. But still, this end left me satisfied. Both combatants fought well, and their battle provided a death worthy of a king.

Keeping an eye on the torch-bearing interloper, I offered a silent prayer of gratitude and prepared to escape into the night. I would not feast on my own son's flesh – let others claim that prize! But then, for reasons I cannot explain, I stopped. For the human, despite his obvious mental limitations and that short-sighted heritage of his kind, this man-cub whispered thanks to the Maker and praise to my fallen king.

"Well done," shouted the keeper of the flames.

Simon made no reply, occupied as he was with his prayers.

I waited then, not wanting my movements to attract attention in the flickering torchlight. But also, I had a growing curiosity about these humans. I wished to see what else they might do.

The torch bearer paused a moment before glancing about for a descending path. I chuckled, thinking the Tongue might yet claim a victim. But that thought overlooked the hawk-sighted man below.

Eyeing the shifting light, Simon must have figured out its meaning, for he soon called out, "Stay there, Reuben! Do not come down. It's a treacherous walk. Wait for me. I will meet you in a moment."

"But you need help with the carcass!"

"No," said Simon, working free his rod. "I will take nothing from him."

"Oh, surely his claws at least."

"No."

"But father —"

"No!" Simon insisted. "He was strong, and sly, this one. A worthy foe. I will not dishonor him in death."

Laying down his staff, the young man gathered rocks to lay about Seth's body. These actions puzzled me until I realized that Simon meant to entomb the corpse. Oh, how my bile flowed at that thought! This barrier would mock Seth's life and defy our Maker's plan! But as I pondered this, my burning fury dissolved into confusion of equal depth, and something even more peculiar. For as I watched Simon at work, and I debated over and over just what his actions revealed, I felt my love for my son transfer to this human. This shocked me not just for its oddness, but its objective. For I grasped how the Maker valued Simon and his destiny – which lay now in my care. And that placed us all in great peril.

Chapter 2

Decisions

Overwhelmed by these mysteries, I was slow to notice the two brothers descending to their sheepfolds. Simon took cautious, restful strides alongside Reuben, who walked as if his concerns lay behind him.

"You did well," said that older one. Like Simon, he was a fine specimen of mankind, his limbs rested and honed, his articulate speech reflecting a well-developed mind – two years his brother's senior, by my guess. Perhaps that explains how he could hold that flaming branch with calm assurance while its consuming hunger brought me nothing but fear.

Simon kept his reply short: "The Lord is gracious."

Though pressed to his limits by my son, this man-cub sounded ready to renew the contest. His heart carried a steady beat. His breath filled his lungs with gentle ease. His sweat came slow and flowed clean. His muscles flexed with little strain, his limbs relaxed yet prepared for action. All that amazed me. My nerves stayed alert observing these two, yet this young man walked in peace, almost as he had before all this started. I doubt I could recover so fast from a deathmatch!

I suspect now he lived each day this way.

"I saw you circle back twice," said Reuben. "Must have been quite a chase."

"He led me on. Goaded me, as if he'd plotted it all out. I might have fallen to his traps twice, but for the Lord's insight. And your appearance. Our God truly blessed me with you, my brother!

You're always there when I need you."

Reuben smiled, then paused to look upon their three sheepfolds, each guarded by a hound. Two female humans and a young lad also watched over the enclosures, each bound in patched, multicolored cloaks and other dusty wraps like those Reuben wore. The sisters stood at rest, contented, as if they knew the danger had passed, but their hounds acted confused. It worried me until a shift in the wind revealed Seth's strong scent clinging to both approaching shepherds. That made me smile, for I knew his mark would mask the humans for days.

"Must have been a fine beast," Reuben reflected. But Simon had his mind on other things.

"Who is here?" he wondered aloud, his gaze locked upon a flickering smoke trail drifting to the stars. My eyes followed that meandering wisp to a small crackling fire circled by stones within what the humans call a tent. Beside the covering stood two beautiful horses, their backs marked by old saddle burns. The great stallions rested, their heads bound and tied to a stake. About their shoulders and necks hung cloths bearing the purple hue of human cavalry soldiers.

Any other night, I would look upon such steeds with hunger, especially if the air bore no scents of their masters. Indeed, just seeing these beasts spurred me to creep closer to that camp, though I did have mind enough to not alert the dogs. Then the wind shifted.

"Wait," Reuben advised. He stood still a breath, then pivoted to look over the dark, rocky slopes. I froze as his flaming light flashed by my hiding place. His eyes passed over me once, twice. My blood grew hot.

"There is another," he whispered.

His caution came with a smile… a subtle passion for the hunt. I gripped the earth with my claws, then pulled them back, ready to spring away. But Simon was not distracted.

"Yes, an older one," said my bondmate. "He watched me battle the young lion. Pay him no mind; I doubt he will act."

Taking a deep breath, Simon pulled his brother about to head once more toward the tent. Like Reuben, I fought to regain my calm. It was difficult but necessary. Flexing my claws, I murmured thanks to my Maker for the reprieve. It reminded me once again just how kind He is.

"What is this?" Simon asked his brother.

Reuben looked to the steeds, then that enclosure of draped cloths, its waving sides aglow from campfires within and without. Having no answer, the older shepherd shrugged and said, "Let's find out."

At that point I did the first of many stupid things. With bold strides the siblings proceeded to camp, where Simon took time to wash and prepare himself.

I raced to the tent.

Oh, I was careful – you can bet on that! Having engaged horse soldiers in my past, I respected the perils of human knives and arrows, and the pain a bold hoof could deliver. While I saw two stallions, I could smell others, no doubt standing somewhere in the dark with other riders.

And yet something drove me on… I look back on it now and wonder why, but for the Maker's prodding, I would take such risks.

This tent was a simple contraption, a square of leveled soil blocked off on two sides with brushed hides taken from goats and other worthy prey, their skins cleaned, honed, and sewn together. Some humans must have hung these sheets over poles connected by dried woven vines, which humans call rope. The hides overlapped the squared earth to shield the seated men from the sky, then hung down from the ropes to form two makeshift walls. Wood stakes anchored their edges, though not too tight, leaving the cloths to flap in the breeze. The humans created a third windbreak by piling their bundles, boxes, saddles, and other things along an open side of that square – and this gave me an opportunity. With my scent diminished and concealed by the wind, I crept behind the loose, flapping wall sheets to hide among the hoarded baggage.

In the center of that square, beneath the tent's waving roof, crackled that smoking fire ringed by stones. The flames warmed a charred iron pot suspended from stakes bending under its weight.

Around that bowl sat four men taking turns dipping chunks of some pastry –

What is a pastry? Well… they also call it bread, or a loaf, if those terms help you understand. Whatever the name used, the pastry is something they eat, made by their own hands. This one was round like a stone yet flat as a leaf – a thick leaf, mind you, like your tongue. Or his tongue.

Anyway, these humans sat there dipping torn pieces of flat bread into some sort of bean stew boiling in that pot. It gave off a hearty fragrance that warmed my nose yet left me discouraged, for the broth held no meat.

As these men ate these drippings, their attention drifted more than the breeze. It seemed not one of them wanted to be there. Troubles dribbled from their voices, one in regret, one in sadness, one edging on contempt, and one trapped by anger. I doubt this misery drew from the stew's lack of flesh. Two of the men apparently held little use for tents. They didn't like the rippling cloths or the stale smoke or that burning broth. I could tell they preferred the open sky – even in rain, I would guess. But most of all, they grumbled in their hearts over these intrusive horse riders. The soldiers endured this, occupied as they were by their own burdens. Most revolved about concerns to be elsewhere, and yet behind that I sensed an impending doom, one that chilled them to their core.

"I can offer a third," an aged voice said, his words hard as the rocks I had just crossed. I could not see the speaker clearly with that haphazard mound in my way, so I crept closer, hoping to find a better view.

"Two-thirds," said an older, softer tone.

"All," came a firm reply.

In the silence that followed, I found a gap between these loosely piled things, one that offered me a good look at all these humans. That's when I spied a third soldier, who stepped around a hanging wall to address the four in the tent.

"Two more shepherds approach," said this sentry.

"My sons," explained an elder.

"Let them pass," answered a voice of authority.

I thanked the Maker for this. Simon and his brother must have caught the guard's eye, distracting him from me.

Of course, I had long suspected those elders carried Simon's blood. They bore a shepherd's distinctive stink, and wore weathered tunics and goatskin cloaks like others whose sheep I'd feasted on. Both elders sat with legs crossed, their laps filled by the curling ends of gray, tangled beards. They smiled at Reuben and Simon, but beyond that, their lives told different tales. The oldest one bound his well-traveled feet in unraveling leather sandals and bared his balding, spotted scalp to the chill night. The younger father left his callused soles open to the earth but kept his crowning hair pulled off his tense brow with a mud-caked cloth tied about his skull. The eldest's pale flesh drooped below his eyes, two patient orbs that stared with sorrow into the stew. His companion's hazel orbs sparkled in the faint light, alert to the smallest details of their visitors. The eldest relaxed with his hands in his lap, knowing his life was his own, while the other – his son, I guessed – gripped his knees with crusty fingers, determined to protect his domain from any challenge.

Opposite them sat two cavalry soldiers, their muscular trunks protected by thick, embroidered cloaks that stank of horse and sweat. Beneath these wraps I glimpsed leather armor dried to cracking by long exposure to the sun and wind. One rider still wore his headgear, a dust-speckled sheet of faded purple wool banded by three strands of old rope. Both soldiers kept a sheathed metal sword and two scraped knives tethered in readiness about their chests.

By their cynical stances and bitter stares, I knew these men sat about this pot with arms and legs ready to attack – although their preference most likely was to get this meeting over with so that they could sleep and depart this wilderness before dawn.

Their readiness prompted reminders of my own longing to leave, to forgo this adventure and stand proud in the night breeze once more. Too many times had I put up with meddling humans. I did not want to endure their antics yet again! But my calling to Simon answered this reluctance with power, holding me firm. I watched the four men gaze long upon each other, weary of talk.

Only the oldest among them, that balding shepherd, offered any hint of compromise.

"We are bound for home," said the younger father, even as Reuben chose to rest behind him. I was surprised to see both brothers had found time to wash before entering, and Simon had replaced his tunic, though their sire paid this no attention. "We have no time to backtrack," he continued. "And we have no sheep to spare. We sold half of our surplus at Samaria last week, and most of the rest at villages or caravans along our way. Only our breeding stock remains."

Simon sat down beside the post upholding the tent's open corner. Drawing his feet beneath him, the lad leaned back and looked me in the eye.

What a moment that was!

Yes, I should have run – but I felt no fear! None at all! I hid among my enemies, with this young Simon but a leap away, and I knew no fear! For in this man-cub's clear gaze, I saw the heart of the Maker. I sensed confidence, peace, and love.

"We need them all," said the older soldier. Having long ago discarded his turban, this weary warrior wiped his stiff fingers through his short black hair, rubbed his aching eyes, and admitted, "We have little choice."

The elder shepherd smiled but gave no ground. "They are our family, captain."

"Jonathan," the soldier offered.

"Captain," the shepherd repeated.

To his credit, this warrior took no offense at that abrasion.

"You will be paid," he assured them.

"Not enough!" snapped the younger father. "Raising a flock is the toil of generations!"

"You learn their strengths, their natures," the eldest said, trying to reason with these grumbling intruders. "We raised many of them from birth, nurturing them, winning their trust, even their love."

"They are pets to our sisters," offered Reuben, showing no fear of the newcomers.

"Yes, that is true," the eldest agreed. His comrade smiled.

"They feed them by hand, tell them stories," said the younger father, the thoughts he shared bringing a smile to his dry lips. "It is something to see! Truly, these sheep are like family to us. Hannah, my oldest daughter, she named them all, and often sleeps among them. So does Anna!"

Simon laughed, and others joined in. The sound amused and thrilled me!

"We learn from our flock, and they from us," said the eldest. "We teach them to mind us and our hounds, and for the most part, they do."

"Oh, yes!" said Reuben.

"In this way we weed out the bad seed and nourish the best lines," continued his grandfather. "In time, they come to live and move together, as one."

"They learn what we want of them," Reuben said, "and they respond at our commands, sometimes before we need them to. A few even understand enough to teach their young. Oh, that is so good to see."

"It is our life's work," whispered the elder.

"Yes!" barked the other father, his anger returning just that quick. "Our lives! What you ask would make us give all that up. Start over!"

"I am sorry," said the one called Jonathan, which irritated the younger soldier.

"Why barter with them?" he spat.

"Because they speak the truth!" the captain stated, at last releasing his own harbored anger. He tried to ease his stance, glancing first at the stew, then Simon and Reuben, but as this man turned back to the older shepherds, his eyes remained hard.

"I can pay you what the crown allows," he said. "No more. Maybe it is not enough, but I doubt you will get much better anywhere else."

"Why?" Reuben said, leaning into the torchlight above the eldest. His young face looked quite handsome in the waving smoke and glowing dance of the flames.

"Hoshea turns upon us," remarked the younger father.

"Not so, Elon!" the captain shot back. "Our king – King

Hoshea – he respects your rights. But the Assyrians march against us. Again. Their lord, this Sargon… he demands blood."

"He demands servitude," the one called Elon answered. "Hoshea rebelled."

The irate soldier bristled. "King Hoshea!" he insisted. "King!"

"Enough," growled the captain.

That young one ignored the order. His eyes burned with threats.

"You think your homeland safe?" this soldier said to taunt the shepherds. "Judah may soon face the same Assyrian whips. As will its people."

The eldest scowled. "Yahweh rejects you."

"All the gods reject us," scoffed the youth.

"Fool!" snapped Elon. "There are no others!"

The hot one stiffened. His brow knotted, his eyes smoldered. His commander snapped a cold command, but that brute still cast unspoken warnings.

These shepherds remained still, unshaken by this tension.

"You never learn," the eldest said in gentle, guarded tones. "Yahweh foretold this. He warned us of the devil's coming, through Amos, through Hosea. We rejected Him. All the tribes… we all failed. All."

"You," interrupted Jonathan, "you are in the heart of Israel, not Judah. It is the law of our king you must obey, not Ahaz. And I tell you now – we need your flock. All of it. Sargon will surely put Samaria under siege. His troops draw closer each day. We need your sheep to survive."

The eldest smiled. "And if we refuse?"

Wrinkles fled the captain's brow, but then his gaze tightened. "Then, Gilead, I will return with all my men, and we will take your flocks – without payment – or have them slain."

Elon drew his hands into fists.

"I will not see Assyrian dogs feasting on your stock," vowed the captain.

"They would not catch us," Reuben injected. He leaned on Elon's shoulder. "Father, resist. We will take to the hills."

The younger soldier sneered at that.

"You could guide your beasts, on foot, beyond the reach of our cavalry? I think not."

Reuben stood, his form a flickering gray pillar of strength in the tent's smoky shadows.

"Simon can track anything," he declared. "And hide anything."

I tensed in sudden realization of what all this meant. Yes... this was what I was supposed to hear through all their stubborn debates. This signaled the burden on my heart. But what did it mean?

The Maker provided no clues. And few of these human words made sense to me at that time, though all those demands and threats – the fear, anger, and terror they held – those emotions I grasped quite well. Indeed, I could feel them in my heart.

His frustration no longer manageable, the soldier captain slapped the earth with his right hand.

"You do not understand!" he insisted. "Our king has men scouring the hills for all the supplies we may find. Our soldiers will take everything! If you were one of his subjects, I would not even ask you for this. I would march you into the fortress, claim your flocks, your dogs, your clothing... all you have! And I would arm your sons for battle!"

"But we are of Judah," said Reuben, a sly grin crossing his lips.

"You think that will stop us?" snarled the young soldier. "Truly?"

"This summer draws to a close," continued Reuben. "We've already traded our prize stock. We could return home now with no time lost."

"You would be caught," the spiteful horseman growled. "If not by my men, then the Assyrians."

"They would respect us," Reuben asserted.

"They respect nothing!" the captain snapped. With a wave of his head to Simon and Reuben, the soldier said to the eldest, "You resist, and I assure you, your grandsons will be armed for battle, your daughters scattered, and you two will get posts atop Samaria's walls, or worse."

"Do not threaten us," Elon warned.

The captain met their eyes, squared his shoulders, and rose to his feet. The other horseman followed his example, a sinister glare upon his face.

"Decide," said Jonathan.

Elon looked to his father, a lifetime of understanding shared within their gaze, then stood, drawing his cloak about him. That move cast his sturdy frame into a dark silhouette.

"Reuben?" he called, both as a command and request.

"The hills," answered his oldest son.

Elon nodded as if he had expected this.

"Simon?" he barked.

I drew still closer. The elders might have seen me then had they found any reason to glance at the baggage, but I gave them none. The young cub sat calmly upon the earth, holding their attention.

"Samaria," he said.

Reuben stared first at his brother, then at his own feet. In that brief time of reflection, I understood the honor and respect they shared. Reuben would not question Simon's decision.

Stroking his beard with his right hand, Elon acknowledged his younger son with a cautious nod, then turned to his father. But Gilead kept his eyes focused on the stew, saying nothing.

"Very well," decided Elon, who now, at last, spoke as sheik. I felt some comfort at that, having wondered just who would take command of this brood. He turned to the captain and asked, "We'll be paid in gold for our whole flock?"

"At Samaria," Jonathan replied.

"And then we may leave?"

"If the Assyrians will allow it, so will I."

"If those devils are there," stated Gilead, "we will head for home."

"No," said Elon. "I will not risk that much. Gideon will start for home tonight with his sisters. We four will take the flock to Samaria."

The captain peered into the elder shepherd's deep-set eyes, then nodded. I, too, delved into those patient orbs and Simon's strong gaze. And I wondered how I would follow them to that human fortress they called Samaria. For if I were caught...

Chapter 3

Reflection

Let us pause a moment to understand one another. Though destiny drums within my heart and the winds sing their calming harmonies, soothing my troubled soul, I must confess this truth: I care nothing for mankind. My memories bear too many scars from their whips, their ignorance, their savagery. That my fate – my heart – would discover honest love for a human... that does not blind me to the evil spilled upon the world by man's foul hands.

Let us be clear: I did this not of my own will but at the Maker's prodding. It is His design, His will, that I embrace Simon, just as He moves me now to share this tale with you.

Ah, but that is not the whole truth. The Maker did give me a choice. I could have followed my hatred for mankind and refused. I still can.

Why, then, do I reveal this adventure? For your soul, and my own. For the lessons the Maker teaches us mean nothing if not passed on to others. In this, He made me the instructor and you the student.

And to be honest, I must do what the Maker places upon my heart – not because He compels me, but because I love Him.

This did not come easy, my learning to accept and understand humans. It took most of my life to grasp why they do what they do. Their speech alone took years to sort through. The sounds they sputter – "words," they call them – those things flow quickly enough from their lips, sometimes, though most humans use way too many of them. The meanings often cause me to stumble and pray for guidance, for the intent behind most words may change from speaker to speaker or place to place, or it may vary due to other things spoken or signaled. And you must pay attention not just to those terms, but the different ways humans may utter them, the order they state them in, and all the things they may use or add among them, for those elements may change what a word means. It often maddens me, the number of factors you must consider! Humans do this on purpose, you know… or at least the smart ones do. And they have words to describe these modifiers of words: gestures, they call them, or expressions, pauses, inflections, distractions, reflections, inferences, influences, attitudes, pressures. Something as simple as a twitch can change the intent of an entire breath's speech. So may the wave of a finger, or a smile, a wink of an eye. Even a cough! Oh, I could go on and on. Believe me! Observe humans for a short time and you will learn these truths yourself.

And that's when you discover how many of them employ such tactics by accident, never meaning to change the meaning of what they think they said. And you notice the habit many humans have of just jumping totally off the subject of their talks at any time, or to laugh or cry or scream, for reasons that make no sense at all. And that's not to mention their mixing all this talk with whistles or wails or other such harmonies they call music! That can be so beautiful and yet bewitching. You may never know if a song carries any meaning at all, or importance known only to a few. For that's another thing – they sometimes mix secret messages within open speech, for they are devious, these humans!

Truly, if I had not felt prompted by our Maker to follow Simon and learn all this myself, I would have padded away from the whole mess before that first sunrise. But at His bidding, even when lying among all that baggage, though confused and bewildered by all that talk, I started recognizing hints of meaning in the garble these humans spouted and the faces they cast. I grasped few actual words at first, and what I thought I knew came together more from the tone or force of their voices and eyes or gestures… all that made more sense than any actual speech or symbols that seemed familiar. Still, it did not take long to put together a basic understanding of those shepherds, even as their tongue-waggling confounded me. You see, not only do the words themselves vary in all their moody ways, but various tribes use parallel yet wholly different forms of speech. The learned humans refer to this as "language." I first encountered this while observing those feared Assyrians, though some among that tribe also spoke what is called Hebrew. Coming to terms with such alternate talk amplifies the confusion, for that's when you learn that these tribes not only speak differently but think differently. Yes! The human tribes display wild changes in logic and decision-making, depending on where they come from. Their languages demonstrate this.

Now remember, I wasn't truly aware of these things for a long time. Years upon years, to be honest. But take heart, for I compile knowledge each day on how these humans talk and think, and what they say and do, and as I observe new things, I revisit my memories and piece together what I know from what I knew. That often-corrected tale I share now. You may trust me on this, for the Maker does, or He would not have asked me to instruct you.

Those subtle changes, they often direct the pattern of human lives. Seemingly everything comes down to details, sorted by the smallest of distinctions… in effect, humans deciding what they like from what they don't. Some of their picks make perfect sense, such as their safety or weather fears, while other choices appear rather arbitrary. Take purple, for example. That's a color, deep and rich, like the stalking night as it gorges on each day's last light. Humans seem to revere this shadowy shade, yet only a few adorn themselves with it, which seems to be by mutual choice. Few are deemed worthy of this purple, for some reason. Compare that to brown, arguably the most common hue in our Maker's creation. All mankind seems to accept this soil tone in whatever form it appears, but they rarely desire this hue unless it glitters. Indeed, brown sometimes draws ire or even hatred, just for its color.

Sometimes what humans value comes down to simple commonality. The more frequently something appears in their lives, the less humans seem to appreciate it. The parched may spurn water for sour juice, even if that nectar binds their stomachs or rattles the mind. In that same way, they often turn from a gentle breeze to breathe deep a smokey stench. Such recklessness makes no sense, I know, but such reasoning often guides their actions. Remember this when you try to guess how a human may respond.

Their eye for detail also reflects an inventive side. That tent, for example – it resembled a cave, but one these humans may set up or take down with but a little time and preparation. They make tents from cloths they stitch together, stretching these skin-like sheets over posts and vines, or they tie them to spikes… yes, spikes – paw-length pieces of wood or stone that humans sharpen at one end to pound into the ground, all to hold things in place. Posts are much longer, like that rod Simon used, though rougher – not worn smooth or carved in those curious ways some humans cherish, with no knobs or points. No, that's wrong; posts may have points, but not as sharp as… well, that I do not know for sure. But they can be sharp.

And then there's that bread, which they do indeed make. You see, they get these heads of grains, or seeds, leaves, and such. Humans crush them all into grit, then mix that in water, blood, the milk of animals, or oils, and other such things. This they roll and mold and pound and… well, I only watched the pastry-making efforts once because it is more boring than anything I can think of. But they beat that damp mass until it's a mindless mound and then they set it in the sun or put it in a fire, and there it sits until, well… oh, enough of this! I can see in your eyes that my explanation makes no sense to you. To be honest, I don't really understand it either. Still, it shows the human's creativity.

Imagine... finding ways to create food to eat from things our Maker provides them. Humans see freedom in this, relying upon their own efforts instead of Him. That concept once worried me, for you watch these humans long enough and you realize they pursue this freedom in just about every way possible, providing their own nourishment or clothing or shelter. At its heart, this freedom reflects their pride and arrogance. You see, they come to imagine that they have no need of the Maker. Indeed, some see themselves as "makers" all their own.

Sickening, I know. Not all humans fall to such delusions. This I also saw. Some emulate our Maker's love, giving all they have to His calling, as I witnessed in Simon and his brood.

Let me speak more of this, for that revelation is so important.

It is never easy, deciding what is worth one's life. Oh, you may argue protecting the Maker's works merits such a sacrifice, but swinging that tail sweeps few flies away. After all, are not all things His works? Of course they are! Even those gnats pestering my ears and the mites chewing my ribs… even they are His children, for whatever reason – one I doubt I will ever understand. But that's not important. I need not know everything; I leave that burden to the Maker. But I do see a truth in this, for every life our Maker creates is a sacred gift. Every single one.

This knowledge leads to another truth, one that strikes ever deeper as we become more aware. Consider my life, my essence. It is indeed sacred, a true blessing, but no more so than any other our Maker devised. Even humans. For all such life gifts are bound together – and not just through His grand creation, but by intent and action, both His and ours. This I learned over time… a revelation of hindsight, you might say, but also of inspiration. You see, all His gifts prove far more entwined than we ever want or care to admit.

As Seth discovered, it's a sacrilege to part with our lives under any circumstance less worthy or noble than what the Maker gave us. One should not waste or rob another of that gift. And yet this truth has two sides, for how we give our lives reflects the Maker just as much as how we sustain or preserve them. To view this another way, sacrificing one's life may prove as important as keeping it, if not more so.

No simple answers rise to such questions, which I suppose is fair. After all, even mud lacks consistency. One must roll deep in the muck to judge its merits and find just the right flow and feel. So it is, in considering whether to give one's life, you may pray the dilemma does not come up often – however slim a chance that proves. For these harsh scenarios rarely allow time to ponder your options. Indeed, such challenges often demand rash acts of faith – which reveal just where your faith lies.

This I can assure you: your first confrontation with death is always the worst. Believe it. Having a loved one at risk may bolster or ease that burden, though that did not impact Seth's tale. His choices led my son to his death. And he made some fine choices, all worthy of his heritage.

Actually, his fate extended beyond those limits, for once his wives preyed upon Simon's flock and suffered their humbling defeats, Seth had to face the human. A king may not ignore such insults.

And, I suppose, it was much the same for the shepherd. If protecting his flock meant giving up his life, I suspect Simon also had no other choice. At least, I think he viewed it this way.

That's one reason why it angered me, seeing Simon bury my son beneath layers of lifeless, heartless stone. This mocked Seth's decisions and defied our Maker's primary purpose in death, preventing others from feasting on Seth's flesh.

Hear me now, for this reveals His truth and heart! Death follows all life, by His plan and blessing. I don't know if it was always that way, but it is now. Death renews and replenishes our world. All creation depends upon it. Even more, death reflects His very self, for our Maker exists in both life and death. His eternal essence flows from one to the other, over and over, for both are part of His nature. And yet this cycle does not limit Him in any way, for while our Maker created these states from His very core and substance, so does He exist and stand beyond them. The Maker is supreme unto Himself.

Yes, that is hard to grasp. I hope I explained this quandary well enough for you to clutch its heart. Some of this knowledge I absorbed at conception, as the Maker nurtured me within my mother's womb. Some my parents taught me, some I learned from events I endured, some from His presence in and about me, in the wind and soil, the trees and grass… and some came woven in answered prayer. Some I grew to understand by lying beneath

His warm sun, contemplating what I observed, or lounging in a muddy pool, cooling my flesh and drowning pests to my skin. And some wisdom took root in my heart as my love formed for Simon, for I realized that, by building that mound of stones, these humans meant to honor my son and esteem the Maker. Indeed, they often use this same process to honor their own dead. Curious thinking, I know, but true nonetheless.

Observing such things taught me a valuable lesson. When dealing with heartache, these humans often claim the Maker directs their actions. But in times of joy, or just situations with little stress, they may choose to do what pleases them, whether the Maker supports such activities or not. Indeed, with many things they do not appear to consider the Maker's wishes at all.

This, I believe, reveals an ability the Maker gave them: to make decisions on their own. This the humans call "freedom."

When I first pondered that, the whole concept spun me into mental circles. All things honor the Maker by doing His will… or so it was meant to be. That is an essential part of life. Creation itself cannot function otherwise. Yet the Maker gave humans the freedom to choose their own path in all things, even down to ignoring His will. Remarkable, yes, and difficult to understand, for that ability enabled many of the pains I've endured from human hands. Trying to grasp this truth makes me ponder the realities of sin. I ask you: how can it be wrong for humans to deny the Maker or His ways when the Maker Himself allows this to be done? That notion seems so illogical… repugnant even. Yet how else could anyone even have this ability to choose if it did not reflect our Maker's will? Indeed, is that the essence of human freedom… freedom from Him?

I now see truth in this, though to even consider breaking His heart offends me to my grit and marrow. Yet this concept spurs a deeper quandary: how can it possibly be the Maker's will for anyone to go against Him?

I ponder this often, for try as I might, I cannot grasp all it suggests. The Maker crafted us from Himself – His very essence – because He loves us. All creation assures me of this, with every sunrise, every breeze, every rainfall, every breath. Would His love extend so far as to allow us to rebel against His will? Does it even encourage such sin?

My mind condemns such ideas. To say the Maker defies creation suggests the Maker defies Himself. And yet His love for us is so strong, I suspect it exceeds even His own natural law. After all, He created this world for us – not the other way around. And He can break it, or its law, if it suits Him.

That's when the hardest revelation hit me, for it wasn't just humans who bore this freedom. Upon long and deep reflection, I realized that I, too, had this power of choice. Indeed, nothing else explains how my heart could reach out in love for this man-cub… much less abandon my son's lion family to follow a human. Such awareness chilled me to my core, and yet even as dread and revulsion flooded my heart, the love this exposed warmed and uplifted me. For I recognized that this, too, fell under the Maker's will, whether I understood it or not.

Chapter 4

Pursuit

The sheik proved true to his word. As the shepherds stepped from the soldier's tent, Elon summoned his third son. The youngster Gideon argued against his father's will but a moment, for though he didn't wish to leave his beloved elders or their sheep, Gideon took pride in this calling to command his sisters and take their family treasures home. But those females protested with a fury beyond any I endured from my long-missed wives – which I had thought impossible. Even after the daughters gave in, allowing Gideon and a few hounds to lead them south, the oldest girl – Hannah, I believe she was – shouted her righteous anger to the hills. Gilead chuckled at this, as did Reuben and Simon, though her cries saddened Elon.

"Just like her mother," he whispered.

My heart trembled at that. Is there any force more adamant than a determined woman?

As her wails faded in the night, the shepherds bound their few possessions, gathered their tired sheep and goats, and started for Samaria. Simon guided them north with caution, for their animals whimpered in their weariness, hesitant to travel within the blackness shrouding their paths. But my bondmate led them with confidence, knowing his way by moonlight and memory, having crossed through these craggy hills many a season. I observed their steps until I felt some understanding of how these Judeans kept order among their restless flock and mindful hounds. Then I took my first of many departures, slipping away to relieve myself and contemplate my future. That's when I discovered the ruse.

Since Elon left by night, the horse soldiers smothered their fires, folded their tent, and went their own way – or so it seemed. In truth, they tracked the shepherds till daybreak before finally riding off. I guess the herders also knew this, for once the warriors truly departed, Reuben spoke of retreating. But his father determined to hold their course for Samaria. The soldier omens came true that night as Simon spied eight mounted horses closing around them. These warriors also wore the purple of Hoshea but claimed no knowledge of Jonathan or his offer. Words ran fast and hot between the humans, on things I did not fully understand, but Elon calmed his sons and these dusty interlopers by speaking of their agreement, which he repeated several times. Only when the sheik called his grandfather as a witness did these road-weary troopers accept the tale. Their departure left everyone with a sour stomach, but Elon pushed on.

Our passage grew discouraging as I trailed Simon and his brood, their reluctant pack pausing neither day nor night in their northern trek. Foul omens haunted our steps as we crossed through Ephraim's stubborn foothills. An oppressive fog spread forth each evening, creeping across our paths as shapeless specters, only to hide each morning behind rocky crests or within black caverns. I felt tension riding the uncertain breeze and resentment in the troubled waters, turning flowers from the sun and birds from their nests.

Elon rampaged throughout the hours, ever fretting his decision to give in to the soldiers yet holding himself bound by his unbreakable word. Reuben often sought to calm his father, displaying harmonious skills with a hollow stick. Whenever the young man put that tube to his lips, it whistled in ways a songbird would envy. Gilead also tried his hand as a peacemaker, spouting pleasant wisdom on all things. But nothing eased Elon's troubled soul. Simon said little, as I soon learned was his way. His eyes remained on the flock and the horizon.

I followed at a distance, having little trouble evading their hounds. Seth's sweat still marked Simon, confusing the dogs' delicate noses, but it little mattered, for long ago I mastered the skills to hide from shepherds and sheep, keen though their ears and eyes may be. I needed that advantage, for often I had to rest my aging bones, eat, and pray. Food proved difficult to find, for most of my usual meals cowered in their dens these days. Imagine how frustrated that made me, forced to hunger in the wake of those tired, complaining sheep! Many a time I wanted to mix within the baying mass and silence one or more voices, though for respect of Simon – and fear for my life – I managed to restrain myself.

My bondmate's quick pace and refusal to rest also made it difficult for me to dwell daily with the Maker as needed. Pausing to bless the rising sun for His mercies and the setting sun in thanksgiving... all this forced me to catch up by running in the midday heat and the evening chill. Not that their pack was hard to find, even in the fog, but the strain of this discouraged my famished soul. I was not as strong as I used to be, and I missed lazy moments spent basking in the sun's warmth or a soothing mud bath. And, if the truth is known, I guess my body needed those times of meditation and prayer. My limbs ached, my paws stung from cracks and burs, and my stomach seethed.

It saddened me that these humans would not pause in His honor. Passing by hill and vale, I wondered if I had misjudged their hearts. But as twilight bathed the dark horizon that second morning, Simon let loose his anguish. Even as he walked – at the front of the flock, as usual, picking their course with patience through that cool, thin mist – my bondmate spoke to the Maker.

"Blessed is Your name, my Lord, God and Father of all things," he said. "Thank you for Your vigilance! Your eyes guide our path. Your hands guard our way."

Turning to follow a descending ridge, Simon lifted his left hand and whistled to the hounds, pointing his fingers to the sky, then toward his destination. These signals amused me, for the lead sheep always kept at Simon's heels no matter what the dogs did. The flock tailed those before them in a wavering line rarely more than two to four animals wide, which strung the drove across a fair distance. But every few moments a restless lamb or goat might stop, get bumped aside, or just wander away from the pack, leaving the hounds to bark and nip them back into place. Elon and Reuben guarded their flanks, as did a few other hounds, while Gilead and his mutt watched over their line's tail end. This allowed Simon to stay focused on his goal.

"Into peril we walk," he told the Maker. "Soldiers of the Evil One close about us, but our hearts are at peace, for You go before us. In You we trust."

"Simon!" came Reuben's distant call.

My bondmate stopped with a sigh. The sheep followed his lead, creating a restless gathering as the slow-marching flock piled up around Simon.

Reuben soon made his way through the drowsy beasts. His soiled tunic still bore traces of Seth, which disturbed those animals he passed, even though they had detected my son's scent many times from both lads since that encounter. Reuben held a thin staff in one hand, a bag of some skin or cloth in the other. He handed that pouch to Simon.

"Father sent them," Reuben said. He knelt to hug a lamb rubbing against his legs. That brought several more of the baying beasts to his side. He scratched one's forehead, another behind the ears.

Loosening its ties, my bondmate sniffed at the bag's contents. His eyes soured. I guess he wanted those dried beans no more than I did. Simon took a few bites on those hard seeds, then spat them out and tossed the rest to the winds.

His brother groaned.

"That's the last time I bring you food," Reuben said. "You can eat what our trail provides from now on."

A few older sheep grew restless as more of their flock pressed against their encircling congregation. A gray mist passed among them, adding to their frustration. A few lambs sat down. The more obstinate ones started to spread out as another cloud slipped by, but the hounds herded the wayward minds back.

A lonely lamb pushed her nose against Reuben's chin. He laughed, lifting the little one into his arms.

"Now, Idan, you must be patient," he scolded. "Rest yourself when you get the chance!"

"Adina," my bondmate said as a correction.

"What?"

"That's not Idan."

"What? Of course it is!"

"See the spots on her flanks? The curled hair along her neck?"

A thin red beam pierced a distant cloud. It soon spread into a fiery glaze that burned behind the horizon. Reuben used the welcome rays to again examine the weary lamb, which wagged its fat tail and mewed, all in appreciation for the warm refuge this shepherd provided.

"That is Adina," Simon said before spitting out more bean chunks.

"No!" Reuben stated. But then he looked closer where Simon instructed and laughed at his mistake.

"You can't even tell a boy from a girl," Simon chided his brother.

Reuben hugged the little one, then returned the lamb to the others and stood, happy to stretch his tired legs.

"It's been a long night," he whispered.

"Nights," Simon said. "And days."

Reuben nodded, then motioned to Adina. "It's hard to see those things in this dark."

Simon rested against his staff. It made me smile, for my bondmate rarely displayed weariness.

"I'm surprised Hannah did not sneak Adina away," he mumbled.

"She tried," Reuben said. "But Grandfather stopped her."

"I wish I'd seen that."

"He had to draw that line, with the soldiers watching all we did."

Simon reached down to pat one lamb, then another. Two restless ones slumped against his legs before lying in the beaten grass. Simon lifted them into his arms, cradling one against his staff.

"They have not walked this long before," said Reuben.

Simon lowered his head, then closed his eyes. "We could all

use a rest. Time to eat a real meal. Pray."

"Yes," his brother allowed. "But what choice do we have? Do you want Hoshea's sword in your hands?"

"Father should leave such fears to the Lord."

"Tell him that."

"I have!" Simon peered into the shifting fog and whispered, "I have. And he agrees. But he feels this is the Lord's will."

"Well then, why do you resist? Besides, I thought this was your choice."

"It was. Is. And yet... well, I have doubts."

Reuben nodded, then smiled as the emerging sun brought forth a new morning.

"Take your own advice," he urged. "Leave it to the Lord. Do what you're told."

Simon met his brother's loving gaze with hardened resolve. Saying not a word, he returned to the trail. The sheep whimpered in sadness but followed, brushing against Reuben's legs as they passed by. He patted a few bowed backs before stepping out of their way to observe the brightening landscape at either flank. I recognized that face: his thoughts focused once more on protecting their flock.

As that third day passed into night, I spied several distant blazes and one very close – the shimmering fires of Samaria, each glowing through low, drifting clouds. Despite the scars of four lengthy battles endured in the last three generations, this capital of Simon's distant kin remained a daunting fixture upon Manasseh's western hills. Stout walls surrounded the city and its highland fields, the barrier a thick mass of limestone blocks, dried brick, and fitted stones, its winding length enhanced with towers, stone mounds, angled gatehouses, and other earthworks.

Though protected by rolling fog, I knew enough to hide from those ragged cliffs and their toothy parapets – for human watchers hid there, each one able to hurl deadly wood shafts that challenged the wind with their speed and silence. In the past I had more luck scaling the smaller walls about the higher fields, though these also sheltered guard hounds and mounted bowmen.

You see, this city had long prepared for battle and siege. Water flowed into Samaria from rain-fed pools atop the steep hills, providing fluids, grass, and grains for its residents and livestock. I could hear them even at this distance, the bellows and grunts of cattle and sheep, horses, camels, and humans. Thousands of humans, clustered in tiny caves or stacked boxes of still more stone and brick. Within the darkness, I sometimes saw outlines of people against the light of their fires and torches, or livestock reflected by that dim moonlight. All seemed content – which made sense, with the wind blowing from the west, hiding the smoke of Assyrian campfires and the stench of their camps. But from my perch above the fortress, I could look beyond the eastern canyons to the shrouded signs of the invaders, thousands strong. Simon and his brother also witnessed this. They stood in shadows atop a rippled crest of rock just below me, gazing into the black horizon with concern.

"They will be here in two days," noted Reuben. "Maybe one."

"Tomorrow night," Simon declared.

His brother's voice turned cold. "Hoshea's bodyguard said Sargon himself comes."

Simon pointed to the center of that dark, shuffling mass. There I saw a ring of campfires. Within its dark hole I spied the rippling hints of a sizeable tent… I wonder if Simon could make this out as well.

Reuben squinted to study the mirky horizon.

"That circle?" he wondered aloud. "You think it is him?"

"Whoever leads them is there," Simon insisted.

Reuben pointed to small patches of flame scattered between the large camp and Samaria.

"Hoshea burns his own fields," the elder brother remarked with some disbelief, or perhaps admiration. Or both.

"It will not slow them," said Simon.

"But it takes away their food."

With a deep, exhausting sigh, my bondmate tilted his head from one side to the other as he studied the distant campsite, as if those slight shifts improved his vision. Simon paused to sip what must have been water from the old ram's horn hanging from his neck and shoulder. Then, with no warning, he left for the dark rock pile where his fathers rested, guarding the one passage to a basin corralling their spent flocks. Reuben stayed behind a few moments before following his brother.

The elders surprised me by rising at Simon's approach; obviously they heard those soft steps, or perhaps my bondmate signaled them somehow. Oh... I overlooked how their dogs slipped ahead of him, as is their way. Silly of me! But I am tired. No matter. In speech I couldn't quite sort out, the man-cub shared all he had learned. Reuben affirmed these observations with brief grunts, sighs, and other such messages they conveyed from time to time, leaving the four to stand in silence, little more than glimmers in the cloud-filtered moonlight. Finally, Elon made his decision.

"At first light, we will go down."

"That is best," Gilead said.

Reuben revealed opposing thoughts. "You still mean to do this, with the Assyrians but a day away?"

His father nodded.

"We have no choice," their grandfather reminded all. "We will find no shelter until we stand in our homeland once more."

"That's what I said," Reuben countered.

"Yahweh has opened this place to the Evil One," continued his grandfather. "We must finish this and flee – now."

"Samaria will fall," Reuben said. "We all know this."

"As the Lord decreed," Elon stated with harsh assurance. "The prophets warned them to repent –"

"He warned us all," Simon pointed out.

"Indeed," Gilead said.

Reuben took that as agreement. "Then why give them our flocks?"

"Because," began Elon, though his eldest son was not finished.

"It is madness!" Reuben said yet again. "A waste!"

Gilead called the boy's name as a gentle appeal, to no avail.

"This whole trip – a waste!"

Elon motioned for his son to calm down, but this time Reuben did not heed him.

"I have put all my life into our stock," he said. "We all have!"

"We will start over," his father assured them.

"But why? These people will die no matter what we do."

Pale light drifted across Elon's brow. It revealed how his gaze burned, but when he spoke, his voice stayed patient… enduring.

"I gave them my word, before God," Elon reminded them. "I will not break it. How can I, Reuben? Honestly, how can I possibly do what you ask, take back what I promised in good faith, when every day, with our every breath, our Lord gives us all we need and more. Can we do otherwise?"

"Watch what you say," Gilead warned. "All of you."

Though offered with caution, that soft comment seemed to raise Elon's fur.

"You think I don't?" Elon put to his father.

Gilead proved he, too, could cast a menacing glare. Pulling back his hood, I imagined his deep-set eyes and sharp nose casting shadows as black as death.

"Are your sons also given?" the eldest questioned.

"What?"

"You send your youngest son and daughters away, and you withhold what Samaria needs most."

Elon folded his arms across his chest. "Four more warriors will not bring them victory," he stated.

"Indeed," his father allowed. "But as you said, our Lord offers us everything, holding nothing back, and freely gives what we will take. In truth, He provides what we need before we ever know we need it, while we, in our blindness, or selfishness, we withhold much here that we treasure. All of you know this."

Elon frowned but said nothing. His father nodded.

"That is why I caution you," said Gilead. "Choose your words with care, my sons, I beg you! For our Lord's example is difficult to follow. We cannot honor Him with but half our hearts or minds. To love Him is to trust Him with all we hold dear. We must never forget that."

Chapter 5
The fortress

Deciding not to wait for daylight, Simon guided their flocks down that rocky slope to the human vale. I held my breath to hear all that moved in that blackness, for the natural trail twisted about that plunging shelf with many a hazardous ledge and stumbling shoal. Such a path could unnerve a veteran traveler even under a bright sun, but Simon descended without fear through the night shadows, threading around thorny brush, gnarled roots, biting stones, and scattered sand pools, choosing careful steps his sleepy sheep and goats could master with ease. Winded myself, I held my place, pondering the best spot to observe these shepherds approach those dangerous city walls. Then something spurred me to stay close to these men, so I flexed my claws in defiance and went down, clinging low to the fog-blanketed earth… for one never knows what eyes might be watching.

An unnerving stillness descended about me as Simon left the rocks to approach Samaria, a fortress built into the eastern slopes of this old mountain. Scorched stubble, dank pits, and ragged scars scoured the earth around the citadel, demonstrating how these humans would rather destroy their homeland than leave any refuge or sustenance for the invaders. I slid into those newly carved ravines, guarding my steps to avoid all that charred, brittle straw. My paws uncovered all sorts of bones and flesh in that loose soil – the bowls of an ox, the torn flanks of a hare, rotting remnants of serpents, rodents, birds… things to make my stomach bellow and roll. But I bit back my urges and brushed the debris aside. On less burdensome days those leftovers might provide a minimal meal for a desperate beast, but not today.

Simon wasted no time on the wounded land, pressing his flocks forward to approach a damp gravel lane leading to the city. Even that path bore rips and holes, meant no doubt to break a leg, cripple a foot, or trap a human's cart, but Simon paid the obstacles no mind. His trail ended at those weathered walls of brick and rock. There rose two new barriers: massive blocks of dry, charred wood, their planks bound together by rusty iron bolts and bars. These stout barriers stood against the layered walls, which soared to hovering ledges aglow from hidden flames.

A cold wind swept around the exhausted sheep. As the hounds gathered the shivering flocks into some sort of order, Simon waited at the wooden slabs for Reuben or his fathers to catch up. I crept ever forward within those ditches until I reached a sticky pool parallel to the lane. It offered the best concealment I could find, so there I hid, wondering why I could not hear the other shepherds. Questioning that reminded me of their tendency toward silence – which then ended.

"You would think someone would answer us," I heard Reuben say.

"I'm sure these gates are always closed this time of night," said his father.

"But why no challenge?" Gilead wondered – which I also pondered. "And no torches?"

"The enemy draws near," said Reuben. "They secure their fortress for war."

Simon tipped his forehead to the west, where the torn trail curled around two earthen slopes to rise out of sight. A band of horse soldiers approached, some bearing bronze-tipped spears, others holding hooded flames that cast flickering slivers of light upon their road. Dangling tails from purple capes rippled in the crisp breeze.

"The king's bodyguard," said Reuben.

I sank my nails into the damp soil, daunted by visions of blackened blades bobbing against the night sky. My ears rang from echoes of hooves crushing frail stones and snapping charred stubble. The sounds ground on my heart as those stallions drew near. I could feel the heat of their exertions through the misty air.

"They will be busy tomorrow," Reuben muttered. The rich texture of his voice carried those sad words through the horsemen's clatter.

Some hounds growled at the newcomers, but at words from the men, these canines divided the flock to clear the gravel path. This allowed the riders to halt not far from Elon and his family. Some steeds stopped before me, others to my left. One proud stallion caught my scent and stomped sideways in a nervous, awkward gait. His ignorant rider kicked back his heels to steady the mount. That horse pouted but obeyed, as did the others.

All praise the Maker! These steeds ignored me!

"May our Lord be with you," Gilead offered the soldiers, though they seemed not to care.

"Who are you?" shouted one.

A drifting cloud allowed dim moonlight to fall upon the elders. Their beards fluttered within shifting gray wisps. I thought it somewhat captivating.

"Shepherds from Judah," answered Elon, stressing the name of his homeland. "Here to sell our flocks."

The mounted ones mumbled bitter tones. Their leader barked a harsh command. His men went silent.

"You've little time," snapped the grizzly-bearded warrior. "Guide your sheep to the upper fields."

Elon nodded. "There is room for all?"

"Of course! But you need not worry about such things. Just follow my orders and move on."

Reuben tapped his staff against the black gates. Elon smiled at the muffled thud, though I don't remember why. Then he gazed into Gilead's confident eyes, drawing comfort from their strength, and turned upon the horsemen.

"Once we see the assessor," Elon told the lead warrior.

That man bristled. "We have no time for that!"

"We were promised payment."

"By whom?"

Elon planted his crooked staff in the earth.

"Jonathan," he stated.

The soldiers glanced at one another. Their voices flew.

"Captain of the First Wave," continued Elon. "The Royal Guard of Hoshea."

"I know who he is!" snapped the leader of these warriors, though I heard surprise in his tone. Turning to a comrade, he spat a summon for this esteemed Jonathan. To another, he ordered the gates open. That rider guided his steed to the iron-banded wood and pounded a distinct pattern against the braced door. But their leader saw none of this. His eyes returned to Elon and the other shepherds, their defiance intact.

"I will count your stock as they pass through the eye," he decided. "Each head." Sounds of sharp impacts echoed from somewhere beyond that wooden barrier. The warrior bristled at the interruption, then continued, "You will lead your flock to the high fields."

"And our gold?" questioned Elon.

"On that, you may deal with the captain."

A horse shuffled in place near me. I ignored his nervous snorts and hugged the earth, concentrating on what these humans said. I grasped few of those words at that time, but the tension in their voices rang true.

Simon's father looked to his sons, the older at his side, the youngest near the gates. Their muted responses worked to calm those rustling, impatient sheep. I could see their anguish in those sleepy eyes, all faintly aglow beneath a mist-shrouded moon.

"Very well," Elon said. "May our Lord's will be done."

Something started grinding within the darkness. Firelight burst from a small gap in one of the wooden walls these men called a gate. That breach widened into a rectangular hole fit for little more than those sheep... humans and horses would have to bend low to pass through. I felt a moment's thrill, for the chasm gave me my first limited look within those walls. But my eyes could not adjust enough between the light and darkness to glimpse what lay on the other side. Another burst of light came through, followed by a soldier bearing a writhing torch. Elon had Reuben take his place, so the elder son went inside, followed by Gilead and several hounds. Simon then directed the sheep and goats into that tunnel, one by one, as he and the stout horse soldier counted heads. When finished, Simon debated with the helmeted one until they agreed upon the number 87. Frustrated but satisfied, Simon led the last hounds into those dark walls, followed by Elon and the torch bearer. The small portal closed with a dull shudder and a sharp, piercing ring, imposing night once more upon those who remained. These warriors sputtered a few brash remarks and rode off, leaving me to cling to the cold, dank earth.

A sudden chill rocked my heart. My bondmate was gone, locked in the fortress Samaria.

Chapter 6

Betrayal

To my surprise – and onrushing fear – I felt a sudden, gripping urge to leap those imposing walls. That's how desperate my need was to stay close to my bondmate, to think I could bound up and over that towering ledge! But this time, that persistent spur proved easy to dismiss. Built and rebuilt from times well before my birth, these manmade cliffs of rock, brick, and mortar reached for the heavens as only a construct of fallen men would dare. And though Samaria's walls fell far short of that stellar goal, their sheer heights defied my feeble skills, with exposed ledges and parapets shielding many watching eyes. Archers would surely spear me long before I ever scaled those stones.

Shuddering at that thought, even as I imagined Simon's misery or imprisonment, I looked to the heavens and prayed the Maker would renew my strained hopes. He cast my gaze instead upon Samaria's slopes, where in the dim moonlight I spied not just stone walls crossing those distant heights, but traps set by the humans. Wisps of fog flowed through dark trenches dug around the bastion, the vapor threads often breaking around sharpened wood spikes piercing the soil.

That stunned me. To think such obstacles surrounded the entire city! It made my heart weep, pondering how long these men must have labored to torture His blessed earth this way. But as I considered this, I recognized these snares could signal possible weaknesses. Those highland walls lacked the size and towers of the lower city, and while I sensed sentries hidden around those protected meadows, there did not seem to be as many watchful eyes as menaced the main gates. Perhaps these humans considered those remote areas less vulnerable, their surrounding cliffs and rocky precipices working to Samaria's advantage – though that did not stop the soldiers from scarring the earth.

With a whip of my tail, I drew in my claws and picked a careful path toward those pastures. It proved oh so frustrating, for studying that western climb renewed all those cries for sleep from my aching limbs. My heart longed to bask in the warmth of His sun and forget all about these hateful humans. Yet Simon's noble spirit still beckoned me. I listened to that summons and knew I could not abandon him.

I took my time to reconnoiter those shadowy ledges and bridge the earthworks protected from moonlight. I did not wish to raise any alarms or lose my footing among all those dangers. Be that as it may, my efforts seemed fleeting; before dawn I found myself at Samaria's upper rim. Up close, I found only a ramshackle stone hedge circled these grazing lands, a barrier I could scale with ease. Beyond it waited a noisy gathering of cattle, goats, sheep, land birds, camels… even a few horses and hogs!

Yes, that was an inviting sight! A sumptuous feast requiring little effort, and with that prevailing breeze from the west, those few watching shepherds had no idea I hid nearby. Oh, I know they could call on a hound or two, and at least one mounted soldier securing the perimeter, but those guardians did not worry me. The chaos brought by my strike would provide more than enough time to escape with my choice of meat.

I contemplated that and almost gave way to my blood yearning, but that longing became an irritation reminding me of my true purpose. My heart returned to my quest for Simon – and for once I was instantly rewarded. Far across those protected grasslands I saw the beasts brought by my bondmate, but not their masters. I looked again and smelled the faint shifting currents for hints, but I found no trace of my shepherds. That could mean but one thing – Simon and his family had come and gone.

All my weary patience burned up then in a deep, boiling anger. I had worked oh so hard to keep track of Simon, as was my calling and desire, but when the lad and his family entered the depths of Samaria – where I dared not go, and I think the Maker understood this – I had no choice but to approach from the heights. They should have been here! Even at my age, I could outpace men herding tired, blustering flocks through those filthy stone streets, no matter their shorter route! I have not seen the day when a meandering mob of sheep and goats could best me. Never!

Oh, the frustrations of that wrathful morning.

Then the winds shifted, and I detected trace scents of competitors. A family of lions, males and females, working together.

I huddled against the earth, shutting out all other thoughts to focus on my senses. My claws extended by instinct, and my limbs primed to attack or flee as I smelt each breeze and listened to the leaves, grasses, and stones, searching for any hint my brethren drew near. And when nothing beyond those busy Samaria fields offered a threat, I waited still longer, pondering the warnings inherent in such signals.

At some point my selfish suspicions gave ground to active thought. Sifting the roots of my risks, some bits of common sense reminded me that I could not protect Simon throughout this quest without crossing some lion's territory. To be fair, that peril shadowed any lion going rogue, as the Maker called me to do. But in my heart, I must have hoped this danger would not come this early… and certainly not so close to a human stronghold. That's when my eyes fell once more upon the wall encircling the fortress fields. My wisdom heckled me, for what more would bring so many kings and queens together than the bleating of man's livestock? My nose also warned of lures hidden among the rocks and timber above me, so I scampered from the Samarian barrier to discover a human path leading to a ragged pile of stones and ash. Blood stained that soil, residue from uncounted sacrifices.

Gazing upon this trampled sacrilege, I felt great distress and anger from the Maker – a burning in my gut to match the fires that once scarred this ugly scene. And yet His directives gave me courage in the face of this pressing danger, telling me these horrors were not my concern. Then I detected more lingering traces of my brethren, again with the odors of more than one male. They reminded me how such a coalition would not tolerate a newcomer preying within their lands. If they sought me out, their interference could disrupt everything I felt called to do. But these traces matched the clues I detected earlier, so with the Maker's comforting hand, I put aside my fears and turned back to His calling – even though I knew not what happened to my shepherds or where they had gone.

Perhaps all these rash, bustling straits drove me to seek hoofed and feathered help. At most times I would not ask their assistance, for birds and beasts may prove oh so fearful and timid when I request aid. But facing all these pressing concerns and my need to move, I saw no other options. And in this, I also felt the Maker's prodding.

Oh, I detect amusement in your eyes. Now I admit that, just perhaps, some of the Maker's children have reason to fear my kind, though my brethren usually limit our meals to the sick and aged... or panicking squawkers who need silencing, if only for sanity's sake. But that's just one of the headaches lions face.

No, what I'm referring to now is how some of the Maker's other children resent my kind as the bearers of authority in His creation. Yes, most such rebels suffer smaller frames than us, and I can see how that could make them fearful and fickle, but some reach our size or even stretch beyond us. And then there are those among the Maker's creations that simply distrust our power and authority. A few even resist it.

But in those highlands, one may usually find hunting birds observing all that move among those rocks, trees, and vales. I figured one such eagle or hawk would deal with me, for few of their kind fear my claws. Many also kept eyes upon Samaria, which I should have expected, having seen those approaching Assyrian fires. I've spied raptors following human armies often, and why not, if you prefer dead flesh? A meal may not come for days on such a trail, but when battle begins, a bountiful harvest follows. I had no stomach for such meat, but some of my kind have, along with hounds, hogs, falcons... the hungry may thrive on such harvests for days or even weeks.

Once I found some birds and beasts who believed I sought not their blood, they did not mind searching out the humans in Samaria and telling me what they had seen, among other things. From their tales, plus those of some sleepy camels, two fearless bulls, and a legion of mice that roamed the Samarian streets, I soon pieced together Simon's exploits.

As the moon slipped below the horizon – and I took my last steps to Samaria's lofty borders – Simon and his family reached those high fields. Theirs was the shorter route, after all. A small fortress held that ground for Hoshea's herds and cavalry, and in it rested Jonathan. Garbed in a girded wool tunic and belt, its tones faded to browns in the dim light, the weary warrior seemed mystified as Simon counted out the flock to the king's awaiting shepherds.

"Truly, I did not think you would come," the captain admitted. "With Sargon's troops just before us...."

His words stumbled to a stop as he contemplated events.

"We gave our word," Elon told him.

"Indeed," the captain decided, yawning. His eyes turned away. "That is beyond question. I only wish –"

Elon stiffened, even as Gilead and Reuben turned to hear the soldier.

"I count 87," interrupted a young Israelite, his uniform more complicated than Jonathan's. He bowed to Simon, adding, "As you said."

"As I said," injected Reuben.

Elon ignored them. "What do you mean?" he put to the captain.

Jonathan took a deep, settling breath, drew up his shoulders, and turned to face the tired elder, who was not cowed by his presence. A camel cackled on and on about that spectacle, though the hawks thought little of it. Still, I wish I could have been there to see the fire in Elon's eyes, the clarity of Reuben's steadfast determination, or the peace in Simon's patient concentration.

"You are a day late, my friend," explained the captain. Stroking his beard with his left hand, Jonathan looked about them and reflected with sadness, "All of you. A day late."

"How so?" Elon stamped his feet in unrest. "Speak clearly!"

"We cannot leave," whispered Gilead.

Jonathan nodded. "Sargon is here. Marching upon us now."

"His camp remains a day away," Simon said.

"Ah, so you know this? And you came anyway?"

"We could do nothing else," Elon muttered, each word as cold as Assyrian steel.

"Such nobility." The captain gazed upon them with newfound respect, though the glint in his eyes suggested he thought it misplaced. "You must know then what weighs upon our king."

Gilead spoke first. "How depleted are your ranks?"

"Ours, little. But we are the bodyguard. The foot soldiers, they run short."

That drew Reuben's rage. "Foul deceiver! You never meant to release us!"

"Not so!" The captain spoke with wounded sincerity. "This is the king's command."

"The king be damned." Elon squared his shoulders and wrapped his arms about his chest, meeting Jonathan's surprised stare as an open challenge. "We will not stay."

The sheik was firm, but so was the captain, who reclaimed his authority with a single, drawn-out breath.

"You cannot leave," he stated.

"Have you no honor?" Reuben drew his staff before him, angling its gnarled head towards the captain's sharp nose. "We have done as you asked. More!"

"Yes, you have, but I can't help you." The captain turned against the lad with reluctance, his allegiance torn by a command he did not wish to follow. But his words remained firm. "By the gods, it is beyond me."

That drew their full fury.

"Blasphemy!" spat Gilead.

His son settled like a rock before the soldier, his countenance hot as fire. "Say no such things in my presence!" Elon demanded. "By our Lord, I will forgive many things, but nothing that affronts Him."

"You," the captain hardened, "will do what you are told."

An amused bull braced for a stampede at this standoff; apparently human fights often spooked herds up there. But this bovine had not reckoned on Simon. My bondmate – who by my estimates was undoubtedly the most capable fighter among those humans – he stepped between the arguers with harmony upon his mind.

"Our payment," he said, repeating himself as first Elon, then the captain, gave Simon questioning glances. "Do we have it?"

"No," the captain stammered. "Yesterday the treasury was packed and hidden in the caverns."

Reuben swore his frustrations anew, drawing Gilead's angry echoes, but Simon remained undeterred.

"But you," he said with gentle, persuasive tones, "you are the captain of the First Wave, the Royal Guard of King Hoshea. You are an honorable man with access to all his resources. You will deliver what you said."

"I would, yes, if it was possible. But this is beyond me." He looked into Simon's eyes and added, "I am not king."

Simon hesitated to accept this. "Surely you do not think we deserve this?"

"None of us deserve this. Blame Sargon."

"I blame no one. We came here of our own free will to help you. We kept our word. We only wish the same from you."

"I cannot release you."

"Then take our gold as a bounty."

The captain stepped back. "Stop there."

"Release my fathers," Simon continued. "Reuben and I will stay."

Elon objected at once, as did Gilead, but Simon spoke over their protests.

"My grandfather is too old to carry a sword or serve the walls," said my bondmate. "And my father must return home to my sisters. They need him. But Reuben and I have our lives before us. *Our* lives, father. To give as we please."

"Enough!" To my surprise, the bull I trusted to share these events said it was Jonathan who interrupted this. The captain turned to my bondmate and snapped, "You think I could be bribed? I will not enslave you! Nor would I steal from the treasury!"

Jonathan swore as the sun's first light slipped above the horizon, casting a bright flare on the human's chill brow. His eyes ground over Simon, who remained impervious to such agony, then softened toward Elon, whose example had long taught Simon of strength.

And that, I think, broke the Samarian.

Sending his assistant away, the captain lowered his voice. "I can get your fathers through the gate."

"How?" Reuben demanded.

"Leave that to me. They will be cast out, though what happens then is up to your god. You will have to trust him."

"That we do," Elon affirmed. "My sons –"

"Are mine," the warrior proclaimed, cutting him off. "I will do with them as I see fit."

"Agreed," said Simon. "Before the sun peaks, our fathers will be freed?"

"It will be done."

So spoke the captain, with words as hard as granite. But as his squad leader returned, with twelve soldiers bound in leather armor, they revealed their intent with sharply crafted bronze blades – all drawn against the Judeans.

"Manacle the older two," the captain commanded. "They are my prisoners. Enlist the others."

Chapter 7

Cornered

Though his heart raged against his patience, Elon held his tongue as soldiers secured his wrists behind his back with cold metal shackles. Gilead took his chaining with a deep, resigned sigh.

"Our Lord's will be done," he whispered.

Jonathan emerged from a room of shadows to stand in the early morning sun, his form now a figure of terror. Half an orb of scratched and dented bronze shielded his skull. Sheets of tanned black leather protected his chest and thighs. Those he covered with a purple cape, its edge flowing with the breeze around a sword hanging from his leather-encircled hips in a pocked hide sheath. With those adornments establishing his position of power, Jonathan led Simon's fathers into the streets of Samaria. Elon and Gilead stumbled in his wake, followed by two soldiers, Simon and Reuben, and the rest of the squad.

I did not get to see any of this. Even as I reached the high fields, these humans passed beyond the eyes and ears of the bull and his cattle. To my fortune – or our Maker's grand design – a pair of hawks decided to follow the awkward marchers, thinking or hoping their prisoners might soon shed their lives and provide a bountiful feast. Our stumbling group led the increasingly frustrated raptors through the city until they reached the king's armory, which sat atop a foothill overlooking the temples of Samaria's false gods. At that point the humans paused, their captain deciding to cast the prisoners outside the main gate.

"I don't advise it," a subordinate put in.

"King's orders," Jonathan snapped.

"But it's wrong to throw these two outside the walls for the Assyrians' pleasure," another protested.

The birds missed a word or two here, which happened often as they recounted this tale. These hawks didn't seem to care about lost details; their ire centered around trying to keep track of men stalking within those manmade canyons and rockpiles that humans called a city. Back and forth the raptors soared, crossing through twisting winds and waves of heat, winging past unruly hounds and a few entranced cats, never able to stay in any one place too long, as is their nature. But I didn't mind their excuses, for they reminded me why I appreciated not being there. Excrement festers and bakes on those stones alongside the wastes of decay and death. Such scents choke my lungs.

An older soldier wiped sweat from his eyes as he watched Elon and Gilead strain against their bindings.

"You know what will happen to them," he reminded Jonathan. "Whatever they've done, it can't deserve their tortures."

The captain took a deep breath. "You know nothing of what they're accused."

"Accused?" His subordinate jerked about in surprise. "Just accused? No decision?"

"The king requires no trials when judging Judean lawbreakers. Or anyone else he chooses."

"Give them a water sack at least," put in Simon, who hid his pleasure at Jonathan's moves. "The midday sun can burn away one's life."

Irritated, the captain turned to face the group.

"A water sack," he repeated, his voice drawing upon all the authority he could muster – which was considerable. "All right then. But nothing else." He paused to meet the uncertain gaze of every soldier in his command. "This is the king's order. Get on with it."

Those bristling eyes ended their debate. The humans separated into two groups. Two warriors joined Jonathan to lead the shackled shepherds down to the outer gates. The other soldiers formed around Simon and Reuben, guiding them to a stone tower in Samaria's black heart.

From the hawk's description, that citadel rises several levels above the surrounding structures, its walls a mix of chiseled limestone, blocks of dried mud, and rough stones bonded with mortars, tar, and clay. At street level it opened with a room of many passages, each blocked at different places with wooden doors, reams of iron bars, or stiff hammered plates. It took several moments for these humans to emerge from all those corridors to reach a spreading yard of fitted stones, a few bubbling fountains, and lush green gardens. All that wondrous splendor the hawks knew well, for they often retreated there, among the brush and trees, to catch a moment's rest, bathe, or enjoy a dove, pigeon, or some other simple feast. So pleased were they to return, my hawks almost didn't see Simon's band reach the three buildings at the center of their haven. These structures fit this paradise, their walls decorated with potted flowers and gorgeous blossoms, hanging vines in glorious diversity, elaborate paintings of things the birds could not even guess at, and carvings of creatures glittering from an abundance of oiled woods, chiseled stone, and hammered metals. As amazing as these things sounded, the artworks made little impact on our squad. The warriors led our prisoners through this vast park, apparently with one of these buildings in mind, but they never reached it, for the brothers bolted.

"Slings!" someone shouted. By his ready order and steady tone, this squad leader must have been used to people trying to escape. But his actions did not seem necessary, for stationary guards blocked each building entrance. All of them moved to converge on the young shepherds.

Now when the older hawk told me this, I could not help but chuckle. From my experience, I envisioned these soldiers, and even the raptors, underestimated Simon. But then, it's unfair to judge those troopers too harshly, for all the world would fall in surprise before my bondmate's genius.

For whatever reason, the shepherds turned toward the narrow

doorway to the grandest of these structures. Five eunuchs rushed against them, their thick, hairless arms brandishing swords of gleaming bronze and broad wooden shields painted with images of trees, clouds, and stars. The first guard reared as a great bear defending its young, raising his double-edged blade with all the power of a charging thunderbolt. But Simon had already left his feet, propelled forward with the deadly grace of a thrown dagger. Folding his arms to protect his face and chest, Simon's shoulder speared the guard just below his ribs. Together they fell, but the shepherd twisted up like a rambunctious cat while the guard slumped in agony against the worn stones.

"Down!" Simon called.

Nodding, Reuben dove into a fluid shoulder roll. A wave of slung stones split the warming breeze above him to strike the pursuing guards. One collapsed in violent spasms, having been hit in his neck by a smooth, sailing rock. His fall tripped two others who might have tumbled anyway from the nuggets that slammed into their leather cloaks. That left one guard standing, unsure whether to confront the rising Reuben or his crouched brother. Simon decided for him, springing against the guardian's sword arm even as the eunuch sought to block him with his conical shield. Snapping the man's thick wrist against the steps, Simon wrested the blade from his grasp and sprang through the artisan's carved doorway. Reuben followed to soon reach his side.

"Where now?" the older brother barked as they ran past four surprised sentries. Simon sprinted on without answering, through a grand hall to a room full of hot stoves and cooks, then beyond that to a passageway connecting places staffed by servants bent to various household chores – mending garments, scouring waste kettles, cleansing vegetables, and other such things people do. Reuben wished to pause in a shadowed spot, winded as he was, but they had no time to rest with their noisy hunters close behind. Simon led his brother up a stair that wound past three levels. My hawks spied the lads racing by windows on each floor, their soft footfalls masked by the bellows of chasing soldiers. On the fourth deck, a warrior who must have guessed their approach made the mistake of confronting the brothers. He soon tumbled down the steps in their wake, sidetracking the pursuers. That allowed the shepherds to emerge unhindered onto the terrace of the princess.

That servant's stairwell opened at the northeast corner of that top floor, just inside the barrier rope strung atop the short parapet. Drawing near, Simon and Reuben took in the city's most exquisite viewing point. Although a distant cloud bank blocked the shepherds from seeing the vast Plain of Sharon and its sparkling border along the Great Sea, that terrace still provided our escapees wondrous overlooks of all Samaria and its awakening landscape. The brothers made a quick study of the streets and alleys, looking for possible ways out of their predicament. Few options seemed promising. Simon pointed to missing guard posts along the outer wall, signs that Jonathan spoke truly of their shortages. A dark spot caught Reuben's eye in the shadowy gardens far beneath them. A few hours still lay ahead before direct light would reach those parklands, but the elder spoke in anticipation of sunrays bouncing like shimmering gold upon that pool, its edge licking their tower's base.

"Marvelous," said Reuben.

"Truly," Simon whispered, "she is."

"She?"

Reuben pivoted, his eyes glancing past the hawks settling upon the ropes to see the lady captivating Simon. She was Rachel, the beloved daughter of Hoshea, and thus the focus of all affections near the crown. Even had she lacked royal blood, her natural attributes would have commanded all anyone had to offer and still more.

Merchants would prize her cotton robe, dyed a luxurious purple, with golden braids about its length and embroidered designs along its seams and folds, and yet its fine weave paled against the alluring form it hugged. Lush as the greenery of Sharon, more enticing than the dazzling reflections of His sun, Rachel stood as the crowning achievement of her lineage. Long, black strands of silk formed her fragrant hair. Skin softer than rose petals lined her proud brow, patient chin, sculpted shoulders, and those sweet, oiled hands.

Polished black leather graced with gems bound her forehead, wrists, waist, and small, elegant feet. An enticingly thin veil accented her nose and garnet lips.

Truly, I am not one for appreciating the designs in human flesh – and I have little patience for those who do. But when I beheld her with my own discriminating eyes, I found the hawks' descriptions more than on target. Rachel was most pleasing, in every way. Even for a human.

If I faulted Simon for anything in this escapade, it would be his falling into an almost mystical trance at seeing her standing statuesque at her bedroom door. For that caused him to not notice at her side a soldier most rare. Captain of a Thousand was his title, which I learned meant a man who would have commanded ten Jonathans and all the men under them. This esteemed one resembled an echo of Simon, though far more refined – his brown hair and beard groomed with style, his hazel eyes all-encompassing, his ears inquisitive, his brow analytical, his limbs well honed, his trunk athletic, his hands reliable and skilled. By the purple cape about his marbled shoulders, he too was of the Royal Guard.

Unlike the shepherds, this man did not suffer surprise at this encounter. Taking notice of the brothers' arrival, the captain rose with a stare as warm as winter's fiercest gale.

"What brings you to these chambers?" he said to the shepherds. Then he heard the rumblings of the trailing soldiers and drew forth a sharpened bronze spike nearly as long as his arm.

"Why are you here?" the captain shouted.

The lady moved behind him. She spouted something the hawks could not hear.

"Have no doubt, my love," said her champion. "Stay here."

While his tone demonstrated affection, her bewitching emerald eyes focused on Simon with something resembling curiosity and interest, or so the hawks guessed. They also detected fear in her stance and tone, though they struggled to describe it. They sensed nothing like a normal response to predators or dangers, but more defiance or denial, or perhaps a rebuttal.

Her warrior placed his arms and legs in a protective stance, one the hawks often witnessed before battle commenced. They appreciated the poise in his ready sword, held aloft with nary a waiver. That alone told of this captain's formidable skills, the hawks believed. I did not doubt them, having seen such humans prove their capabilities time and time again, though mostly from a distance.

"Be still," the man ordered. "Stay your ground."

Simon turned upon him.

It must have been a grand duel. Simon lifted his captured blade as he raced toward the captain. The Samarian also charged, waving his metal shaft back and forth through the warming air. They met in the terrace center, two titans matching each other stroke for stroke. Neither scored a hit.

This concerned me, for though I admired Simon's skills, I feared he suffered a distinct disadvantage with his scarred weapon. From my observations of human rage, my bondmate's stubby sword could not match the captain's longer, lighter blade, its polished sides flashing in the sun. The hawks also voiced worries about the soldier's device, but I could not grasp their meaning.

Scouting the ledge for an escape, Reuben tried to call his brother off, but Simon ignored this, consumed with a battle he had neither anticipated nor desired.

A loud bang echoed from the staircase. Reuben pivoted to see the door bulge outward, only to snap back amid shouts of frustration. Reuben slammed into the rattling wood to keep it shut, then jammed the tip of his staff between the door and its frame.

"You handle that blade well," the captain told Simon. The warrior darted beneath my bondmate's fluid defense, only to see Simon counter that move with ease. That earned a smile.

"Surprising skills for a goatherder," the captain said.

The door shuddered. Reuben yanked his staff back and forth to break off its stuck end, then shoved the remainder back into the gap. The wood slab shivered anew, but he ignored it to make a second plug. Reuben repeated his tactic again and again until most of his shaft stuck out of the wall, wedged in four places. Each one worked to pin that battered door shut against those trying to break through. The hawks watched the wood shake once, twice, expecting it to burst at any time.

"We must go!" Reuben shouted to his brother.

"To where?" the captain replied, taking pleasure in the words and, perhaps, the fight. Then he pulled back a step and lowered his weapon. "Let us stop this and talk. Tell me why you are here. For there are but two ways out, and you have blocked one. I'll not let you use the other until I know these things."

Simon smiled at that, then pressed forward, slashing his thicker blade back and forth across his battle zone. Sliding back once, then again, the Samaritan placed himself in the bedroom's entrance. There he stood firm, proud of his accomplishment.

"You cannot get by me," he said, his voice a statement of calm assurance. But then he heard shouts from the walls at his back. He glanced into the darkness, then froze.

Simon stepped beside the princess, his sword down, his gaze almost blinded by her beauty – or so the hawks put it. Something she said had yanked his thoughts from the battle, though just what was spoken the birds missed. She met his eyes, troubled but undeterred.

With his free hand, Simon touched her chin, her cheek. The first grazed her flesh like a rolling tear, soft and silent. Her eyes flared, but she remained still, as if abashed that anyone would dare such a thing. But when the second stroke drew near an eye, she reared like a viper, though the contact lasted no longer than a blink.

"You dare?" she cried out.

This outraged the captain. He charged, his blade poised to attack or defend. Reuben darted in, swinging the knobby remainder of his staff to bludgeon the soldier's sharp nose, but the warrior slipped below that club and slapped Reuben's scalp with the flat of his blade. Simon pressed forward, sweeping his sword against the captain's chest. The Samarian pivoted, parried the blow, and turned it aside. His blade darted into the vacuum to nick Simon's left arm.

"Give up!" the captain demanded.

Simon slashed his sword back and down. His opponent sidestepped – and collided with Reuben's stout bludgeon. That blow to the head felled Rachel's defender. A desperate groan slipped from his lips as he slumped to the floor.

A flurry of shouts sprang from the bedroom and the stairs. Reuben looked to both, then to Simon, who glared down at the fallen one in readiness to continue.

"Come on!" Reuben urged. "We must flee!"

"Where?" Simon snapped. "He was right – we are trapped."

"No, he's not," Reuben insisted. Looking to the sky, he offered a quick prayer to the Maker for guidance, then hugged his still-numb brother.

"Follow me," the older one said with confidence. Then he threw himself off the terrace.

Startled, the hawks sailed down in pursuit. That angered me, for I did not want them to abandon Simon like that, but I guess they had no choice. They watched Reuben plunge into the depths of the cold, dark pond. Waves splashed up, then rippled outward.

The birds circled, waiting for Reuben's emergence, but the spreading rings only grew smaller. Then a second force collided with the waters. The surprised hawks dove to see Simon's tunic disappear beneath the shocked surface.

Neither lad returned.

Chapter 8

Confrontation

I saw them emerge from a dank, leaking pool just outside Samaria's outer wall. Reuben first broke its muck-pocked surface, gasping hard for breath, followed by Simon clutching a desperate, gagging Rachel. He pulled her struggling form onto the scarred earth and upheld her until Rachel's liquid coughs stopped and her breaths came easier. That's when she thrust him away with foul-sounding mumblings. He let her fall to the earth, where she lay sobbing in exhaustion. Only then did my bondmate drop to the torn soil. He rested a moment, then lifted his eyes to his brother.

"You knew of this?" Simon wondered aloud, his tone one of awe and praise.

"Guessed," Reuben answered.

"How?"

"When we walked the flocks in," he said in short, sputtering takes, "I saw – you did, too, I know! I saw they had filled many of these ditches – these pits here – and the ruts, the troughs… the Samaritans filled them with mud." He held up an arm to watch the sludge drip from his skin. "Water, that is. But I couldn't, could not see where the runoff came from. So, I figured it had to draw from somewhere in the city, or above it."

"Yes! I should have realized that."

"Yes. And yet, as we walked along those streets, we passed no creeks… no running water at all. And when we reached the fields, I saw only one stream coming down the peak. It wound across that field and filled several ponds before it flowed into Samaria."

The woman struggled to her feet, muttering angry words over and over while flinging sticky muck from her arms and hair. Unbalanced by all that, she tumbled back to the earth with a pitiful groan. Her frustrations then burst forth anew as she noticed the many gemstones missing from her clothing, the soddy tangles in her hair, and other such disasters from their plunge. The brothers stopped for a moment to hear this, but otherwise ignored her, which surprised me. Rachel was handsome, even when covered with soaked cloth and soil. But why Simon would risk his life to capture a strange female, I will never know. It should have been the other way around.

My bondmate was the first to stand upright; as against Seth, his strength returned oh so quick. But his brother was not far behind.

"When we escaped those soldiers," continued Reuben, "and we reached that tower, I saw that pool and how it lined up with the slopes and walls beneath us. We had a pretty good view from all that way up there, and yet I couldn't see a canal or stream anywhere around. Nothing seemed to feed that pool, outside the one stream we saw rolling from the fields. It must have reached that pond, but it just ended. And I couldn't see any place else for that water to go. So, I figured it must escape under the walls. That had to be the source – the water source, I mean – for all those traps, those pools they made outside Samaria. Or some of them, at least."

"That pond?"

"What else? These things had to be connected, it seemed to me. They must have diverted the water under these walls, at least for now, with the Assyrians coming. Most likely they used an old outlet for flooding, when that ever happens."

Simon stood there a moment, marveling at his brother.

"So… you just jump in, thinking you could swim through."

"Why not?" Reuben allowed himself a delightful grin. "It works that way in those caves you love. You taught me that! And

I figured, if I was right, that pond had to be deep. Enough to jump into, anyway."

Simon laughed. "That was one good guess!"

"Well, we didn't have much choice," Reuben reasoned, dismissing the little pride I perceived in his eyes and voice. "I figured, even if I was wrong, we would be off the tower. To be honest, in the back of my mind, I figured a city like this must have several such ponds to provide enough water for all these people. We probably just didn't see them."

The woman chuckled in scorn. That drew Reuben's gaze. His tone grew cold.

"Why bring her?" Reuben asked his brother.

Simon tried to turn that aside. "Had to. She saw us leave."

"You had to?" Reuben rubbed his toes, then stepped out of the mud and stretched. "All she could have seen was two men diving to their deaths."

Simon gave an awkward shrug and changed the subject. "Let's find our fathers."

Reuben stood still. "And her?"

"We take her along. Otherwise, she may see where we go. Give us away."

"They will see us from the parapet soon enough, if they haven't already. We'll be dodging arrows by midday. After that, their riders."

"Then we better get going."

I must admit, little they said made much sense at that time until the word "riders" registered in my heart. Then I remembered how I sat in muck just outside that imposing human city, the sun arcing for its midday point. Samaria's swift horse soldiers would soon rampage down my tracks, with the Assyrians not far behind.

A more stupid predicament I could not conceive.

Swearing under his breath, Reuben tried shaking the mud and water from his tunic, but the futility of that led to a frustrated sigh and the decision to start walking south. Simon watched him take his first steps, then bent to pick up the princess. She slapped his face. He ignored her, so she hit him again, a solid blow that gave his jaw a firm shift in its sockets.

"Don't touch me," she spat, or tried to, before his strong hand sent her reeling. She lay there, nursing her left cheek until he approached a third time. Then she kicked him hard.

You must give Simon credit. The human stood there, stiff from that painful blow, not saying a word. Surprised, the female and I both waited for him to act. The difference was I foresaw the catlike speed with which he scooped her up. Bracing her arms against her sides, he secured the lady against his chest and started tracing his brother's steps, all before she understood just what he had accomplished. She shook her torso in protest, and when that failed to get her loose, she focused on her voice.

"Put me down!" she snapped. "I said put me down!"

The shepherd made no answer.

"Let me go!" the princess screamed. "You cannot touch me! The king will cut off your arms for this!"

Simon started to run.

Aggravated to a fury, Rachel started screaming for her freedom, all the while mixing in more foul-sounding things than I had ever imagined. Only when I sensed her throat aching, and she realized she had to conserve her voice, did some rationality enter her thoughts.

"Why did you take me?" she questioned. "Why?"

When Simon still ignored her, she repeated herself. He remained quiet, jumping over a pit in pursuit of his brother. Angered, she cursed.

"Do not abuse the Lord's name," Simon warned her.

"Finally! You can talk!"

"When I must."

"What does that mean?" When Simon still didn't answer, she spat, "Do you always ignore those you kidnap? Or is it just me?"

He smiled, which she despised.

"Answer me!" she howled.

Simon skipped over some rocks, glanced at her stern face, then muttered, "I would rather not."

Those words seemed to surprise her. Seeing this, my bondmate muttered, "It scares me, talking to you."

Her face twisted as if she might laugh, but then the princess recognized he meant what he said. That's when her eyes spread wide in astonishment.

"I scare you," she pondered.

"No, not that. Well, maybe a little. But I… I am just afraid I might not speak right. In front of you." When she scoffed, Simon added, "My grandfather often says: 'Opening my mouth increases the chance I'll say something stupid.' That's what I mean." He paused to catch his breath, or his thoughts, before adding, "I don't want to say anything that might hurt you. I do not want you to think badly of me."

It took a few breaths for her to grasp this, but as the words took root, she warmed with a hesitant smile. Simon did not see it, focusing instead on the path. Picking careful spots for each hard footfall, my bondmate charged full stride several steps, then leaped across a dark, deep rip in the earth. Rachel cringed in his grasp, fearful of tumbling into that dank crack, but Simon achieved a gentle landing on the other bank without losing a step.

I saw then what the hawks must have witnessed in the city – a reluctant admiration reflected in her eyes, on her brow.

"Wow," she whispered. "That was well done."

Pleased, Simon picked up his speed to reach Reuben, then pass him. The older brother soon matched that pace, which carried them past a ragged crest where the fortress walls turned east. There, across the horizon, awaited their fathers and four camels.

"So… Jonathan kept his word," remarked Reuben, falling a step behind his brother. The princess turned her gaze upon the older one, only to look away when she drew his stern eye. Reuben chuckled, which annoyed her even more. Then that anger changed to astonishment. Pulling herself up in Simon's arms, she pointed behind them and shouted, "A lion!"

I knew I was getting careless, running in the open like that, but I figured I had no choice. Had I gone straight west, or south, escaping the city and its damaged fields by the most direct courses, I might have lost Simon and his family. Still, all this climbing and chasing had brought sharp, stinging pains in my legs, and my footing grew less sure. I dropped to the earth when she spied me, thankful for an excuse to rest.

Her alarm did not move Simon. "Quiet," he whispered as he pressed on.

"He's gone!" she marveled. "Just like that – he's gone."

"Not now."

"Did you see all that hair? I've never seen a lion with a mane like that!"

"Be quiet!" Simon snapped.

From the scowl on her face, I could see she was not used to taking commands. Or perhaps that hatred reflected who gave that order.

Reuben glanced back, then hurried to catch up.

"Surprised they have not seen us," he whispered, though I did not understand what he meant. "No horns, no shouts, nothing."

His brother offered no reply, his eyes focused on their fathers. Reuben matched his resolve, and so the brothers sprinted forth, stride for stride, until they reached the pitted and scarred roadway just beyond the main gate. I caught up with them by slogging through a newly carved gully that meandered quite close to their point.

As I expected, Reuben embraced his fathers at their reunion. Simon nodded their way, then tossed the female down to examine the camels – some of the strangest four-legged contraptions I've had the "pleasure" to eat, which is not often if I can help it. "Warm flesh is good flesh," Seth liked to say, but in my aging, I find almost anything chews better than those desert mumps. But enough of that. Smiling at Simon's attentive mind, the older shepherds turned to Rachel, not knowing what to do. She frowned at their stern gaze and turned away, yet made no effort to flee. Sliding down beside a shallow puddle, the woman spouted more harsh words while swishing what water she could find over her feet. She kept her eyes on Simon as he examined the hooves, eyes, teeth, and hides of each mount. He then ran his fingers over their bridles and looked under their blankets, expressing surprise at their cleanliness and little wear.

"They will do," he decided.

"They're a gift of Jonathan," said Elon, though his attention remained on the woman.

"May the Lord bless such an honest man," Gilead remarked. "Still, I would rather walk. Camels can shake the bones right out of you."

"We need their speed," Simon said.

"You look better," Reuben told his fathers.

Elon smiled, his beard fluttering in the breeze. "The captain released us once we reached that gate. Said he regretted our treatment but thought it necessary."

The sheik looked first to Simon, then Reuben. When neither spoke, he drew upon his authority and asked, "Who is this woman?"

"We had better leave," Reuben said. "The Assyrians come."

Following the lad's gaze, I saw dust from the horde closing upon the eastern slopes. In the soil I could feel their pounding steps. The winds carried the bloodlust of their mounts. It mixed with their warrior songs and drums to chill my heart. The earth wept at their approach.

Elon stood his ground. "Who is this woman?"

"The wall guards will notice us soon," Reuben added.

Their father brushed that aside.

"There are none here," he said. "Only the eastern walls are manned. The others rest and wait." He strode past the girl, burning her with his eyes, and took Simon's shoulder. "Who is she?"

Ending his examination of the camels, Simon embraced his father, then stepped away.

"I do not know," he said.

Elon softened at the simple honesty in that statement, studying first the face of Simon, then Reuben, and finally the girl. To my surprise, this drew forth kindness in her eyes, if but a moment.

"Then why did you bring her?" Elon pondered.

"She saw us escape," Reuben pointed out as two bored mounts reclined on the sandy earth. "We had to bring her, to keep her quiet."

"A beautiful child," said Gilead. Welcoming her in the Lord's name, he apologized for her treatment and expressed sorrow for not having a dry blanket to offer her. Reuben suggested she use a camel's riding blanket, which drew a bitter sneer.

Gilead accepted this with grace.

"I take it drowning did not still her tongue?" he asked Reuben.

The young man laughed. "We had to swim under the wall to escape. Through the channel they used to fill these traps. We may be filthy, but it got us out of there."

Elon considered this, then hesitated as if divided on what to do.

"You were lucky they remained open," Gilead said. "The Samaritans will soon close those outlets before the Assyrians arrive."

The sheik turned his cautious eyes upon the woman and asked, "What is your name?"

That brought a smile to her lips. Perhaps she recognized his authority… that would make sense for someone born into power. Whatever drove her, the beautiful one straightened her back, her eyes glowing, and answered with pride. "Rachel, daughter of King Hoshea and Samantha, his most beloved wife."

"The princess!" Elon whispered.

"Hoshea's only daughter," Reuben said, speaking what they all must have thought.

She nodded with grace, but her eyes remained on Simon. My bondmate met her stare without pretense.

"A strange twist," Gilead reflected.

"Strange?" Elon spun in anger towards a camel. "Abominable!"

"We'd best depart," Simon advised, even as his father looked to the heavens and wondered aloud, "Why, Lord? Why?"

"Question not our fate," Gilead scolded. But Elon did not listen. Taking his seat on the back of the largest humped wonder, he whistled that wheezing mound to its feet. The creature responded as one trained well. The others soon followed.

"We have little time," Elon warned. He watched the others each pick a mount, Simon having the passive woman sit before him, then growled, "We will drop her off at the first haven we find."

Rachel offered not one word of protest, even when Simon put

his arms around her to take the reins of that smelly beast. He soon led their four camels into the mountains of Ephraim as the sun rolled into the afternoon. They pushed hard, pausing only when they regained the heights of Samaria's southern foothills. There the Judeans rested, to my weary delight.

As I fell into the soft grass, my back to the full sun, I watched Simon lead their small group into the shallow dip of a circular crest. There the four men inventoried their remaining provisions. Outside of their slings and Simon's water horn, the brothers had lost all but their soggy tunics in Samaria. Thanks to Jonathan, their fathers retained their slung pouches and staffs along with one full water skin. Elon also claimed a water horn, although it was nearly empty. They gave thanks for this, which surprised me, although I should have expected it. As shepherds, they usually lived off the land while traveling, just as I do. Simon and Reuben scouted their refuge for workable staffs but found no suitable tree limbs.

Rachel used this time to bemoan all the jewels washed from her wraps. The shepherds smiled at this, giving thanks when she relented. Even so, I sensed they pitied her, for they prayed the Maker would uphold her in whatever hardships lay before them.

"We could all use this," Gilead added before giving thanks.

Deciding everyone needed a moment to rest, Reuben and his fathers drank from Jonathan's water sack and spoke of odds and ends, their plight through the city, the loss of their flock, and hopes for the women they had sent home. Each one cast straying eyes upon Rachel from time to time, as if hoping their words might pry loose the princess's distant thoughts. But her silent gaze remained on the crest overlooking Samaria, where Simon sat in the shadows of an obstinate granite boulder, watching their spent trail for pursuit. While everyone regained their breath and composure, putting into words all the curiosity that burned their thoughts, he remained still, vigilant. I watched and waited, my paws keeping pace with what moved around us. Thus I knew what transpired when Simon spoke one thing: "There."

Reuben responded at once, sprinting to his brother's side. Cresting the hills framing the eastern horizon reared a few

Assyrian horsemen, the first claw of Sargon's army. From its dust echoed thousands of chariot wheels scorching the earth.

"It has begun," Simon whispered.

"Samaria will not survive this time," Reuben thought aloud.

Horns rang from the Israelite capital. Angry shouts roared from the eastern walls. Crimson banners unfurled in the shallow breeze to drape the gateway towers.

"Proud Hoshea," Reuben said with both admiration and pity. "He knows Sargon will not relent."

The main gates swung open. The first wave of the Royal Host, twelve of Hoshea's finest black corsairs, bounded into the wind against the gravel road, undaunted by the hazards marring their path or the coming waves of death.

"I don't believe it," Reuben whispered, leaning forward. The beautiful horses inspired his awe, charging against the sun in rich purple riding pads. "He can't mean to contest the Assyrians outside his walls!"

"Wait," Simon cautioned, even as their companions came to see what moved the older son. "Do you not recognize him?"

The horns blasted once more, and the gates crashed shut. To my surprise, the twelve horsemen continued alone, racing not against the Assyrians but towards us. The lead rider held aloft a silver sword blazing in the sun. His long brown hair flowed unrestrained in the breeze.

The princess came to rest a step behind Simon, looking over his shoulder with a soft, triumphant smile.

"The captain," Reuben muttered in sudden recognition.

"What?" Elon snapped.

Simon turned to Rachel with a face both chill and uncaring.

"Did you think he would abandon Samaria like this, in its time of need?" Simon put to her. But she did not answer, her eyes locked upon the approaching horsemen.

As she watched, the pride that had filled her faded away.

"They come for her," Reuben realized, rising to his feet. "We must leave."

"Into the crags," ordered their father. "Simon, lead us."

Together they looked over their camels one last time. The

woman glanced first to the spires of her home, then to Simon.

Strange, I saw indecision in her eye.

"You think you can outrun them?" she wondered.

Simon lifted her onto the camel's broad back. Rachel did not resist. Slipping behind her, he chose a path into Ephraim's rough interior.

"They will not travel where we go," he said.

When the shepherds passed far enough ahead, I followed.

Chapter 9

Bathing

Simon seemed determined not to rest before reaching Judah. That nearly killed me. As the carved moon neared the top of the sky, my pads screamed each time they settled upon the earth, and even the least used of all my muscles threatened to cramp. Many did. May the Maker forgive me, for I endured pain enough to forego this destiny, had I any real choice in the matter.

The lad led us southeast into the bowels of Ephraim, choosing little-traveled passages in deep, overgrown valleys or narrow channels between limestone outcroppings. Though we saw no sign of Samaria's warriors, evading settlers proved difficult. Several times Simon circled around terraced farms, though once he crossed a well-maintained field to avoid hitting a road. Twice my bondmate backtracked to bypass clustered homes.

Such was his design. Simon would have traveled on through the second night from Samaria, the woman sleeping against his chest, had his father not signaled an end. Which was good, for my paws burned and my throat felt covered in dust.

"The Sabbath," Elon called with a soft voice.

No one responded, but I think all understood this warning. As the crescent moon peaked, Simon found a cove within a similarly shaped ridge of brittle rock that seemed hidden from just about everything. Within its walls they camped, their camels left to lie down behind its entrance. I curled up in warm sand just above their heads and watched what followed.

Sharing water and fruit found along their way, Gilead led the shepherds in giving thanks to the Maker, whom they called The Lord. The female Rachel sat outside their circle, partaking in their food but not their worship. Indeed, the princess seemed confused by this acknowledgment of Him, though she offered no substitute. When the men finished, Simon took a seat in shadows at the mouth of their inlet, keeping watch on their camp while the others rested. Rachel chose that moment to approach him.

"We passed a stream just over that hill," she said with short, choppy speech. I could not tell if this betrayed her weariness, caution, or distrust – all three, I suppose.

Simon nodded, his head but a shaggy, pale form in the dim moonlight. The woman waited as if expecting more. When nothing came, she blurted out, "I wish to bathe."

"Why?"

It was a simple question, spoken with honest innocence, but her ire rose nonetheless.

"So I will not smell like you!" she exclaimed.

If that bothered my bondmate, he did not show it. Simon made but one reply: "You will not run?"

"Would it do any good?"

"I doubt it, though I am not The Lord."

She hesitated. "You wouldn't stop me?"

"Would you tell anyone where we are?"

"At my first chance!"

"Then I will stop you."

Her response taught me something. With one dismissive glance at Simon – or, at least, upon what her weak human eyes could make out in such pitiful light – she tossed back her hair and strode down the embankment. She never looked back, though from her measured stride, she must have expected Simon to stop her at any moment.

He didn't.

Her sense of freedom increased as she walked past a natural wall of stones to gaze upon the shallow brook. Emboldened by that precious sight, Rachel ran to a sandy pool where the gurgling waters rested. There she waded in, both chilled and purged by the cold stream. She rolled in the light waves, rinsing her hair and clothes with the wholesome liquid. Milky white in the moonlight, her lithe form seemed at home in the brook. When content, the princess lay still, a natural island in the stream, until a distant hawk split the night with its challenge. Only then did she seem to realize her opportunities. Gathering herself up, Rachel struggled into her wet undergarments and cloak – always a strange sight, watching humans wrap themselves in such things – and waded into the grass to slip on her sandals, pausing first to beat off the last clinging soil. Her head glanced about as she wrung out her hair, her eyes glowing with hope. Finally satisfied with whatever moved her thoughts, she ran headlong towards the vale.

Simon awaited her atop a lone boulder just beyond a crest. Focused on her backward gaze, the princess almost ran into him.

"Damnation!" she cursed, accepting her capture with a frustrating halt.

Simon made no reply as he dropped to her side, which increased her anger.

"You watched?" she spat, folding her arms across her chest.

"No. You are not mine."

That surprised her. "Then how did you know I was here?"

"I have ears."

"But how did you know I'd come down this side of the stream?"

"Your soles are of fine leather, so I suspected you would wish to save them from another dip in the water. That encouraged you to get out where you entered the pool."

That spurred her to swear, which brought a wily grin on Simon's lips. He offered her a wool blanket but she shoved it away, angered he would ever think of wrapping her within a camel's pad.

"I shook it first," he said.

"And the fleas?"

"Fleas, hairs, they're all gone. I hope."

Those last two words slipped out as he placed the sheet about her shoulders and led her back to their camp. The whole scene amused me… with two holes, that cloth could double as a human's tunic! But then I looked anew at Simon's worn clothing and realized that might explain many things.

The princess seemed to soften as she yanked the warm cloth tight around her form. Her brow relaxed, and her eyes calmed. She looked at his patient face, which remained ever glued to His horizon, and allowed a brief, fleeting smile.

"Why give me this?" she asked with a nod to that blanket.

"You may get cold."

"Why would that bother you?"

"You are of our Lord."

Flaring her shoulders, she acted rebuffed, defensive.

"I am nothing to you," Rachel whispered.

"We are all of The Lord."

"I know nothing of your god."

"Then you must learn."

They passed by the pool where Rachel had cleansed her form, and perhaps her worries. Her voice turned bitter. "How could you care anything about me? You abducted me!"

He shook his head.

"No?" she scoffed. "Then how did I get here?"

Simon pivoted to stare into her eyes. By her fluttering lashes, her steady stance, his move did not alarm her. Indeed, his speed probably impressed her.

He made one direct inquiry: "Would you have told your soldier friend how we escaped?"

She hesitated but a moment before nodding. "Benjamin was there. I would have had no choice."

"That's your answer, too. I had no choice." He started once more for their camp, yet said between steps, "Still, I did not steal you."

"No?" She rushed to keep pace, forgetting perhaps how she had sought escape moments before. "He wouldn't agree."

Again my bondmate stopped, driving his heels deep into the earth. "What is he to you?"

"My betrothed," she said, stumbling in both form and thought at that unexpected question. "Father chose him."

Even to someone sitting a fair distance away, smelling her

breath, her fresh sweat, listening to her heart flutter, her speech floating upon a helpful breeze... in all these signs, her repressed fears were as clear to me as all those twinkling lights in our night sky. Simon also noticed these reservations but did not press them.

"He pursues you when your city needs his sword," said the lad.

"He's trying to save me!"

"So am I."

Those short, gentle words unlocked something within her. Drawing alongside Simon, taking his left arm with hands pressed by concerns, she turned him about and said, "From what?"

His eyes met hers, revealing his open, patient heart.

"A doomed city," he told her in soft, faithful tones. "Unwanted passions. Your own blindness."

They stood still, staring at one another, taking measure of their resilience, their souls. His cheeks twitched in the chill breeze. Her scarf fell from her head, revealing her face to him in all its splendor. She wet her lips, then drew several fluttering hairs from her eyes.

I crept forward, curious at this. Their gaze remained locked, their hearts coming together, their wills closer than a physical embrace. I wonder if either one noticed Reuben's somewhat quiet approach, or his fond smile. I doubt it.

"The Sabbath," came his soft reminder. When neither moved, he repeated himself twice.

With the third interruption, Simon broke contact. He looked to Reuben, then the female. With a slow, withdrawn sigh, my bondmate entered their cove.

Reuben took Rachel's arm as she tried to follow Simon.

"We go to pray with the morning's first light," he said. "You may join us, if you wish, but sit well behind us and do not linger."

"What?"

"You cannot stay long."

"Why not?"

"You must prepare our food."

"Me?" Anger flashed from her tongue. "You dare –"

Reuben maintained his patience.

"We have gone four – no, five – five days without a good meal. You may prepare us one."

Indignant, she threw her shoulders back and laughed. "I am a princess of Israel! Not a servant!"

"You are with us now," Reuben reminded her. But she was not daunted.

"That can be changed," she told him.

Meeting her gaze with a gentle smile, he whispered, "May our Lord's will be done."

There, beside a limestone boulder just inside the entrance to that narrow canyon, Reuben left her. And there she stood, hungry but defiant, when they emerged from a morning of prayer.

Accepting this in silence, the shepherds decided not to travel that day. Perhaps this, too, was to honor the Maker. Simon and Reuben took turns watching different approaches to their camp, relieved by Elon and Gilead from time to time. When resting, they sat in discussions I could not hear. But this I learned: never again did they ask the princess to perform such a task, though to my surprise, she later volunteered her services, even when she apparently did not know what she was doing. But it little mattered, for like Simon, from that Sabbath morn I too had fallen in love with her.

Why, I do not know. Harboring such feelings for Simon made no sense to begin with, but to share such heartstrings with a human woman, and a strong-willed one at that... believe me, it has not happened since. But with Rachel, my love was real, vibrant, and fulfilling. And I thank the Lord for it.

Chapter 10

Escape

That next day remains an odd pinnacle in my life. I still struggle to explain it. The attractions of that woman, the beauty of Simon, the strain of the chase… all these strange, disturbing charges echoed through me like rolling thunder. They agitated my mind, and to be honest, somewhat excited me. And as our escape progressed, I found myself getting far more involved in these endeavors than I ever expected or wanted. The emotions spread throughout my flesh until, at some abrupt moment, I became part of it. I started thinking of these five humans on the run as "we" instead of "they." From the beginning I had identified with Simon, but never the rest. Then things changed, and with a swing of my tail, I joined them, in my mind at least.

It remains a strange, uncomfortable sensation, picturing myself as, well, a human. Weird – and unsettling. Somewhat sickening, actually.

Perhaps it was destiny, for our – their – troubles began in earnest that day.

Emerging from morning prayer to a bright sky, the five had just mounted their camels when a low, moaning horn echoed from the eastern peaks. Recognizing that signal, Elon directed them into a series of chasms heading the opposite way.

"Makes little sense," Reuben offered. "We passed but one road, and it led to Shechem. It should be in Assyrian hands."

"Must be," Simon agreed.

"So how did one of Hoshea's men get east of us?"

They had no real answer for that. Elon suspected the horse soldiers may have circled around their camp on the Sabbath.

"Not that it matters," he reminded us. "However it happened, they are there."

That spurred Simon to pick a southwestern course, choosing the unknown peril over the Israelis. The princess worked with him, agreeing to whatever he asked, which helped everyone get by, for passing unseen along these trails required all their diligence. Rough and winding, this route slowed our travel as it increased our efforts. The terrain seemed to disapprove of these humans, rising and falling at a whim, the trails often turning every which way except what they wanted, sending rocks to tumble across their dusty paths and dislodge loud, angry birds from their nests. Such things frustrate weary souls. Reuben considered the unrest a reflection of their anxiety, but Simon feared it was more than that. Twice he motioned all to stop, looking and listening for signs of pursuit, though Elon ever waved him on. I understood the elder's haste, for I also heard nothing. But as the day came to its close, we found before us a valley with many tilled fields, its channels running south between high limestone ridges. That, to Simon, was the worst possible turn.

"We dare not enter the open hills," Reuben agreed.

"Have we much choice?" their father said. "At this rate, it will be winter before we reach Judah."

"Wait," urged Simon.

We waited. I welcomed it, for these rocks bruised my pads, and the dust clogged my nose and made me sweat far more than I wished, but Elon grew ever impatient in his desire to move on. Just as he pushed again to leave, they heard the horn. This time it was high-pitched, rippling in the breeze. From across the valley came a low, pulsing answer.

"Quick!" shouted Simon. "Follow me!"

He chose a sharp climb through twisted, broken rock, one the camels approached with care. Simon's mount suffered the greater hardship, managing two bodies on its back, but my bondmate gave his servant no rest. After topping the high crest, Simon sent his dank beast down a sandy channel to a dark, narrow cut in the rock. Shadows fell upon the rough surface, making footings difficult, but their mounts crossed through without accident. That's where they finally rested, in a shallow bowl of stone, though Simon and Reuben soon crawled back up the crag to watch their path. Across the fields they spied two members of the Royal Guard emerging atop a western slope. Within the valley they saw another pursuer racing from the south on a black stallion.

Not one followed the shepherds' trail.

"We were lucky," Reuben whispered.

"For now," Simon agreed, "but father is right. At this pace we will never reach Judah. They will catch us at their leisure."

"You see any alternative?"

"The valley." Simon took a deep breath as if reconsidering his words. "We rest here, then go back once they have moved on. Perhaps we can catch them in a blind spot."

"Between scouts," Reuben said, considering it. "It could work."

I knew not what to think of that. Elon disagreed with their suggestion. Though moments before he had been itching to hurry, their near miss renewed his caution. The sheik now wished to distance us from the horse soldiers. When his sons bowed to this, we resumed our travels with the night, heading along a deep, winding path that, to our regret, provided no suitable outlet but the valley we had sought to avoid.

Girding their tensions, the elders drew everyone together and led them into prayer. That lasted a while, but it proved worth it, for conversing with the Maker renewed their peace and restored some unity. At the sun's rise, Elon agreed to risk crossing the tilled lands.

This concerned me, for the morning brought a clear sky. Any eyes atop these high ridges could see across great distances, and our tall camels would stand out whether walking or running across this valley floor. I had not felt so vulnerable since I navigated those manmade scars in the earth outside Samaria. But

my fears proved false, and our passage uneventful. Elon took
heart at the Maker's fortune while Gilead basked in fond
memories of this vale's lovely details.

"Best pasture I've seen this way," he commented more than
once, praising its creeks, pools, terraced fields, and shady groves.
In time this spurred Rachel to say, "Is that why you came up
here?"

Those words, her first significant offering since her bath,
caught everyone off-guard.

"We usually summer in Israel, or even farther north," Elon
answered once the shock of her speech wore off. "Over the last
six years, the markets here have paid more for our wool and
flocks than have other markets."

"We just overstayed our welcome this year," Reuben offered
with a smile.

"But how," she wondered, considering these things, "how did
you end up in Samaria?"

Reuben laughed. "Prisoners of our stupidity. We believed one
of Hoshea's captains would pay us if we delivered our flock to
their hands."

"As they ordered us to," Elon added.

Her cheeks flushed. "They refused?"

"Unless you consider forced labor and chipped swords proper
payment," Reuben said with a stiff smile. "Yes, they refused.
Simon and I were looking for a way out when we, well, found
you."

Shamed by this, Rachel retreated into her silence, her eyes
withdrawn, her brow wrapped in self-condemnation. At one point
Simon tried to nudge her into a conversation, but she resisted.

As the night fell, Simon spied a stretch of worn soil crossing a
valley opening just before us. After debating our options with the
others, he led their camels forward. It took many anguished
approaches before that trail lay at our feet. We stopped as Simon
dismounted to examine the grounds.

His report startled them.

"Are you sure?" one of the elders wondered aloud; I do not
remember who.

I leaned forward to better hear this expert tracker explain the signs he found in our setting darkness. The fact that I had already made the same conclusions did not make his logic less attractive.

"The prints are true," Simon said, kneeling in the sandy, night-shrouded roadway. Taking care to not block the moon's light, he pointed to varied hoof prints going in all directions. "There are few signs of traffic – a donkey pulling a cart, a man walking, taking his time. Some wildlife." Simon straightened his back, choosing his words with care. "A single horse has passed by three times since the midday… heading first to the east –"

"The Shechem road," Reuben told them. "Towards Jerusalem."

"– then the west, then back east," Simon continued. "He paused each time, first atop the left hilltop, I would think, then to our right, and the last time here."

"How long ago?" Elon said.

"Not long. Less than a day."

"Then he will return before sunrise," Reuben guessed.

"Yes," Simon agreed. Then he shifted his stance, his eyes still on the road. "Possibly."

"You see more?" Gilead wondered.

"Another rider." His words cooled. "Not one of Hoshea's men."

"How can you tell?" Rachel cut in, gazing down from Simon's patient camel.

"The shoes," he explained. "They're different; better made. Its gait is wider and more regular. Deeper. A larger horse, more seasoned. A stallion, I would think, like the nomads ride, most likely… a true bloodline." He glanced at his fathers, but neither spoke. Not that they had to – I know what they feared. "He also was here since midnight."

"We better move," Reuben urged.

Elon hesitated. "Perhaps we should find a retreat just off the path to wait and rest ourselves. Our trail could give us away."

"That it already has," Simon stated. "We have mixed our marks here, atop the rest. Whether we cross or not no longer matters."

"We shouldn't have left the crags," their father reflected. "I am sorry."

"No, you were right. We needed faster movement." Simon steadied his mount and swung up before Rachel. "They are timing us, with riders at each road."

"Driving us," Reuben observed.

"True enough." Simon kicked his camel to begin. "With skill. By now, they have two riders behind us, at least as many before us, and I would guess there are three at either side. If we don't go forward, they will contain us."

"It makes little difference," Elon mumbled. "Their trap will spring when they see this."

"Then we will trust in our Lord," Gilead told them, "and go on. His will be done."

That's how we ended our fourth night from Samaria – on our feet, holding back our fears with each step. By morning I felt so weary I doubted I could continue. All told, it was just over a week since Seth had fallen and this endless journey began. A week and a half, perhaps. As I lay atop a cool slab of limestone, absorbing the emerging sunlight, my limbs felt numb from exertion and my footpads screamed in constant pain. But I was not alone in this. Gilead was short-tempered and ready to drop, while his son fell ever deeper into regret at forcing his family through such a trial. And the female, confused by her emotions, often spat bitter venom a poisonous viper would have difficulty matching, although she released this more against herself than the shepherds.

It fell on the brothers to push their group south, even as their pursuers grew ever near. Reuben was a charm, his spirits positive, his insights often extraordinary. I must have underestimated him before – he seems to have a unique ability to reason with his own kind. Simon remained the solid rock, master of himself and his terrain. Even when the gruff camels balked or just stopped, and the woman babbled about stinks or her filthy wraps or bathing or other such things, my bondmate strove on, never bending from his objective, confident in what lay ahead. I have no idea how he achieved this clarity of mind. I doubt his moments of sleep over this entire escapade added up to half a night – yet his focus only sharpened.

The way he selected their paths, I wondered if he knew these trails better than he let on. While I had nothing to pin this suspicion on, it seemed ever more apparent that the more they pressed south, the more he recognized each ridge, grove, and gully.

Now I do not mean to dawdle over him, but honestly, after watching Simon as I have, I cannot help but wonder if ever this world has seen his equal. A stupid thought, I am sure, as many humans as there are or have been, but if his race could claim many such Simons, or even Reubens, then why is it so chaotic?

I can only believe that reflects the rippling wake of Eden.

No matter. I may praise Simon's endurance, but it was that shepherd's stubborn resolve that aggravated most of my wounds. Sometime that night their recurring anguish overwhelmed me, and I dropped to sleep. I suppose it was inevitable, for the Maker knows I age, and with that comes some weakness. I doubt I could have kept pace with them much longer. And sleep proved a blessing. The morning sun found me upon a warm, round rock sticking from the earth, my flesh aching but somewhat refreshed. Across many fields below my platform, I spied my bondmate leading their camels south.

Though these dusty round knobs and grassy vales were easier on my feet and joints than those past stone mounds, my muscles had just about died. And with each breath, I hungered for a real meal, a kill I could snuggle up to and feast upon for a day or more. That would have been oh so good!

As the sun's warmth lulled me to renewed sleep, I drifted off with no regrets. Simon, I knew, would push on. I would just have to catch up as best I could. But the shifting wind brought a nightmare to life: the scent of my kind. I rolled my head up, opening my ears and eyes wide to identify my brethren. The soil told no tales. Neither did the winds. But my heart still held fear, for I could smell their presence... out there. Then came the horn.

It was a shallow blast, high-pitched and hollow. Though it echoed from across the horizon, I knew its origin. Probably everyone did, and if not, the princess soon told them.

"Benjamin!" she exclaimed, twisting on her seat to look back. The road lay behind three rolling hills, but that did not stop her from a futile search for the source of that irritating sound. "That was his own!"

"Why do you care?" Reuben spat.

"He is my betrothed!" she snapped. "Captain of a Thousand – the youngest so honored in all the armies!"

"Is that why you love him?"

"Who spoke of love?" She took one last look at the northern hills, then turned in slow frustration to Simon's sweat-damp back. "I did not say I love him. He is my betrothed. My father paired us."

On that note, I forced myself to shake off these fears and pay more attention to my family. Though it meant rambling down the thorny slope after them, I did not want hesitation to put me in the way of Simon's pursuers.

"Quiet!" my bondmate urged. "Listen."

Their talk ended. I slowed, choosing my steps with care, but I think the woman still saw me. Reuben did, I know, but he said nothing. His cares centered on Simon.

The shepherds pushed on through the day, pausing only to refill their drinking horns or water sacks at a shallow brook. There they got a bit ahead of me, for desperate as I was to stay awake, I followed the woman's heart and rolled in the stream. The sensation was awful, mixing relaxation with frustration, but it did invigorate me.

As I shadowed them anew, Reuben tried to start Rachel in discussions of her betrothed, but Elon curtailed each attempt with a bitter look or command. Simon welcomed that, wishing for silence at all times.

At his father's urging, they left behind the central valley for the rocky steppes of the eastern Ephraim hills.

"That should slow them down," Elon hoped.

"And us," Reuben pointed out.

"Yes," the sheik answered, "but these rocks better suit our camels."

"Perhaps not," Simon cut in. "Our mounts are weary." His father frowned, spurring my bondmate to nod in agreement. "Still, it may not matter, since these ridges force us one way."

"They could be waiting for us at the end," Reuben speculated.

"Then we will change paths," Elon said.

"Over these rocks?" Gilead scoffed, kicking his camel forward to better hear them.

"Dangerous," Simon warned.

"We go west," said Reuben, finishing for his brother, "and probably find Hoshea's cavalry. Go east, and we hit Shiloh."

"Could be worse," Gilead told them.

"I doubt this Captain Benjamin would risk that," Elon reflected.

"You speak foolishness," the princess interjected. "For me, he will risk anything."

"Shiloh," offered Reuben, "has probably been hit by the Assyrians."

"Never!" Rachel snapped. But Reuben was undaunted.

"Do you understand Sargon's power?" He pointed to the sun, now far past the midday point. "For all the time we have fled Samaria, the Assyrian army has marched its troops through the mountain approach to its gates. It will do so for many days to come – the horde is that large. And that is just part of it! Many troops have marched north and south, to secure the land and isolate Samaria. They'll strip food away from every settlement along Ephraim's eastern lands, those they do not destroy, all to feed their men. Who will stop them? Hoshea is holed up in his fortress."

"Not for long," Rachel proclaimed. "He has 10,000 chariots! I have seen them!"

"Not that many," said Simon. "Not even close. Most of those he lost months ago in battles at Aphek, Beth Shan, and Ramoth Gilead. We heard this from your own soldiers."

She quivered at his words, her face displaying honest surprise.

"The Assyrians care not for Israel," Elon growled. "Your father was a puppet of that bastard Tiglath-Pileser."

"Language!" scolded his father.

"Had Hoshea not snapped against Shalmaneser," continued Elon, "had he not stopped those bribe payments, your pretty capital might still thrive. But your father's defiance started your destruction. Sargon will finish it."

"Dare we enter Shiloh?" said Reuben.

"By my heart..." Elon paused as if checking his soul. "On this I would risk all. If we could trade our camels for others, or horses – not pack animals, but fresh stallions – we could sprint south along the road and soon reach our homeland. That is worth the risk, I think."

I did not. Camels were one thing, especially in meandering gorges of broken limestone. But there was no way I could keep up with four steeds galloping down open highways. If they made it through that town they called Shiloh – a place I did not know, or want to know – my role in Simon's destiny was finished.

Of course, that did not concern them, if they even knew about it. One by one, these men agreed with the head of their family.

"And what of Rachel?" Reuben pondered aloud.

Elon looked into her still-shaken eyes. "It depends on what she wants. But," he confided to her, "I would not remain behind. You cannot – must not – trust the Assyrians."

"You speak from experience?" she said, her voice still touched by doubt.

"They are the Evil One's sword," Gilead explained, "and yet they tear at us with The Lord's blessing. Oh, if only Jonah had not reconciled Nineveh! I fear that took away our last hope."

Reuben scoffed. "Don't tell me you believe that story?"

"The Lord still works in our world," their grandfather warned. "Every day He labors for us. Yes, I have heard many people speak of the Dove's tale. The words ring true in my heart. Repentance is indeed blessed."

"Not for Gentiles!" It was Simon who now spoke. "They are murderers!"

"So they would have us believe," Gilead said.

"So they will prove at Samaria," Simon shot back.

With a slow, regretful nod, his grandfather allowed that Simon could be right.

"Fire would have best suited Nineveh, but for Jonah's testimony," he said. "But it was done, and its judgment withheld. The Lord made his choice. Indeed, The Lord sent Jonah, if I remember all of his tale. And now these Assyrians are more vicious than ever."

"You're scaring her," said Elon. Smiling with confidence, the sheik reached over and hugged her shoulder as he might embrace his own daughter. "Consider well your freedom. Should they find out who you are..."

"My freedom," she stammered, a bitter edge sharpening her words. "You make my days sound numbered either way."

"Not so," said Simon, bending back to best speak with her. "We could release you now, within these hills. With The Lord's hand protecting you, you would survive. Or we could release you at Shiloh, where the Assyrians are sure to come, if they have not already. Or you could come with us, to Judah."

"And what," she pondered aloud, "what would await me there?"

"What would you want?"

She looked with warm eyes upon my bondmate, then whispered into his left ear. Laughing, he kicked his mount into a reluctant sprint.

Chapter 11

Disaster

Creeping to the summit, Simon and his family looked across the lazy slope to find Shiloh's outer walls pierced many times. A smoky haze clung to the stone ruins of that once-proud community. Disfigured heads atop blood-stained poles haunted its gates. A dozen or more corpses hung from the citadel's one tower.

"May the Lord have mercy," Simon prayed, even as Elon slapped the earth in anger. Rachel said nothing, her eyes spread wide in horror.

"Sargon," Gilead whispered in sorrow.

I almost turned away, for Shiloh's death throbs made the winds unbearable. Such indiscriminate killing, such wasted flesh… it is an outrage to the Maker! But Reuben, as usual, had his eyes open to opportunities.

"There are no guards, no garrison," he cut in. "They may have gone."

"Or they're dead," said Simon.

"What good is that?" Elon whispered as he turned away. "There can be little left."

"We must make sure," Reuben insisted.

"You dare enter that?" Elon rose to his feet, then kicked his toes into the earth, scattering gravel and splitting his flesh. He stared down at the blood as an atonement for his guilt.

"We dare not give in to fear," his oldest son countered.

Elon did not respond, focusing instead on his bloody toes.

"We must defy these invaders," said Reuben, "if only to redeem those they have slain."

Rachel lay still, as one in shock, her eyes locked onto the mourning scars of what had been Shiloh. Simon slipped a hand about her waist to comfort her. She rested her palm against it, then settled into his grasp, weeping.

"Why?" she cried. "Why?"

"The Lord allows this," Gilead whispered.

She turned up to face him. "What sort of god could do that?"

The eldest accepted her frustration with patience.

"My child, He did not want this to happen. Prophet after prophet He sent among our people, warning those who would listen to repent, to turn from these false gods and heathen practices. But most did not. This is a doom we have brought upon ourselves."

Those words stroked against the grain of my fur. How strange is humankind to defy the Maker, their true Father, even at risk to their lives? Our One God would give His life to save them, yet they forfeit their lives to defy Him. And they call such insanity freedom, or intelligence.

Stupidity is more apt.

"We," Simon echoed, deciding then to stand. The others soon followed him.

"Yes," Gilead muttered. "This awaits Judah as well."

He almost choked, so wounded was his spirit. The woman absorbed their words, then gazed again upon the defiled city.

"But you follow your god!" she said in weak protest.

"We follow the Lord God of Abraham, Isaac, and Jacob," agreed Elon, "Of Moses, David, of our fathers and family. He who led our peoples out of bondage to His land. This land. But many in Judah have turned from Him, just as your people did."

"Our nation will also fall," confirmed Gilead, "if not to the Assyrians, then to some other terror. But if we follow our Lord, He will provide for us, whether we live in exile or captivity. For great is the Lord! All praise His name!"

So awesome was the power of his speech that I expected the

Maker to open the heavens before us! Instead, those words pried open a door even more difficult to reach.

"Your god," stammered Rachel, "he must indeed be special."

"He is God," declared Simon. "There is no other."

She looked into the depth of his heart and nodded. "If that is true, then I must meet Him."

"I will teach you," Simon assured her. "After we search Shiloh."

That last thought horrified me. The winds, the horrid cries, all should have warded us away. But the men seemed determined to fulfill this foul destiny. Sharing a silent understanding, they rode their camels toward the hilltop ruins, picking each step with care.

They did not scan the horizons for watching eyes, which surprised me. Perhaps they thought the risk of entering Shiloh far outweighed meeting their pursuers. Perhaps the stench of decay overwhelmed them. Perhaps Simon just is not perfect after all. Whatever the case, that oversight triggered the trap.

I stayed behind a sharp crest, tucked under a limestone outcropping. I had a clear view and no wish to draw any nearer to that cursed land.

My bondmate and his family approached a hole in the wall away from the gatehouse, avoiding the Assyrians' horrid stakes. Simon was the first to dismount, followed by Reuben, then the others. Rachel came last, tying her facial scarf tight as if to block whatever foul odors she met. That left Gilead alone outside the tumbled walls, watching their camels as Elon managed the difficult passage through the fortress rubble. Simon and Reuben disappeared within the streets.

It did not take long before they returned. They traded terse words with Elon before he sent them to search different paths. Other movements caught my eye. I extended my claws, ready to charge, but then I caught the scent of other humans… scared, wounded, hungry, all emerging in slow, haphazard steps from behind stones, burned walls, buried holes, and other hidden places. Elon met them with a smile, as did Rachel, sharing what little food they had. The victims then retreated to Gilead.

"Survivors of the Assyrian carnage," Elon stammered.

"The Assyrians must have taken everyone else," growled his father.

"Those they did not slay."

That hinted of meanings I could not understand, but the grandfather did.

"Where?" he inquired.

"At the eastern gate." Elon bit his lip. "We must not go there."

Rachel sagged as she shared their water with these beaten, trembling souls. The guilt gripping her heart made these burdens intolerable.

Wise old Gilead also noticed it. "You must not take this horror upon you," he told her. "The Lord will be our avenger."

I heard a menacing thud – as did Elon, who turned to the sound to see his father stumble forward as if pushed. No one looked more stunned than Gilead. He crumbled to the stones about him, not knowing why. Then I saw the bloodied arrow extending from the back of his left shoulder, and I heard his painful cry.

Truly, I never would have thought those dank horse soldiers could surprise me. That attack proved me wrong.

As Elon knelt beside his father, from the north and west emerged five members of Samaria's Royal Guard, two with arrows spent, two primed to fire. They held their bowstrings for a sixth rider who approached unarmed, racing his black stallion toward the shepherds.

Shiloh's refugees fled back into the wreckage. Elon ignored that, turning instead upon the last interloper. Anger filled the sheik with savage power, but I sensed similar fury in the rider, though he shielded his face beneath a black headwrap bound with gold braids. Calling his mount to a halt, the brash man leaped from his saddle to pin Elon against the rocks with a strong left hand. His right drew a polished dagger ready to cut into the shepherd's bearded chin. Elon resisted, but the warriors offered no quarter.

"Stop struggling!" he warned. "Do you wish death?"

Staring into his black eyes, Elon stated, "You will if my father dies."

Rachel rushed to divide them.

"No, Benjamin!" she cried. "Let him go!"

"Stay back, my princess!" the newcomer warned her. Only as the other soldiers dismounted, with seven others riding from the hills, did this Benjamin release his hold on Elon. Two of his men renewed it.

This time the sheik did not struggle, though his defiance remained. "Help him!" Elon demanded for his father.

Rachel was already there, holding Gilead's head as the elder struggled to probe his own wound.

Her weeping eyes flared with hate.

The Israeli captain seemed to measure the old man with his gaze before ordering the arrow removed. As his men bent to the task, Benjamin turned to the princess.

"Your Highness, I apologize for being late," he said, his tone bitter. The wind shifted, carrying the wispy smoke through their ranks. Gilead coughed.

"Late?" she exclaimed, throwing her anger at his feet. "Look about you! What of these people? Who will save them?"

"I know not," Benjamin said, taken aback by her rebuke. "I was sent to rescue you. Your father would accept nothing else."

That seemed to soften her – until Gilead groaned as warriors tore the arrowhead from his body. Benjamin eyed the elder with little care, thanked his men, and turned to the ruins.

"There were two others," he told his squad. "Fan out. Find them."

"Why?" the princess demanded.

"Why?" The captain kept his eyes on his ten soldiers entering Shiloh. "To bring them before the king."

"No, Benjamin."

His voice remained hard. "I have no choice. They abducted a member of the royal family."

The princess took his sword hand and held it against her face. "No," she purred. "You must not."

He turned away, revealing a vest of metal scales beneath his cloak. The woven rings sparkled in the sun. That sudden shimmer blinded me for a second.

"Let them go," she said to his back. "They fed me, protected me, even taught me some things." She swung to his right side. "Let them go. Please."

Even from my great distance, I could see she fought a lost cause. Benjamin's heart was not on her but the destruction at his feet. Hatred strengthened the fortress of his resolve far beyond her vast abilities to weaken it.

Still, he did not condemn her. "I cannot" was all he said. That left their party in relative silence, broken at odd times by the whimpers and moans of the wounded. Then the first of Benjamin's fighters returned, followed by another, and two more, their eyes humbled, their ropes empty.

The Israelis waited for more, but no others appeared.

The captain swore to himself, then focused anew on this situation. His determination took root once more.

"Kaleb!" he called. "Saul!"

When the winds overcame his echoes, Benjamin sent the four warriors back in, along with the two who had tended Gilead.

I found myself regretting that foolish move. Not that I expected Elon to do anything rash. Once freed, Simon's father bent beside Rachel to comfort Gilead. But the soldiers, as I expected, had no chance.

One fell before he could climb the rubble, knocked unconscious by a spinning stone impacting his forehead. Another suffered a disabling hit before he made it into the street. The last four members of Benjamin's Royal Guard charged the slinger's likely refuge. I heard signs of commotion, then silence.

Two shepherds emerged, each armed with a new staff.

"Simon!" cried the princess. "Be careful!"

The captain almost stumbled at that, though he soon steadied himself.

"You must be exhausted," Benjamin said, choosing words to awaken but not scold her. Then he drew forth his small sword, one with a base wider than his hand, and faced my bondmate.

"No need for that," Reuben cautioned. The brothers scaled the rubble of that broken wall with care, their staves serving as braces. "We only want some horses."

"No," stated the captain.

One stallion swung his head to the horizon. A hoof stamped against the dry earth, scattering dust into the foul breeze. His nervous jitters spread among the other steeds, their heads bobbing, their tails swatting against the wind.

The humans did not notice.

One camel climbed to his feet, his head glancing about. The others watched this, then decided to join in. That surprised me, as camels thrive in a state of patience, so I hid against the earth and looked to see what could alarm them, all the while condemning my carelessness in not knowing all that happened around me.

To his credit, Simon spied these cautious actions and looked to our horizon. But then he saw Gilead's wounds.

"See to our grandfather," he told Reuben. Simon then faced the captain, his arms crossed, his will blunt.

"We will take five horses," my bondmate decided.

"Five?" Benjamin glanced about, his eyes stopping on the woman as she cradled Gilead's head. That sight brought realization and rage. Spinning to Simon, the captain swore, "Never! None of you will leave – except by my hand."

"Appropriate," came a low, cutting voice. "For I too desire your hand – upon my vest."

Only then did the Hebrews discover themselves surrounded by a tightening circle of at least 30 Assyrian horse soldiers, many with bows primed and aimed at the Hebrew hearts. Upon a black charger came a thick-chested man bound head to foot in leather sheets and iron scales, his scalp topped by a conical helmet of black iron outlined with three stripes of shiny bronze. A wavy charcoal beard hung from his chin to his dagger-studded belt. Against his chest clung a net full of hooks sunk into dark, bloated hands.

"Murderers," Benjamin scowled.

"Guard your tongue," the Assyrian barked, "or I will gouge it out."

Chapter 12

Destiny

The Assyrian chuckled. It sounded like a misshapen growl, twisting up and down in awkward jumps. I hated it.

"Bind their hands," he told his men, his eyes never leaving Rachel. A hungry smile claimed his lips. "The woman is mine."

The shepherds tensed, hearing hostile tones in a language they did not understand, but Benjamin apparently did. The sturdy captain of Samaria's Royal Guard stepped between Rachel and her assailant. Aiming his sword at the chief butcher, Benjamin declared, "You will not have her."

That act of bravery I shall ever remember.

As often happens, such defiance drew a savage response.

A black shaft pierced Benjamin's metal links to lodge in his right shoulder. The captain fell back a step. Rachel screamed. A second bolt, narrower and longer than the first, tore into the Samarian's left breast, knocking him back still more. His face contorted in agony, his brow burning red in his anguish, but his eyes stayed bright. Words struggled from his lips amid bubbles of blood – "You... will... not" – until a singing shaft split his chest bone. Its bloody point emerged from his back.

Benjamin fell to his knees. His eyes dropped in stunned agony to view this last wound.

"Coward!" Simon shouted. "You fear facing him?"

I cringed, knowing what would result. But whether by skill or fate, Simon shifted his makeshift staff to meet the soaring arrow, which buried its jagged head just under the rod's knobby crook. Simon yanked free the shaft and lifted it high above his scalp, all while keeping his eyes locked on the Assyrian leader.

Sargon's chieftain dismounted, then drew his thick broadsword with his right hand. Simon stepped forward to meet him, ignoring shouts from his father and Rachel. But my bondmate stopped when a blood-stained hand grasped his left knee.

"No," Benjamin whispered.

The wounded Hebrew coughed. That shallow, gurgling sound hung in the air. I could hear death's approach, and yet this warrior stayed on his knees, supported by sheer will.

"I saw… saw her love," Benjamin stumbled to say. "For you. I envy you that. She is… she is everything to me."

Snorting like a boar, the Assyrian leader stepped toward them. Benjamin shuddered. His hands fell limp to his sides.

"Protect her," he asked my bondmate.

Simon stiffened as their adversary drew near, but the chieftain shoved him aside to focus on Rachel's betrothed. Simon braced his feet to charge forward, only to feel Reuben's hand on his shoulder, urging caution.

The Assyrian ignored that threat. Focused on Benjamin, the interloper bellowed, "You still defy me?"

A strange look of surprise lit all the Hebrew faces, for the chieftain now spoke their language!

Benjamin struggled to lift his head, but when the effort overwhelmed him, the defiant Israeli spat blood upon his opponent's dusty iron scaling.

I found myself starting to really like this Samarian. The Assyrian also smiled, offering a nod of admiration. But that did not stop him from lifting high his sword to shear off the captain's head.

Rachel screamed as the skull rolled away. Blood gushed from his open wounds, but Benjamin's trunk did not topple.

"A worthy man," the chieftain declared, kicking the corpse aside. "But even the strong must fall before us."

"Then I am next," Simon stated.

"No!" Elon called over Rachel's shrieks and tears.

Simon planted his staff in the earth before the killer. The Assyrian laughed.

Reuben pulled on Simon's shoulder, most likely to turn his brother's gaze from his adversary. It didn't work.

"Wait," Reuben urged. "Not now."

"They are an affront to God!" my bondmate snapped.

Gilead's weak voice startled them.

"Are you God," he said, "that you know His will?"

Simon seemed stricken by that.

"You saw what he did," he muttered.

"All the faith in the world will accomplish nothing without His blessing," their grandfather warned. "It is not His will, this fight. This is His judgment. Let it be."

Rachel fell upon Gilead, sobbing. This diminished Simon's rage a bit. He stepped back, no doubt weighing one word against another, but when the Assyrian leader took another step forward, Simon stood his ground.

"Ah," said the chieftain, chuckling that arrogant chortle of his. "I have heard of this god cult of yours. Indeed, I once met one of your... what was he called? A prophet, I believe. I was but a child then, yet he amused me, parading around Nineveh as he did. Such brazen arrogance! Foolishness, it was. Yes... foolish."

He laughed at his own thoughts, but when no one joined in, the bold one steadied himself.

"Another day, perhaps," he decided. "No matter."

Turning his back to Simon, the commander shouted a new order to his men: "Round them up."

Though spoken in his native tongue, Elon seemed to understand these Assyrian words.

"No," he stated.

The chieftain turned towards our sheik with slow precision, as I might when confronted by a viper, bear, or some other nuisance. Every fixture of this killer's being presented a warning to his enemies. Then he smiled... as vile a look as I have ever seen.

"Do you know what this is?" he said in terms the Hebrews knew well. Holding aloft his thick, bloodied blade, the Assyrian said in honest appreciation, "Damascus steel. A treasure!"

Back and forth he waved the weapon, across his front and over his head, amused as the lingering blood crawled down one path, then another.

"You saw its strength," the chieftain said. He pointed to the headless corpse. "Look! Thick bone it parted as smoothly as the wind does blades of grass, and yet its edge remains sharp, unblemished."

He laughed while slicing imaginary foes, then pulled his blade back, satisfied.

"Yet with the will of Ashur – the true god – even mighty Damascus, the great capital of stubborn Aram, fell before my soldiers." This savage let his words weigh upon their souls before asking, "Do you pitiful Israelis still oppose me?"

"We are not of Israel," Elon told him.

"Then why are you here?" the Assyrian roared, irritated that anyone dared answer him.

"We are traders from Judah," said the sheik. "We were traveling south to our homes when these soldiers stopped us."

"Ah, but you have Hoshea's daughter with you." The chieftain switched his sword to his left hand as he walked to her kneeling form. I saw Simon cringe as the Assyrian ran his thick fingers through her silky hair. She trembled at his touch, almost dropping Gilead, but remained silent.

"That's why they trailed you, is it not?" the chieftain said with a nod to Samaria's fallen warriors. "It's why we did. Oh yes," the Assyrian gloated, "we saw these riders storm out of those gates. We even spied her gown atop one of your camels, though from that distance, we were not sure it was Hoshea's purple. His is a rare one, you know. I wondered how he could afford it… probably left over from old Jeroboam's riches."

The arrogant one wiped his blade against his palm, then slipped its cold metal back into the leather sheath at his left hip. His hand he licked clean.

"When you disappeared into the cliffs – and quite well done, I must say – we had little idea what was going on. But," the Assyrian pointed with acknowledgment to fallen Benjamin, "his stubborn search helped me to stay on your path."

"From the east," interjected Reuben.

"Why not? These lands are ours."

"That is your concern," Elon stated with icy decisiveness. I wonder now just how hard that was to say. "We wish only passage home."

Impatient neighs rolled from Assyrian stallions of all colors and types. Most shook their heads, and some reared. The chieftain sighed as his riders steadied their beasts.

"Yes, my beauties," their leader called to them. "Home! If only it could be." But his face turned cold as he walked before Elon. "My home has been my saddle for five years now, and before that, the soles of my feet. Where is yours?"

"A village north of Jerusalem."

"You have a wife there?"

"I did, once."

"And now she is dead?"

"The Lord has taken her."

The Assyrian paused, looking about as if pleased with Elon, or himself. He waved his hand toward Gilead and the brothers, saying, "This is your father... your sons?"

Elon nodded, cautious, not knowing where this conversation headed.

"You have daughters?" the Assyrian said.

"Three. A fourth died at birth."

"With the mother."

"Yes," Elon whispered.

The chieftain took a deep breath, then let it slide out.

"I see the memory is yet fresh," he said. "I grieve for you. But your family is strong. That is good."

With a snap of his fingers, his soldiers released their hold on Elon.

"Take Hoshea's horses and be gone," the chieftain told our sheik. "As Judah is yet unneeded, I grant you this. I, Ashur-jorath, lieutenant of the First Brigade of Aram. Remember that name! Speak it if any of my men stop you, and if they understand your speech, they will allow you to leave. But you must go south and depart this land. It falls under the crown of Sargon."

"What of Shalmaneser?" wheezed Gilead.

The lieutenant chuckled. "A worthy question, one I didn't expect from you. So, you know of that quarrel?"

"I know," stammered the elder, "that Sargon usurps the throne."

Ashur-jorath hardened. "I serve the rightful holder of our crown. No matter his name."

"What of the princess?" Simon barked.

That drew a pause. The Assyrian glared at my bondmate's impudence, though his eyes soon softened.

"You are indeed bold," the lieutenant told him. "All of you. I like that. But I warn you – take care! Such insolence brings death to most of our prisoners. But I will overlook that now, for your father's sake. As for this woman, she is mine. What I do with her is my concern – not yours."

Sinking his fingers into her rich hair, he took a firm hold and pulled it up, compelling her to her feet. Wincing in pain, she struggled to ease Gilead's fall to the hard soil. Then she turned upon the Assyrian, her eyes blazing in fury.

The chieftain laughed.

"Yes," he said, caressing her with his cruel stare. "Yes! You have the spirit of a goddess! A queen!" He turned to Elon. "There are many uses for one such as this. Who knows what Hoshea will do when he looks down from his citadel and sees her in our hands? Samaria's walls will tremble!"

His words brought bile to my mouth. I looked at the shaken girl, her face wet with tears, and dreaded my decision to stay hidden within these hills. I should have followed Simon into the ruins! Then I would be at his side!

My bondmate rushed the lieutenant, only to be shoved to the earth. He would have fallen there, slain by Assyrian arrows, had Reuben not grabbed his shoulders from behind.

Two soldiers dismounted at a hand signal from the chieftain. He kept his eyes on Simon as the warriors bound and gagged Rachel. Securing her hands before her waist, they stuffed her long hair within her cloak. Then they laid the princess across the lieutenant's horse, her stomach resting before his wolfskin saddle. To hold her steady, the Assyrians tethered her ankles to her wrists beneath the steed's waist.

"Make it tight," the lieutenant called. Then he leaned close to Simon. "I don't want to snag a galloping hoof in her bindings. That could hurt her."

The princess did nothing through this humiliation. But as the soldiers finished their last knot, Rachel could no longer hold back her tears. Maddened, Simon tried a move of cunning to escape Reuben's clench, but his brother's grip held tight.

"You want us all killed?" Reuben whispered.

The lieutenant's cackle turned into a taunting laugh. Mounting his steed, the heel on his right boot clipped Rachel's scalp.

May the Maker forgive me, but I felt that blow in my surging hatred.

Simon writhed once more for freedom, to no avail.

"Have faith!" he shouted to Rachel. "I will find you!"

"Forget her," warned Ashur-jorath. "If I see you again, I will bathe in your blood."

With that, the Evil One's mouthpiece rode north in a thick cloud of dust. The shepherds watched these horse soldiers leave, the wind whistling in their wake. Reuben held his grip until even the foul scents of these Assyrians faded, which lasted far beyond their disappearance behind the horizon. Only then did Simon angrily brush off his brother's hands to stride straight for Benjamin's steed. Introducing himself with a gentle caress, Simon jumped upon this stallion's soft riding mat and secured his staff behind him.

The horse seemed to welcome this.

"I'm going after them," said my bondmate, leaving no room for a challenge.

"I'll go with you," Reuben offered.

"No," Elon snapped to his firstborn. "I need help with grandfather."

Simon nodded to his father's stern gaze, then rode off, sitting in the saddle with all the confidence of a master rider. The stallion first headed east, then north, keeping his scent from blowing toward his prey. I asked the Maker to aid him in this, for in his haste Simon gathered nothing for his trip, not even a water sack.

At that moment all thoughts of pad sores, blisters, and torn muscles left me. Like Simon, I, too, charged after the Evil One's minions. At last, my destiny lay before me, and I welcomed it.

Chapter 13

For Sargon

I recall little of that journey north. Nibbling, drinking, sleeping, praying, hiding… all these things blur in my mind. Keeping out of sight was our chief concern, for Simon more than me. I had the shorter trail upon the mountain slopes and foothills, while Simon had to ride wherever necessary to stay near the princess yet evade the Assyrian sentries. But he was up to the task. I doubt the lieutenant even knew my bondmate stalked him. Simon rarely left my sight from my vantage point in the highlands, but I knew to look for him. These horse soldiers did not.

Keeping pace with the swift-footed cavalry almost killed me. In truth, I had no idea how to do it. A lion will never outrun a horse, and yet I had to remain close, all while staying upon the slopes to keep Simon within my sights. I ran, on and on, as my pads split and my muscles screamed for rest. I focused on Simon, for he needed me. And I prayed.

Bless the Maker, these Assyrians love their horses. With their prisoner secure, these warriors rested long and often in coves of plentiful water and grass along the road. I grabbed each opportunity to curl up in the warm sun, nurse my wounds, and give my worries to Him.

That alone ensured my survival.

I was ready to sleep a week by the time we reached Shechem, a small community on the northern foothills of my beloved

Gerizim. The sun slipped behind the horizon as the Assyrians drew near this settlement. Its manmade walls remained stout and secure, for the people of this trading center threw open its doors to the Assyrians – but that's a tale for another day, for I know little of it. Besides, these Assyrians certainly didn't care – this lieutenant and his troops showed no intention of sampling Shechem's treasures. As I settled into the rocks just above these warriors, content to take my rest, the chieftain directed his scouts to a busy cluster of tents and makeshift stables outside the city. Then he dismounted, shuffling bowlegged into one of the larger pavilions.

Simon waited there, lodged in the shadows, hiding from a giant soldier not much younger than Elon. This sweating man – a captain, I soon learned – sat in a folding chair around various packed supplies these road-ready Assyrians coveted. Something irritated the tired storekeeper, which may reveal why he seemed little impressed with Ashur-jorath, lieutenant of the First Brigade of Aram. Then the captain surprised me, complimenting the newcomer on his harvest of hands.

"Those unworthy of death," the lieutenant explained, brushing the comment aside. "Listen to me, my captain. I must reach Samaria by the midday sun."

"Why?"

"Upon my honor, sir, I carry a weapon that will pierce Hoshea's heart." Ashur-jorath stiffened at some affront I didn't understand. "Upon *my* honor, sir."

That drew the officer's attention. He rose to his feet, which brought his tailored frame into my view. Wrapped in colorful robes of wealth and power, this captain felt comfortable in his office. And from his structured brow, analytical stare, and cautious stance, I guessed this Assyrian took little for granted.

"Just what do you have?" he wondered.

"*My* honor," the lieutenant stressed once more.

"Yes," the captain agreed. "It is your deed. You may have the credit. But what is it?"

That acquiescence seemed all Ashur-jorath desired. Smiling in grateful warmth, he lifted a torch from a central tent pole, keeping its flames from the rippling cloth walls, and ushered the captain to where his horse soldiers waited outside. Then he froze.

In his absence, the men under his command had hung the princess by her tied wrists from a hook hammered into the top of a tall wooden pole. These warriors chuckled at her futile resistance as their grime-splotched hands slapped and squeezed her writhing form.

Rage burst open within my heart, and yet I wept as she tried to cry out in shame and agony, her words muted by that rough gag in her parched mouth.

I imagine Simon would have betrayed himself, moving then to defend her, had the lieutenant not charged against his own men.

"Animals!" he scowled, casting them away as leaves in a gale. "Fools!"

"Magnificent," marveled the captain. This Assyrian circled her weary form, admiring her ever-present beauty. "Truly superior. What do you want for her?"

"She is for Sargon," stated Ashur-jorath.

"A worthy gift. I see why you treasure her."

"You know not her true value," said the lieutenant. Proud of his accomplishment, the soldier settled his hands at his hips and proclaimed her heritage. When the captain doubted him, Ashur-jorath detailed their chase and her capture, which raised the captain's esteem.

"You shall have everything you need," he decided, praising the lieutenant's name. "Even two of my stable boys – a gift of my own." Then he gazed in lust one last time at Rachel's distraught form. "Drawing our amusement from her before all Samaria will surely throttle old Hoshea. I think I should be there for that. And if he does not buckle, why, we'll sail her head over his walls! Though that would be a waste."

That thought seemed to disturb the lieutenant, though I doubt his feelings were genuine. After watching these dogs, I questioned whether Assyrians cared enough for anyone to feel sympathy or pain.

Oh, how I wanted to feast upon them! It seemed so appropriate!

So trapped was I by my anger, I thought little of Simon until a pair of dusty stable hands brought forward eight new mounts for Ashur-jorath's riders. There Simon was, wearing Assyrian servant's garb over his old tunic, leading three weary stallions past Rachel's trembling form. I doubt she saw him at first, but on his return, her eyes spread wide with fear and joy. That alone must have given her strength to go on.

But I was not alone in noticing this.

"You there," the lieutenant called to Simon. "Come here."

My bondmate made no response until Ashur-jorath checked himself and repeated his command in the Hebrew tongue. Then Simon obeyed, displaying not a hint of surprise or fear. At his back, just within his belt, I spied a dull carving knife.

"I know you," Ashur-jorath pondered aloud. He peered through the night shadows, seeking a clearer view.

"You have been to Shechem before?" Simon asked, his voice wary.

"No," the lieutenant admitted.

"I have drawn all my servants from here," the captain said, dismissing this talk. "Much easier people to master than those of Shiloh."

"We took almost 3,000 slaves from Shiloh," the lieutenant stated.

"I saw them march by," the captain acknowledged.

"Most everyone else is dead," Ashur-jorath continued. "That makes Shiloh quite easy to master, I assure you."

"No doubt." With that, the captain waved for Simon to leave. "But these locals, they don't mind giving all they have to stay alive. The men cower, the women submit – you should stay a night, see for yourself."

"No," said the lieutenant. He, too, saw the captain's eyes lingering yet on Rachel. "I tell you – this prize is for Sargon."

"But would one night's delay –"

"No!"

Ashur-jorath whistled for his men to pick and saddle these new steeds. The soldiers grumbled, wishing rest and sleep, but did as they were told. The lieutenant used that moment to lower the princess to the earth. She sought to flee, but he threw her over his shoulder as easily as a journeyman's bag.

"Fools!" he shouted, which brought everyone to a tired halt. "All of you! Fools! Don't you realize what we have here? This girl is the key to Samaria! Hoshea must see her as he remembers her, as pure as possible, before we ravage her. We will take her in front of the city. In front of him! That, my friends – ah, that will break him!"

The captain allowed a sly smile. It made me want to vomit.

"You are destined for greatness, Ashur-jorath," the storekeeper said. "Though you return as my superior, I hope to work with you again."

The lieutenant folded his right hand into a fist and slammed it against the iron plates guarding his left breast. Then he jumped with grace upon his new steed, handling his feminine bundle with ease.

"If that happens," Ashur-jorath told the captain, "I will remember your kindness."

Nodding to his men, the lieutenant dropped Rachel against his stallion's broad shoulders, not bothering to tether her. The princess whispered the saddest groan I have ever heard.

"Still, it is a waste," the captain mumbled.

Frowning, the lieutenant led his squad into a ride that passed swifter than the journey here. But this time Simon was among them, a servant atop a dusty white horse galloping at their rear.

Licking my paws one last time, I soon followed them.

Chapter 14

Imprisoned

It hurts me to admit this, but at this dangerous stage of Simon's life, I took a great risk and abandoned my watch over my bondmate. It yanked my mane to do so, but human traffic along his road forced this upon me.

Reuben had anticipated my problem. As Simon's troops neared the highway, I saw their movement slow to a crawl due to a near-endless number of other advancing Assyrians. They clogged the human trail from Shechem to Samaria with their dust and wastes. Yes, I witnessed marching soldiers galore, but they competed with seemingly endless others: horse-drawn chariots of different types, some decorated with blazing colors, others dark as night or bland as the dirt they pummeled. Wagons loaded with boxes, baskets, and jars, piles of rocks, tree limbs, cloths, things they ate, and all sorts of other cargo I could not begin to name. A train of ox-drawn trailers and carts paralleled the main road when the sod proved strong enough. Those heavy platforms bore things I did not understand at the time – pieces of shields, shelters, and other devices they would build to attack those city walls, or things they used to establish those camps that spread across hills and fields. I smelled strange winds from boxes, bottles, and bundles of what they called medicines. Several carts came piled high with swords, axes, bows, arrow bundles, and other weapons I grew to hate, all along with things those sunbaked men used to make and repair their battle arms. Some I soon learned fit within broader activities they called leather and metalsmithing, tools used for everything from vest and bridle making to hammer forging and blade repairs. A select group guarded treasures for the king's court. Barefoot and sandaled shepherds drove herds of sheep, goats, hogs, and horses in the hills and fields alongside these roads – which strained my heart, as you might imagine. But around all these beasts, and the other travelers, scampered uncountable cavalry troops, each one picking its skillful way through gaps between wagons and the livestock.

Gazing upon all this human congestion, which ran from one horizon to the other, I saw no way I could travel among them… and to be honest, once my steadfast faith in our Maker weighed upon my decisions, I did not mind our separation. I came to believe I could indeed find Simon again at Samaria – I don't know how I determined this, but the answer struck me with such assurances that I did not question it. And besides, taking in all this chaos nearly drove me doggy. The dusty stench set my nose to pouring in a hopeless effort to clean it all away.

I hate that, the way it runs through my hair. All the clots and snarls and… oh, let's go on.

Mind you, I did not give up the chase. Traveling southwest, crossing many hills, I reached the trail Simon himself blazed just days before. I then retraced the shepherd's path to Samaria, enjoying the solitude our Maker had designed for our earth. Through this I regained my sense of well-being. Indeed, so great was my satisfaction that I managed a half-day's sleep in the warm sun, giving all my cares to Him. And without the flock to slow my passage, I made the trip to the hills overlooking the devil's destination in under two days – a full day shorter than that by Simon and his family.

If I may boast, that success marks just one more advantage of being a lion, chosen by the Maker to rule His creation. When I must, I can outrun any human, their camels, and even some horses, if need be. It helps if they're older steeds, though the aged ones often did choose more efficient paths.

My perseverance filled me with pride – until I considered Simon's resourceful nature and wondered if he could have maneuvered to arrive before me. That thought swept me from tremendous self-satisfaction to great distress, fearing I might lose my bondmate in this sea of humanity.

I had no difficulty finding Hebrew slaves, for the Assyrians had thousands working outside Samaria's walls, driven by whips to fill scars left upon the earth by Hoshea's troops. The arriving Assyrian soldiers established camps just beyond bowshot from the fortress parapets, their numbers soon spreading to encircle the lower grounds. The invaders welcomed the chance to rest, turning their attentions to cursing the slaves, singing songs of death, or chanting phrases of corruption. Only those troops climbing the mountainous slopes risked battle. They hoped to establish a parameter around Samaria's high fields, where the Israelites used their new trenches as defensive lines.

That was the key, or so it seemed. As long as Hoshea held those crests, keeping the Assyrians from their grazing stock and water, Samaria had a chance. But the Evil One's fist had other weapons. While thousands of the conical-capped soldiers taunted the wall garrisons – and their cavalry units darted back and forth around the citadel, their archers sometimes managing to pick off a careless sentry atop the parapet – Assyrian regiments worked just behind the garrisons to assemble huge siege towers and stone-chopping machines. Once the earth about the walls was patched and dry, slaves and oxen would add more wheels to these iron-plated battlements and roll them to positions against the fortress walls. These platforms could shelter slaves piling up dirt ramps against the barriers, stonecutters pounding axes and rams through the walls, or soldiers ready to scale the parapets. That would begin the true assault on Samaria.

Among these machine builders I spied a hollow iron sphere shaped like the head of a ram, its curled horns dwarfing the bulky human hammering out its shape. A band of men worked beside him, using axes and saws to hew several cedar tree trunks. Later I learned these workers would bond those poles with ropes and belts to form one monstrous wood spike. Once capped with the forged ram's head, the Samaria gates would face a staggering challenge.

One may only imagine the despair these sights fueled among the Israelis atop the fortress walls. Yet all this would pale against what these devils planned for the princess.

My blood simmered at that thought. I began to sprint across the crest, looking for the tent Simon had said was Sargon's – for there, surely, would they guard Rachel. The setting sun turned my jaunt into a race, for I feared losing my bondmates if I did not find them soon. Then there came forth a beat, dark and angry. I froze, pondering this, as other booms joined in rhythm. Rich voices mixed into that storm, Assyrian choruses near and far, all crashing against the fortress like waves breaking upon a shore. Intrigued, and a bit unnerved, I sought reassurance in searching for the source of that intimidating song. Soon I spied a mass of men pounding upon hollow basins capped by stretched skins. They stood a stone's throw from the fortress, their frames draped in the settling blackness by bright fires lit at their backs. I stared into them, giving my eyes time to adjust… and noticed behind that a pavilion of heavy cloth walls ringed by tall, imposing sentries, their armor shimmering in the rippling light.

That, I knew, must be the traveling tent of Sargon.

Renewed in spirit, I looked for the best way to reach that place, but I found no easy path. To evade watching eyes, I had to circle two thorn-pocked hills, scampering from sheltering rocks to sand pools and dry gullies. The darkness slowed my pace, leaving me quite anxious when I finally came to a ridge that plunged to a weathered basin cradling a dusty roadway to Samaria. Far across that passage rose a stubborn cliff, its footing marred with sand falls, limestone boulders, and clumps of sage. Between that slope and my perch meandered at least three flocks of sheep, squads of shifting cavalry, a cluster of wagons, and countless groups of Assyrian soldiers, all heading west despite the night to heighten the siege.

As you might guess, that sight had my tail whipping about in anguish. To my left opened the valley before Samaria, flooded with abused Israelite slaves and the bloodthirsty worshippers of Ashur. To my right, the eastern path wound beyond sight through restless foothills ever crowded despite nightfall. And though they lacked any semblance of organization, this stream of foul humanity offered no opportunities for me to cross over.

That left me one option. Trusting the Maker for my deliverance, I leaped onto the road.

Chaos exploded about me.

The lambs went first, charging in mad blindness under stallions, beneath wagons, or wherever else they could to escape my scent, much less my sight. Several mounts reared, two throwing their riders against the hard earth. A well-stocked cart attempted an abrupt stop, only to see two wheels buckle from the strain. One wagon overturned onto a platoon of torch-bearing soldiers. A band of goats, gripped by some combative fever, tried to butt me. When I dodged from their way, they slammed into a stallion, an ox tethered to a trailer, and a fat Assyrian shepherd already beside himself with woes.

All troop movements along the road stumbled to a confusing halt. As everyone screamed for answers, I rambled through their ranks, then scratched my way up the steep ridge to top the opposite bank.

Ah, that was invigorating! To see stout warriors so terrorized at your approach, they forgot the iron swords at their sides or long staffs in their hands. Rarely have I felt such elation! I considered roaring in pride to send Sargon's hounds baying. I restrained myself, of course – it is arrogant to boast before cowering fools. For it is truly said: few things capture the essence of His Spirit – boldly proclaiming His mastery, instilling terror in His enemies, shouting witness to His glory – like a single lion's roar. But mankind is the one creature in all creation that often fails to grasp this. These freedom-loving simpletons quake in terror at our roars, but rarely marvel at the majesty. So shallow is man's mind sometimes.

But I am off-track. Forgive me.

Confusion flowed strong enough that day to not require further input, or so I thought. As I scrambled through the gravel, the sharp crack of an arrow shaft taught me my error. That missile from a human's long bow smashed into rocks just to my right. Once its iron head carved a new hole in the limestone, its wooden shaft shattered into flying splinters.

As you might expect, that made me hurry. I sprang up the cliff's scarred edge, turned north between clumps of prickly grass, and slid down a sandy bank, pausing a third of the way to slip about a rock shaft and await pursuit. But none came. I primed my claws as the moon rose, but these Assyrians must have taken my appearance as a fluke and found something else to worry about – like gathering their scattered livestock and renewing their travels. When satisfied I faced no further trials, I found a hidden refuge and gave my time to rest and prayer.

Nightfall took on a new meaning under an Assyrian siege, for the valley suffered so many small fires, some parts of the fortress blazed brighter than by day. Human activities continued at the same pace as before; this Sargon cared as little for wasting time as Simon had during his attempted escape. Or perhaps this Assyrian king refused to give any rest to Hoshea, his troops, or the slaves. I understood the wisdom there, for while sleep offered little comfort for those within the city, lack of sleep could destroy them.

Happy to find few hounds guarding this warrior breed, I made my way within the shadowy chaos to thread a path towards my goal. Unlike Jonathan's tent, the fabric tabernacle sheltering the Assyrian king offered no loose flaps or unguarded sides. I gazed upon its expanse – for a surprising number of rooms stood beneath its wide frame – and despaired, wondering how I might find what I sought. But such thoughts were without the Maker, for as I gathered my patience, I found the princess.

Rachel trembled within a shallow wheeled box of wood and metal – one similar to cages the abominable Canaanites often used with my brethren. The sight made me long to taste blood! No one should have to eat and sleep beside one's own festering waste, or to lay in a ball because those walls of bars prevented any other move! But that was how they humiliated my princess. She sat bunched in the corner, her uncovered head between her knees – her only defense against the lewd taunts spat by almost everyone who walked by.

At least she retained the garb I had first seen her in, brown with stains though it was, with all the gems and shimmers torn away. Still, the worn cloth offered some covering… perhaps it helped her cling to some dignity.

I sat in frustration high above her, flexing my claws as one man after another shined his flaming torch against her bars. Rachel refused to weep, trying her best to ignore them. I wondered how long she could maintain this, for I heard her breaths flow in short, agonizing bursts, keeping pace with her rapid pulse. I could smell her agony in her running sweat. But when a thick brute of an Assyrian thrust his hand within the bars to graze a damp cheek, she sank her teeth into his wrist as might a bobcat. I cheered her on as he cried out, yanking his hand – and her head – against the unyielding metal rods. The humiliating laughter of Assyrian onlookers – and the hard stare of one of Sargon's guards – kept the wounded one from retaliating.

As he stalked off and the commotion dwindled, a young lad caked with dust approached her from two horses he had been feeding. Seeing the guards looking elsewhere, he laid his palms upon Rachel's shoulders. I heard a whimper as she dipped her head against his muddy fingers, welcoming the touch with all her heart. A guard noticed this and spat out a harsh command. The interloper bowed and backed away, his head lowered with respect, but his heart leaped, and his eyes burned with hatred.

Only as the lad returned to his horses did I understand what I had seen. Our exhausted, dejected princess had swooned to his touch, almost to tears. Her love relit the coals in his weary eyes, but he mastered those flames through devotion to our Maker.

Only Simon could pull that off.

My heart warmed at that thought until my eyes looked once more upon that cage. Many a time I had seen friends and enemies die within such prisons, never again to stretch their limbs as the Maker meant them to beneath His life-giving sun. I gazed upon the distraught princess and – may the Maker forgive me! – I doubted even Simon could save her.

Chapter 15

Deeds

As the moon rose full over the horizon, the dreaded king appeared. Having seen many men in my lifetime, and feasted on a few, I can declare this: never has a more inhospitable, antagonistic character lived than Sargon. Fearful, even to me – which I have never admitted of any human before or since.

The moon cast a dull white glow like death shrouds I've witnessed upon many a kill, yet this monster seemed at home in its ghastly light. He emerged from his tent at a rapid gait, bound in flowing cotton robes of black and purple. Golden tassels lined each edge, framing colorful symbols of all Assyrian subjects. It was an elegant weave, the patterns circling his arms and neck with such grace the king looked born to wear them. Yet his countenance pointed ever towards war. A black leather girdle protected his trunk and waist. It supported four daggers, a long sword, and his royal scepter, a sculpted rod of gold bearing the head of – of all things! – a roaring lion. In his left hand, protected by a stiff wrist shield, he held aloft a thick, well-crafted bow of dark wood, its shaft engraved with lines and curves I could not decipher at this distance. In his right hand, Sargon gripped a staff carved with equal skill, its tips glistening of black iron knobs. Atop his head rested an iron helmet with streaks of crimson and bands of gold, the circles narrowing to a rounded crest.

His armor and weapons dazzled all with their craftsmanship, each piece chosen and prepared to serve death. They created a most imposing image, magnified by the hulking servants trailing his steps. Foul, grimacing shield bearers protected Sargon's flanks. Between them strode a long-haired man with the scent of a woman, his back loaded with full quivers of black arrows, a spare bow, a crimson spear, and a long wooden handle capped by the widest axe head I ever saw.

The great king extended his broad arms, stretched his muscles, and looked up to the fortress spires, revealing his face. That stubborn, arrogant face.

It was corruption with many parts – a broad forehead curled as a thick shield about his uncommonly large skull, two hazel orbs probing from dark, recessed pits, the sickening shade of pooled blood that colored a beard as wildly raging as my own mane. These made him seem as much demon as human.

This nightmare king turned my way, spearing my mind with a stare of utter domination. I flinched despite the great distance – one could not look upon him and not cringe – and I thanked the Maker when Sargon turned away. Then he cast those proud eyes upon Rachel, whose cage sat in the shadow of his tent. A chuckle ground from his lips… an unnerving raking from the depths of a truly vile soul. I saw her cower as if his gaze burned her skin, but this king little cared, his intent still fixed on Samaria's defiant walls. Striding across the broad ring of desolation surrounding the fortress, Sargon ignored arrows falling about him until he drew within shouting range of the main gate. There he raised high his scepter. Its golden head pulsated with reflections of those raging fires and the moon's ghostly sheen.

The man-woman lifted a hollowed oxen horn to his lips and blew a harsh blast. At its end, Sargon returned his scepter to his belt and reclaimed his bow.

"Hoshea!" he shouted. "Hoshea! Kneel before your master!"

His words tore at the wall's limestone bricks from its foundation to its parapet. Arrows flew in response, striking the earth about his feet. The titan did not seem to notice. His shield bearers rushed forward, their huge leather barriers held high to protect their king, but Sargon did not quail. As his lips curled into a hungry smile, the king primed his bow and let sail a shaft that tore through the neck of an Israeli archer atop the central tower. Laughing, Sargon took aim at a different parapet and split a Hebrew's skull cap. That man's pierced body tumbled down the stonework, delighting the Assyrian host.

A triumphant song roared from at least three trumpets above Samaria's main gate. A rebellious cry soon followed... I wondered if it might be Hoshea himself.

"Leave us!" commanded the opposer. "Depart my land now, or by my hands, you will surely die!"

Brave words, I thought, but Sargon's scornful chortle dissected whatever strength upheld them.

"Fool!" called the Assyrian devil. "You will grovel at my feet before I leave this forsaken place! I will crush your heart with my hands and feed it to my dogs!"

Hoshea did not cower. "Deluded mongrel! How many times have we brushed your fathers from these walls? Samaria has never fallen! It never will!"

Scattered Hebrew soldiers cheered. Sargon reached back for an arrow as if thinking he might aim across the vast darkness for that voice atop its distant tower, but in the end, he did nothing but laugh.

"Hoshea," he called as a parting shot, "how is your daughter?"

Satisfied with that final, grievous blow, this shell of evil returned to his tent, taunting the Israelis by walking within range of the fortress almost the entire way. Many an archer took up the challenge, but no arrows fell near this brash king's broad strides or those of his followers. As cheers rose throughout the Assyrian ranks, their songs of death began anew, giving Samaria and its nervous residents no respite through the night.

Sargon turned his attention to the princess.

She sought solace in the far corner of her prison, her legs pulled tight to her chest, her hands wrapped as armor about her ankles. While the king leered at her, saying things even my delicate ears could not hear, a guard crossed behind the cage and poked at her with a long knife. He urged her to get up, to step forward. She refused.

"Leave her be," the king said after four or five stabs failed to dislodge the princess. His words ground into an icy drawl. "I doubt she will resist once I pour gold upon those delicate wrists, or that sweet neck… her eyes, her lips. You will see, my friends. Before long, she will beg for whatever mercies I offer."

One look into his scorching gaze verified his wretched intent. I feared Rachel would break when she too recognized his madness, but though this horrible cycle repeated itself three straight nights, one a human's Sabbath, the princess survived, her mind and will intact. Hoshea showed signs of breaking in these trials, but not his daughter. She never replied to Sargon's corrupting words, never bent to accept food or drink, never heeded that dagger's point to take even one step from her perch. Only when this relentless king vowed to pare the skin from her nose did she relent – to spit into the monster's left eye.

Fearing retribution, a guard jabbed at her with his spear, though the bars made his frightened, nimble target inaccessible. But this made Sargon smile. Gritting his teeth, he offered but one word – "Tomorrow" – before strutting away.

She glared in defiance at his departing shadow until he disappeared into his tent. Then she collapsed, sobbing against that damp floor as these moments of terror finally consumed her.

Rage and pity poured from my heart. This fair human deserved far better than this!

From the darkness erupted a malevolent fireball. My instincts threw me back as oil-fed flames feasted on the far corners of Sargon's tent. Summoning horns rang through the night. Assyrian foot soldiers and whipped Hebrew slaves rushed toward the explosion, crossing paths with anxious livestock fleeing the fire. Heckling taunts rose from the fortress, answered by far-flung arrows and rabid cavalry teams beating down grass burning under the northern winds.

Sargon and his court emerged from the smoke to watch the hungry flames spread. The king stomped about as efforts to douse the blaze failed. He pressed hundreds of Hebrew slaves to shovel dirt upon the fire. The heat scorched their tools. Many laborers cried out in agony before the conflagration, their shrieks twisting the whistling winds into sirens of death.

It took me some time to brave more of this scene. I do not trust insolent blazes; such things I leave to the Maker. But love of my bondmate and the princess held me in place; with time and forbearance, I overcame my conflicted heart and mastered my fears. Only then, as I edged deeper within the rocks to escape a smoke-clogged breeze, did I spy Simon. He stood beside Rachel's cage, his wiry frame bare but for a loincloth, his sweat-soaked arms seeking to wedge an iron pick between the fire-lit bars. Hooking the tool's thick point behind a rusty post, he pressed his every limb against the metal. One rusty bar stretched outward. The metal cage groaned… another rod bent toward the lad… but not enough.

As I watched Simon realign his tool, only to fail again, I suffered a deep sense of defeat. It was as if my heart was locked in that cage, tortured and near breaking, never to escape. And as I pondered it, this image took fearful reality. For it was my heart – my destiny – that lay before me. Why had the Maker forced me to endure these hardships, to fall in love with two humans, if not to preserve them here? Could I have any other purpose?

Ah, I should have realized that if I had to ponder whether it was the Maker's will, I had failed. Such truths should stand out by instinct if not insight. Yet despite trailing these humans for days on end, despite learning these brutal lessons of carnage, I still had walls in my mind and heart that blocked the will of our Maker. I still carried hatred against humanity that fought His purpose for my life.

"Halt!" came a stern voice. "Get away from there!"

Simon stepped back to find a soot-stained Assyrian poised to attack, a thick short sword in his left hand. The winds shifted, allowing a flash of firelight through the smoke. There stood Ashur-jorath, a newly crowned captain.

"What are you doing?" he shouted, changing to the Hebrew language as he shoved Simon aside.

"Leave him alone!" cried Rachel. But the captain laughed, having already decided to ignore Simon. No doubt he considered my bondmate a disposable slave. But then he looked about, confused.

"Where are the guards?" Ashur-jorath wondered. "Off again?"

"I am trying to get her out!" Simon said. The captain reared at that, so the shepherd added, "The fire is too close. She must not die this way!"

The Assyrian hesitated. "The winds blow south, fool. But I suppose it would not hurt to move her. Get a horse."

Dropping his pick, Simon scampered into the darkness. Ashur-jorath fingered his snarled beard as he watched the shepherd leave, then gave that up with a shrug to inspect what damage Simon did to the cage.

"Little harm done," he mumbled to himself. Eyeing the cringing woman, the Assyrian spoke in her tongue. "Do not worry! This little fire will be out soon enough. Though I suppose tomorrow you might wish it had ended here."

A team of foot soldiers ran by. Ashur-jorath grabbed one and asked how this trouble had started.

"I do not know," the man said, pushing to move on before he recognized the captain's rank. "There's oil everywhere – a lot of empty jars."

Ashur-jorath lifted his head, glanced back to the smoke, then this soldier.

"It was set to burn?" the captain snapped. "No accident?"

"Looks so." The man coughed; from his scorched hair, hard breaths, and sooty clothing, it appeared he had risked much in battling the flames by hand. "I suspect someone spilled that oil all about and threw a lamp upon it. Lit right up."

Ashur-jorath considered this, then nodded, releasing the man to leave. Simon reappeared leading two nervous horses, their eyes shielded to block them from seeing the flames. The captain eyed my bondmate with curiosity as the young man tied these agitated beasts to the bent bars. I did not understand that reaction until Simon settled his crook before him. Only then did I notice the lad had cast himself once more in his old, much-stained cloak.

"You are the one – the shepherd I saw at Shiloh," marveled Ashur-jorath. His words hardened. "You still seek death?"

Simon flexed his knees, his hips, his elbows. His staff held firm before him, my bondmate stood ready for battle. The captain smiled at this. He drew his sword with confidence, enjoying the drama.

"No mercy this time," Ashur-jorath declared.

For but a breath, a wave of thick smoke obscured them. As it faded, I saw Simon reeling, pursued by the aggressive Assyrian. I heard unyielding Damascus steel tearing chips from hardened wood. I saw the blade flash in the dancing light, drawing ever closer to the Judean's damp flesh.

That made me blink, so surprised was I at seeing Simon retreat. Then I watched him strike back, and I understood. The Assyrian was a master swordsman, which meant he commanded his body and feet with as much skill as his blade. For each swing or jab of Simon's staff, Ashur-jorath countered with a solid parry, graceful spin, or sharp, precise dodge and thrust. For each change in my bondmate's position, the Assyrian responded. For each acceleration in tempo, the Assyrian proved Simon's equal. And while Ashur-jorath seemed unable to turn an attack against the shepherd's able staff, his own unbroken defense promised Simon would stand only until my bondmate's wood shattered or someone else among Sargon's vast force discovered this contest and joined the battle.

Then, in a roll of smoke, it was over. Backing into the darkness, Simon struck a wheel on the cage and hesitated. The captain used the time to roll his blade into the crook of Simon's staff, pulling the rod from his weakened grasp.

"Indeed, you are worthy," Ashur-jorath said. Planting his blade at Simon's throat, he smiled. "I enjoyed this. Thank you."

Not one to surrender, Simon rolled hard left, bringing his feet about to kick the captain's knees. But the Assyrian already lay against the earth, for Rachel had thrown a handful of waste into his eyes!

You see, his abrupt recoil threw Ashur-jorath's head against the cart, which made the warrior loose his footing.

Praising her name, my bondmate leaped atop the captain and smashed his face into the earth. That thrilled me, for though the blow did not slay the Assyrian, it left him unconscious. Then another figure closed upon Simon before he could rise. The princess shouted a warning, but it proved unnecessary – Simon had laid his schemes well.

"Need help?" asked the man, a brown-bearded worker bound in the sooty, muck-ridden tunic of an Assyrian slave.

"This," said Simon, lifting the pick, "is more than enough." Taking a deep breath, he wedged the tool's broad iron back between the bars and shoved.

"Do not linger on my account!" he told the newcomer. "Surely they will miss you!"

The slave stepped into the shadows but stayed close. "The taskmasters have more of us fighting your fire than they can count," he said. "Few watch us closely. We are fodder to them."

Now I had thought Simon was just about the perfect human specimen, and I still do, but I will bet this newcomer, who was twice my bondmate's age or more, had muscles and bones far tougher than those of my shepherd. At least he did at that moment.

"You use that wrong," this man said, stepping forward to take the pick from Simon. "With this, you should leverage your weight and roll the edge, not press it. Put your right hand at the tip of the handle, like so. The other just below the head, to keep it from slipping. Then drive your weight against your right palm. Rock the wedge back and forth."

With this technique, the newcomer achieved in three swings what Simon failed to do in twelve: spread the iron bars wide enough for Rachel to squeeze free of her cage.

Oh, did my soul leap at that!

"Next time," the man told Simon, "you might strike the wood floor like you would the earth. That oak probably splits faster than iron bends."

I thought that silly, considering how loud wood may crack, but neither Simon nor Rachel showed a sign they listened. My bondmate worked to lower her weakened form to the earth. The two men then drew her into the shadows as Rachel struggled to stand, her limbs stiff from days of torment. Simon held her side, offering comforting words, but anxiety entered his tone as more slaves dashed by to battle the flames. Then my bondmate threw caution aside and lifted her into his arms. They stood together, huddling in shared strength as he cradled and massaged her flesh. Curious... I noticed their faces drawing ever near one another. A flicker of firelight danced upon their eyes, bringing them together. Something passed then within their thoughts. I did not understand this mix of confusion and interest, but their helper also witnessed this – and he chose to lean back and laugh.

I recoiled, fearing what alarms this might sound in Assyrian ears. And yet I reveled in the experience, for that wondrous sound, full of purity and grace, revealed a spirit fully grounded in the Maker.

"May the Lord bless you," this man said, "and may He speed you away! There is little time."

"Indeed." Keeping his left arm about Rachel, Simon extended his right to the slave, pulling him close. "Tonight we ride for Judah."

"Say no more," their helper urged. "The less I know, the better for us all."

He twisted away to spy out watching eyes. Then he focused anew on my loved ones.

"But I will keep you in my prayers," he said, "for I, too, am from that blessed land."

"So I thought," Simon admitted. "These Assyrian rags didn't seem to fit you."

"Ah, but this is my curse, to wear these things, to walk this earth once more. I never wanted to see this city again, but that was the Lord's will."

Simon hesitated in the swirling smoke. For a moment his weariness showed until Rachel laid her weight against him anew, weeping at last from her torment. He hardened then, supporting her with all his strength and mind.

"I have distracted you," the slave said. "Forgive me."

"No, we need a moment more," Simon replied, "for she is not yet ready to ride."

"But she must!"

Whispering soft prayers, the Judean laid his tender hands upon her shoulders, caressing her. There, for the first time in my life, I witnessed a direct act of the Maker.

Now I had seen His will at work in the creative force of spring, in the showers that replenish our vibrant earth, in the births of cubs and the splintering of the night, and oh, so much more! But never – even though I prayed often for such guidance – never had I experienced His paws working beyond the laws of His nature. And never in my most extreme dreams would I have expected His working through the hands of a human – much less an Assyrian slave!

"The first time I saw you," this man told Simon, "I beheld the Lord in your heart. Never stray from Him, and you shall thrive.

"And you," this blessed one whispered into Rachel's ear, "you are not corrupted. The Lord lives within you, waiting to guide you, though you have yet to recognize His call. Heed Him, my daughter, for He cleanses all wounds, even such as these. Go now and know you are not just forgiven, but loved. Your life is before you. Live in His light!"

At this man's touch, such healing power flowed into Rachel that her soul blazed brighter to my eyes than the flames gnawing at Sargon's royal chambers. Newfound energy and courage rushed through her blood to renew her bones and muscles. She rose like a dancer upon nimble toes, her limbs refreshed, her mind whole. Filled with the Spirit, she kissed Simon, then the Judean.

"Go now," said the slave, slipping from their grasp. With his touch, their troubled horses settled into something close to a patient mind. "You must hurry."

She soon sat atop a spotted white mare, riding bareback as if accustomed to it. Simon could not help laughing, only to realize the brashness of the act. Choking off his mirth, Simon slipped atop a brown steed, even as their helper turned away into the choking haze.

"Wait!" my bondmate called, either not realizing how his voice carried or not caring about the risk. "Come with us!"

"No, I must not. There is no time. And the Lord has placed me here. I may not leave."

Their horses stomped in place, irritated by the smoke,

frightened anew by the flames. But Simon hesitated.

"What is your name?" he sought.

"Go!"

"But I must know," Rachel said, steadying her mount. "I want to remember you!"

"Recall people by their deeds, not their names," said the slave. "But if it will speed you along, know this. I am Nahum."

"Counselor," said Simon, reflecting on that word's meaning. "Fitting."

"Now go!" Nahum commanded.

At his word, the horses bolted towards me – which I should have realized was their shortest route to freedom. Flame-spread chaos ruled the fields at my back, opening the door to our escape. Shouts cut the fire-torn night as these steeds flew by, fleeing over the crest into the darkness. I turned to follow them and so, to my everlasting regret, never saw if those Assyrian masters discovered this helpful slave.

That negligence started a chain of prayers I repeat each night. Indeed, I will call for Nahum's deliverance until I die. For such men rarely think to provide for themselves.

Chapter 16

Trapped

Across the hills I ran, enjoying the terror my marauding shadow cast on those I passed, until I escaped the last ebbs of that bonfire, ever following the trail of Simon and Rachel. But as I scampered over a black crest so that the winding human road flowed before me once more, my left front paw slid upon a discarded garment. By instinct I yanked it up with my teeth – only to be so repulsed by its sour decay, I could not spit the soaked thing out fast enough. That lingering stench filled me with shock and dread, for I recognized Rachel's sweat throughout the tattered covering.

Confused, I leaped down their trail, fearing what tale lay behind this abandoned gown and what my bondmates might encounter on that road. But with the Assyrian army encamped around Samaria, traffic along this path was a pittance of when I last faced this test. Even better, the blaze remained a beacon on the dark horizon that drew all kinds of attention, leaving little to focus on us.

Or so I thought.

At first glance, my difficulties were trivial. No herd animals of any kind crowded this hardened earth, and apart from two wagons already at rest, their drivers speculating on what the fire meant, the only soldiers and cavalry in the vicinity headed towards the city to learn this for themselves. Taking heart at this, I drew in my tail, stretched my claws, and rambled out.

Only then did I find some riders paused there not in transit, but awaiting my return. In my first crossing, I must have disrupted their travel or frightened them far more than I realized. Shouts of "The lion!" echoed among the rocks. A horse soldier charged me, kicking his mount to a fast sprint through the darkness while drawing his bow and a long shaft bundled against his back.

Let us be clear – I have never trusted any human who could direct a horse without touching his reins, much less prime a bow in full gallop. I rambled up the opposite bank as only a lion can, tearing rocks loose with my claws to throw back down my path, hoping to spook that horse and leave the riders behind. It didn't work. As three arrows struck near my paws, I sprang over the southern crest into darkness. Alarmed, I stretched out my claws for some footing but found none. I tumbled down a gravel embankment too loose for even a squirrel to tread. A stout stone struck my skull, ending the whole sad affair.

As you might guess, the sun peaked out – a warm, almost sensual sunrise, reflecting the Maker's brilliant creation with quiet passion – before my eyes could focus again. With my first conscious breath, my predicament made itself clear. My unexpected sleep cost me precious time; Simon and the princess must be long gone, perhaps under dogged pursuit. I might also suffer from trackers… indeed, I pondered how they had not already found my still form. But I could neither smell nor hear any predator nearby, not even a falcon. I can only assume the riders had reached my ledge and, with my fall into blackness, missed seeing my unconscious form. Thank the Maker for that!

My ribs burned, as did my paws, but these concerns faded as the winds played with my mane, the sun warmed my flesh, the birds sang of His grace… ah, that was good. I prayed thanks to the Maker for another breath of life, stretched my aching limbs, shook piles of sand and soil off my back, smoothed out my dusty tail, and decided to get back on my destiny's path.

Then I smelled my brethren.

Throwing myself down, I speared the earth with my claws and focused on these scents. I detected at least three different lions in the shifting winds – no, four: three females and an angry male –

their odors drifting from hills all around me. Gripped by dread, I watched and waited, sifting through what I could see, smell, and hear, until I felt satisfied my brethren did not stalk me. This did not come easy. May my Lord forgive me, but I was too weary to recall if these sweat markers matched lions I knew. I drilled back in my mind to all the lands I crossed in pursuit of my bondmates, revisiting each path, crest, and vista, but no hint of these brethren rose to concern me. And yet uncertainty gnawed at my heart. I clung to the earth and listened to the breeze, rocks, and soil, wondering if any lions or humans lay in wait on my trail. It stressed me, sorting out the road traffic and Assyrian camp racket, until I recognized how this background noise had clouded my mind for days.

All that drew me back to my mission – and my lost bondmates.

Chastened and embarrassed, I thanked the Maker and shook the dust from my fur and thoughts. Though I risk capture or death, I had laid in my folly and fears long enough.

What Simon could tell by examining earth signs, I soon discovered with my own senses. My bondmate had led the princess southwest, as might be thought wise by those who knew him. His strength, after all, lay in his knowledge of those craggy ridges and broken peaks where he had often shepherded flocks to market. Long ago he must have discovered what hidden paths there led south for home. So, I started down this direction, though my heart pondered what sheep trails Simon might know heading southeast, as fitting his proven ability to confound his opposition.

It was not long before the prints of our pursuers scattered, most taking different routes along many separating paths. These humans must have assumed Simon would cherish the speed these passages allowed, not knowing my bondmate had witnessed Assyria seizing those eastern roads through Shechem and Shiloh. No doubt Simon figured Assyrian blades also held the western towns Yaham and Socoh by now, and perhaps even Aphek – meaning that human highway to the south, and maybe even the one to the sea, offered no escape.

If my logic worked right, my Simon would forgo these trails to forge his own path, and where better to do that than in the forbidding hills of Ephraim, which he knew by heart?

I expected no Assyrian to choose that wild land, but I was wrong. At least two groups of horse soldiers headed into the rocks. One pursuer – a lone rider – appeared dead on target.

Drawing in my breath, I made a quick prayer for our safe passage and started south, aiming for a long, steep ridge I suspected Simon would ride around. It was about my only chance of catching them, for if I was correct and he did turn back east, I would cross their steps around a small community the humans called… Pirathon, I believe it was. That, at least, was my thinking. But as I finally managed to top a high ridge offering a revealing view, the sun blazing above me, my optimism faded. For I heard hunting dogs set loose.

From their baying, I knew this probably drew from a few packs of those shaggy wolfhounds the Assyrians trained for vile tasks. Hell's beasts, I considered them – huge, tireless, dark-furred hunters with teeth that could crack bone and jaws that never let go. I had no doubts they were sent for the woman and not me, but I also knew the hounds would catch my scent. Whether they then pursued the woman or me, it meant trouble.

Even worse, as the baying took on a clear direction, the road filled with echoes of pounding hooves. Hundreds, it sounded like. From the dust rising to the north, Sargon had sent many riders to guard these lanes.

Hearing that, my hopes for escape almost died. If not for my faith, I would have abandoned this calling. But with the Maker's guidance, I bore the risk and ran harder and faster than I have ever pressed myself, tackling more steep ridges and crossing more ripped gullies than I can remember.

In some ways this trial seemed futile, for as the midday sun passed and I struggled up a crest overlooking a dry valley of biting grass and thorn-ridden sage, I smelled the hounds crawling among the rocks behind me, howling in their hunger for blood. Whether they saw me or not I did not know and little cared, for they sang their intentions quite well. And, to be honest, after the brutal day's travel I had endured, I also thirsted for battle, and I hungered for meat. Days of evading enemies left me tired of flight, and a desire to give those rascals whatever fury they dared take. Dogs, even hell hounds, little scared me, though the hints of their numbers promised death. But what did that matter? Even if I fell, I would keep these beasts away from Simon for a while, and that offered time my bondmates could well use.

Wondering where I should make my stand, I leaped across a rooting creek and climbed its many banks. Brush grew thick in that pitted earth, and though the brook wound through its gullies in quiet contentment, the tall grass just beyond its sandy shore remained quite dry.

Hearing the pursuing barks climb in pitch as the dogs jumped the stream (I laughed as one whining beast tumbled in!), I crossed back and pressed through a patchwork of prickly shrubs under the shade of musty cedars, their gnarled branches dipping as if to block my passage. I navigated my trail through those limbs to stumble into a hidden crevasse abounding in sharp, crag-splintered ledges. Winding paths formed among those weed-flocked walls and gravel drifts, passing by black caves and plunging holes.

Down in the canyon's depths rode Simon. The princess clung to his back, her beautiful form bound within the servant's garb Simon had worn in Shechem.

Oh, if you could imagine my heartache! I had underestimated Simon's resources to drive himself around the long ridge and back into the heartland this fast. Even worse, I had led his pursuers to him!

The winds rose with the song of these hounds. A new hunger skewed their calls, revealing when those dogs caught Rachel's scent. At that moment they lost all care for themselves – and me – charging headlong through the briars for their prey. Hearing this rabid chaos, Simon dismounted, glanced about the tall chasm walls, and grabbed two aged cedar sticks. He beat these against nearby stones, scraping free their bark.

"What is it?" Rachel wondered aloud. But the rage of their pursuers soon made itself clear.

"A cave!" Simon yelled to Rachel. He started sawing one stick against the other, increasing his speed with each breath. "Find a deep cave. Now!"

Cursing my ineptitude, I bolted atop a high ledge to my left, hoping to draw some of the black beasts after me. But these hounds had been trained well, keeping their noses locked onto their prey. Barking their desires to rend and kill, the lanky wolves charged at full gait over the ledge.

Two dogs stumbled upon loose earth. Three others tripped over their rolling bodies. Seeing them tumble end over end, the last four hounds hesitated before taking the descent, their passage slower, their steps chosen with some care. But as the winds circled about them, burdened with churning dust and sand, the three leading dogs gave in to their fury and pressed on.

I stood still, horrified at what I feared was to come. My bondmate knelt in the sun, his head in that dry, wind-swept grass. I could hear the wood grains grinding against each other. I could imagine the hounds overjoyed at finally seeing Simon's outstretched neck. No doubt their jaws hung open, dripping in anticipation!

"Leave!" my bondmate yelled at Rachel, to little effect. Though dismounted, she stood by her anxious, pacing horse. Her steady hands held Simon's rod – to what hope I could not tell.

How that frustrated me! I wanted to scream at the pair, though my throat could not master those queer human sounds. But it did not matter, for the Assyrian dogs were soon to fall upon them. Simon never lifted his head – nor did he stop stroking the sticks. The fastest, most crazed hound leaped for the lad's sweat-soaked scalp, his lips issuing a snarl as chill as ice.

In mid-flight that cur collided with a blur. The foul dog fell, choking on its last breath, a black arrow penetrating its neck.

Praising the Maker, I searched the canyon for our savior. It was not long coming, for down the opposite wall ran Reuben, his hands fitting a second arrow to his bowstring.

Yet all was not won. As Reuben slid in the sand, Rachel's horse reared, stretching its hooves for the dogs. Undaunted, one hound met its challenge while the other turned upon the princess. She faced the attack with equal fury, swinging that staff to crack the dog's scalp, but the wretched beast brushed her crook aside and dove for the lady's heart. In mid-flight that hound collapsed, a black arrow lodged in its breast.

Two pounding hoofs ended the third dog's life. I allowed a brief smile at that stroke of justice until the rest of the pack drew near. In that timid breath I smelled smoke.

Reuben jumped the last distance and made sure the first attackers lay dead. Planting his feet at Rachel's side, the older brother took aim for the approaching pack.

"Why did you wait so long?" Simon bellowed, not taking his eyes from those hot, battered sticks.

Drawing a deep, steady breath, his brother released a shot that flew straight and true into the lead hound's skull. The crack of that hard bone stabbed my ears.

"You knew I was there?" Reuben pondered aloud, even as the stricken hellhound tumbled among his brethren, scattering the pack for a moment. Yet that disarray brought the dogs within a stone's throw of my loved ones.

Simon did not answer. He thrust the smoldering wood into a clump of brush, then shouted for the breeze to ignite these stalks. One call proved enough; the moody wind came down in its own rage to set the dry grass ablaze.

It was hard to gaze upon that and not run. Though I loved Simon, I feared he'd lost his mind as I watched the lad wave one burning stick through mounds of weeds at his feet. When he tossed the other blazing rod into the sage above the dogs, trapping the now-desperate hellions within a scalding vice, I knew it was over. We were dead.

A sour prediction, true, but one that filled me with regret, for the circling gales soon had the entire canyon ablaze. I heard Simon yell instructions, but I lost his words in the chaos of my age-old fears. Frantic to almost mindless panic, I threw myself north, intent on nothing but escape. I knew the fire spread at my heels – I could feel its crackling embrace! That my lungs were not seared, that my fur remained unsinged, nothing like that mattered. For I had experienced burning in my youth and would not endure that agony again.

132

When the stream appeared before me, its current but a crawl about a lazy pool sleeping at my right, I dove head-first into its depths. That damp, enclosing chill would have rankled my heart most any other day, but this time I welcomed it. I waited in the deepest point as the flames rushed over and around me. But once out of the canyon's swift breath, the fire dwindled and died.

Only then, feeling a fool for collapsing in such terror, did I emerge from the water, my fur soaked, my heart sullen. Though I don't recall it, I suspect I shook my flesh like a beaten cur. It is hard, getting all that water out of my mane, my ears. It demands concentration, which may help explain how I did not hear the sounds of battle.

Once I no longer dripped like a bloated child, I slipped back into the blackened canyon, my tail held close between my legs, to find Simon and Reuben at the mouth of a dark cave, fending off three scorched, surviving canines. Simon delivered crushing strikes with his staff, but only Reuben and his bow seemed able to provide a death wound. Displaying his skill with each shot, this final battle soon came to an end.

Finding a patch of unburned grass, I dropped to the earth, devoting my damp, weary limbs to the sun. The humans did much the same for a short time. Reuben soon decided to hunt down their horses, for they had scattered during the assault. His departure left Simon alone with his love.

That's how it started.

Chapter 17

Law

I do not know if I can explain these human emotions, but I shall try.

This strange situation started with innocence. Anyone who came under the same wind as Rachel knew she needed another bath. Maybe more than one.

Wait – perhaps that's not fair. In truth, I have problems telling such things, for humans almost always smell strange. Like Simon's people, who carry that distinctive stink of sheep. But no matter.

Rachel felt she needed to bathe, or so she said. Perhaps she also wished to get away from all that dead flesh – something I've noticed humans often do. I could tell Simon wanted to leave, though knowing him better, I suspect he recognized these hounds had Assyrian masters following their path. But until Reuben returned, my bondmates could not travel far, and so their impatient waiting provided Rachel her opportunity.

Having seen the stream that saved me, she soon spoke of cleansing her arms, hair, and Simon's cast-off slave garb. And she did not wish to be alone – which seemed to bother Simon.

"Please," she urged at his hesitation. "I do not trust these hills."

"Neither do I," he admitted.

Since Reuben's departure, Simon had leaned stiff as a stone against their cave's blackened entrance… I suspect that deep hole must have saved their lives during the brutal firestorm. While he listened to Rachel, Simon's eyes maintained a sharp vigil upon their canyon's ragged rim, as if he expected to find something. Perhaps he sought me, though more likely he watched for Assyrian hunters. I do not know for sure, for our eyes never met. But as he stood there, resolute, she came to him.

Despite the grit, soot, and stench of her captivity, she remained an alluring human. That grimy Assyrian cloak accented that, for cut to a different purpose, its stiff, splattered skins did not move well with her flesh. Yet as she approached Simon, circling her arms about his chest, hugging him as if she were comfortable with no one else, I wondered if concealing her body no longer mattered.

"Please," she whispered.

Simon resisted her charms. His brow may have wrinkled, but I saw no other response. This did not bother her. Placing one hand on each side of his head, Rachel turned his face toward her, meeting his stare with bold confidence. Flashing a warm, almost playful smile, the princess drew him away from the cave. Together they climbed a drifting path along the canyon wall, walking as if they knew just where my pool was. Exhausted, I lay not far from the waters under the scorched limbs of a cedar anchoring the shore. I hoped the tree's shadow might hide me from my bondmates, but it proved no concern. As they reached that small knob of earth, the scars left by the blaze drew their attention from me. They bent low under the blistered wood, touched by the cedar's haunting reflection on the mirky green water. Leaning against Simon once more, Rachel gave him a quick kiss on his bristly cheek, then scampered into the eddy. Their contact seemed to unsettle my bondmate. Whether surprised at her affection or embarrassed by his presence, he gave up any notion of keeping watch over her and turned away. I feared then he might find me, but if Simon did, he did not show it.

Swimming into the stream's timid currents, Rachel slipped off her wrappings and held them in the slow-moving water, at times squeezing the cloth, other times splashing it through the waves.

"Catch!" she yelled when done.

Hesitant, Simon turned to see what she was doing. Her soaked ball of clothing struck his face to encircle his head. My bondmake stumbled back in shock – something I had never seen him do before. She burst into laughter, a joyous sound that drowned out his embarrassment.

As Simon hung her streaked, dripping cloths upon a cedar limb, she called to him anew, accenting her playful words with splashing water. More than once she urged him to join her, but my bondmate did nothing. Only when she announced she was done did Simon speak, saying he would go look for his brother.

It seemed to me that he was distracted or confused. His steps fell out of rhythm, and his path meandered about as he returned to the chasm's edge. Finding no sign of Reuben, Simon sat down against a wind-smoothed stone. His shoeless feet dangled over the ledge.

Had he been my cub, I would have swatted him for that. Such a needless risk!

Singing in the breeze, her passionate words as sweet as the songbirds of the fields, Rachel soon joined him.

"I do not like heights," she said, drawing close to him nonetheless. Her long hair dangled in a dripping rope about her shoulders, weighing against the cloth clinging to her bosom.

Simon did not shy away. Neither did he welcome her contact.

"Why then," he asked, hesitating, "did you live atop the tower?"

"Father's wish, to keep track of me. But I didn't mind. I came to like it. Easy to get away from things, having my own place in the clouds. And the view… that was magnificent. I could stay away from the ledge and still enjoy it."

"The dive must have terrified you."

"Yes!" The memory turned her countenance dark. "But not as much as that tunnel you pulled me through down there. That fall, it went so fast, but then, those depths, and being under the water that long, in the darkness, and the cold!"

She stopped then, looking at Simon to speak, but when he said nothing, she felt a need to continue.

"I didn't know what to do," the princess admitted. "I almost panicked a few times, but each time I felt your strength. That hold you had, your arms around me so. But I had no idea…no idea, what we were doing there. Did you? How did you even know that pool went under the wall?"

"Reuben guessed. He led the way."

"And you just followed him?"

"He's my brother."

"But you couldn't see him down there! I couldn't see anything! How could you?"

"I did not need to. I knew where Reuben led."

"How?"

"I… I do not know. I just did."

"But why did you follow him?"

"I always do when he is not following me. He figures things out."

"You don't?"

"I trust my eyes, my nose, my heart. My God. I feel my way around. And He leads me. Or He leads Reuben. That is when I follow. In truth, I guess I always follow, either The Lord, or my brother, or my fathers."

Simon kept his gaze on the canyon rim, observing their world. She studied him, then laid her head against his shoulder.

"I couldn't have done that alone," she said. "Not with that darkness, the depths and pressure. Not without you. But you got us through. You saved me."

Rachel clung to him, hugging his chest. Then something made her pause, and her tone changed. Sitting up, shaking her dripping hair, the princess went back to his first question.

"But mostly it, the tower, it was where the king – my father – where he could watch me. Protect me, as he put it. My king could seal off my tower at a command. He appreciated that."

She hesitated, her eyes falling to her empty hands. Her fingers clutched at something that wasn't there.

"You think he will survive?" Rachel wondered aloud.

Simon did not look from the black canyon's edge as he whispered, "No."

For a moment Rachel rested her head in her hands, but then her fierce spirit took root once more and she rose to meet Simon's cold stare.

"Your God," she whispered, her speech stumbling with her thoughts. "I... don't understand all this, what you said. What your fathers said. Your God... He wishes my father dead?"

"No, I doubt it, though I am not God. Grandfather loves to remind me of that. But I suspect the Lord wishes no one to fall, except maybe the Evil One. Our God is our Father, our Creator. He loves us all. But our Lord also believes in law, and justice. In truth, that is His substance, His will, as deep and enduring as His love. To deny His law is to deny His love, to deny Himself, all He is and all He has done. And there lies your answer, I think. Hoshea denied God's law, but even more, he denied God – and he defied the Assyrian crown. That will earn his death."

"And my people."

Simon nodded.

I watched her eyes as this reality took hold. Though Rachel had heard all this before, she now understood the vast, horrendous ramifications of Simon's words. Leaning against him, seeking solace, the princess wrapped herself under his strong wing. His aura of security, of truth, was her undoing. With each breath she gave up a little of her stubborn resolve, her painful anguish. I watched her sphere of regal invulnerability unravel and dissolve, revealing for the first time the wounded human soul that was Rachel, daughter of Hoshea and Samantha, Hebrews born of common blood in the fallen world of our Maker.

Simon's resistance collapsed, washed away by her tears. Slowly, tenderly, he drew her into his warm embrace. They moved away from the rocky ledge to rest within a bed of soft, singed grass blowing in gentle waves under that warm sun. He lay beside her, holding her close, comforting her as agonies flowed from her beaten spirit. As her pain consumed more of her conscious self, Rachel drew ever against him. Within the desperation of her whimpers, their lips brushed.

The inferno started by Simon's hot embers paled before the tempest ignited between their hearts. At that brief contact, she transformed her respect for his sacrifice, her care for his compassion, into a love far more enduring. With an explosion of passion, Rachel welcomed Simon with a commitment that reached past his startled mind to pierce the depths of his soul. Then, perhaps for the first time, he realized the full capacity of his heart to love another. The ardor that had stirred him – feelings he had ever denied, masked in shame or cloaked as one might veil temptation – revealed itself as a glorious blessing our Maker instilled in all His creations. Something to be cherished and fulfilled in His eyes.

Simon joined her in that kiss, recognizing that within his arms he held a precious soul who embraced his heart in a way not even his parents had done – indeed, as only the Maker could. The very idea elated him, which she experienced through their bond. To her it grew even stronger, as an overwhelming fervor for life and all its essence. She drew him ever closer, and together they shared their innermost desires, arousing power of a ferocity neither had before experienced or understood.

And so, as I said, it started – a sad problem born in hearts that meant nothing but good. Yet no one should be faulted. Had I been human, I too would have comforted Rachel in her sorrow. So why should not Simon?

Still, this was something new, as shocking as lightning, as overwhelming as fermented wine. In that light it makes sense to expect both to experience the fears of commitment and sacrifice. It just happened that Simon reacted first.

At least, that is one way to look at it.

As they lay next to each other, their arms entangled, their lips as one, Simon decided to pull away. The impulse swept over him like a heartbeat, and he followed without hesitation, as he would guidance from the Maker. Dazed, surprised, Rachel reached for him to return.

"What is it?" she wondered in a soft, loving tone.

Simon probed his stained tunic as if fearful he had discarded it. He crept back on his hands and knees, saying nothing.

Noticing what he was doing, Rachel tightened her own coverings.

"What's wrong?" she asked him.

Simon didn't move.

"This," he whispered. "This."

Rachel took his hand.

"I don't think so," she said.

"Oh, yes!"

Simon knelt, drawing his arms about him as if he endured a sudden chill. But Rachel seemed content in her warmth. Her eyes were firm, her voice steady.

"No," she assured him.

"But this… we rush things. There is ritual to follow –"

"Do you love me?"

Simon froze. I know not if it was fear or confusion that worked on him, but looking into her patient stare, my bondmate seemed unable to function.

Rachel felt no such limitation.

"I love you, Simon. Do you love me?"

Within his deep gaze, I could see my bondmate struggling to determine his feelings. With those simple words, Rachel put her life before him, a gift for his taking, and asked only that he do the same. For a shepherd committed to his family, his Maker, such a division is not always easy. But when the truth became apparent, with His blessing, Simon hesitated no longer.

"Yes," he declared. "Yes, I do."

"Then let us join," she said, reclining in the glow of the sunset. Her damp gown glistened against her quivering flesh. "Let's begin our lives together. Now."

"Not this way," Simon replied with a strength of resolve he lacked before. "Yes, I do love you. But the will of my Lord, of my family… for that, I would have us wait."

She rose as a striking serpent. "Can't you make me your wife by lying with me? Is that not your law?"

"It may be; I do not know."

"And you do not care."

Her sudden aggravation surprised me – it still does, even as I reflect on it. Only moments before, these two had professed their love for one another, truths I could hear in their hearts, their breaths. But now Rachel spoke in tones I thought she would reserve only for those she condemned.

No… that's not it. She cared for him, her love as deep and passionate as any I had ever felt. But he had somehow bruised a lingering wound. Her defenses undone, Rachel had lashed out, regretting her words the moment she said them and yet too stubborn, or too hurt, to take them back.

At that inopportune time, Reuben called for them. I heard his approach, and with it, the strong breaths and hoofbeats of their tamed mounts. The interruption brought forward Rachel's independence. Surging to her feet, the princess stomped down the charred canyon slope, leaving Simon to trail behind like a beaten dog. Neither spoke. Reuben followed them in confusion. Gazing upon their anguished faces, Reuben must not have known what to say either, for they set off in silence.

Chapter 18

Clarity

Fearing the master of those hounds would soon discover them, Simon led the trio south within the night's rich shadows. Though I suspected our pursuers trailed far behind us, I held my tongue and stayed near my bondmates. Still, I felt growing concerns over Simon's actions – as did Reuben. For Simon's steps were disjointed and irregular, his directions a curious mix of straightforward and haphazard choices. As the trio changed paths twice while climbing a gentle ridge, the older brother suggested they rest.

"No," Simon snapped.

"Then let me lead," Reuben insisted, "for your mind seems elsewhere."

Simon brought his mount to a halt. "You think you can do better?"

"This night, yes."

Drawing his light brown steed alongside Simon's black charger, they shared their views on that and many other things, but Simon's brow remained stern, locked. Reuben drew away rebuffed.

"What is it?" He grasped the young shepherd's shoulder, but Simon hid within his fortress of anguish. "Can't we talk about this?"

Simon rolled his eyes about, his breath sliding away in whistles of exasperation. I doubted he could bring himself to say anything, and if he did, I suspected it would be a diversion, a block… an escape of some sort. Yet as Simon reached within himself, something foul sprang forth. He turned his attentions upon his brother with a look of damnation.

"What took you so long?" he spat.

"So long?" Reuben seemed surprised, though he knew what his sibling meant. "I left at daybreak, as we agreed."

"You were supposed to help me – with the oil, the fire. She was not supposed to face Sargon again!"

The drop in Reuben's voice betrayed his self-conviction. "Her guards turned upon me. I had to slay them."

Simon hesitated. This was unexpected. "But we silenced them."

"They woke up!"

Reuben twisted in his saddle – as if, by turning, he could avoid their conflict. But it did not work.

"Dragging them out of the way took time," he said. "That slave, Nahum, he had to leave for some reason."

"He gave me his pick," Simon volunteered.

"I figured as much. It took time, hiding those bodies. When I finally had the second one there, the first rose." He paused, then whispered, "May the Lord forgive me; I had to do it."

Love for his brother softened Simon's heart. For the first time in quite a while, my bondmate must have turned his fears from himself.

"It was necessary," he said.

"It was evil."

"You cannot condemn yourself. This is war."

"War?" Reuben turned his guilt upon my bondmate. "Was my killing him that much different from what they did at Shiloh?"

"Yes!" Simon spoke with clear resolution. "Their tortures were an abomination. They are not of the Lord. You took their lives to save lives."

"They could say the same thing. Did they not serve their god… Ashur's his name, isn't it?"

"Ashur is not God."

"Tell them that! They do not know."

"Then they will learn! I tell you, the Lord will destroy these people. He allows them to do these things, to pillage our brethren… it is to punish us, not to glorify them! All things are tools in His hands, Reuben, even such twisted spirits as the Assyrians."

Rachel chose that moment to interrupt. "I am tired. I need to rest. Please… let us stop here."

Oh, how I wanted to comfort her then. Her heart bled from her words! Yet Simon met her stare with eyes of equal suffering.

"We shall, but not here," he said. "But you're right; we have spoken enough. Let us go and pray."

Simon kicked his mount forward. I do not know how he did it, such was his pain, yet his response seemed to strengthen Rachel. Reuben looked with troubling questions to the princess, and she answered with the same loving smile she might give a brother. With that silent exchange they descended that ridge, then climbed and departed another, sharing little else between them. But from that moment till sunrise, when they did rest, Simon's directions remained sharp, his choices wise. They entered a stream and traveled far within its chill waves, clearing away their steps and scent. Then they climbed the slopes before them within the moon's shadows rather than under its gaze. Simon paused with every change of the wind to smell the breeze and listen for pursuit, and he kept his eyes on watch for the slightest omens. And as they saw food along their trail, Simon had foresight enough to fill their stores.

It cheered me to see this. Simon was clear and focused once more.

Choosing a narrow inlet between mixed trees, their leaves wonderfully illuminated in the morning twilight, my bondmates dismounted in a restless silence. Or at least I assume it was such, for the draft carried little my way, and I must admit that, in my weariness, I heard even less. I hurried my pace to draw near them. As I regained my breath from that final, stressful sprint, Reuben took their horses unto his care, checked their flanks and hooves, and led them to a sheltered spot on that grassy hill to rest and graze. That left Simon and the princess alone once again, he in an awkward retreat, she torn by her fears and desires. But as they looked upon each other, their eyes shared a wounded love.

"I," Simon stumbled to say, "I will gather some leaves. For your bed."

That unlocked something within her. Taking his hand, she stared at his fingers, nails, and callouses. Then she lowered her head and kissed his palm.

"I am sorry I rushed you," she whispered.

Dropping his gaze to the woods beyond, his words trickled forth. "I will sleep over there."

"I want you near me."

"No."

"Please," she implored him, "do not condemn me. I meant but to cherish you!"

I watched them with my claws extended, fearful of the vast multitude of errors possible in such foolish talk when truth lay at their feet. I could sense Simon's indecision. He strived to harden his voice, to shore up his resolve, yet his heart fought against him.

"I have never done this," he admitted.

"Nor I," she replied, a touch of pride highlighting her words, or perhaps it was a defense of sorts. "I do not wish to, actually, if it upsets you so. But in my heart, I know it is right. Is that not what you said of your faith? Something you feel in your heart?"

Strengthened by her honesty, he nodded. "And more. We guide ourselves by prayer, by the law, by the teachings of our fathers, our priests. And by our hearts. But this, this is not —"

"Simon."

"This is wrong," he decided.

"Simon, my love, those men intended to… break me. Corrupt me. They would have, had you not acted."

He sought to hide his eyes, but with gentle, patient hands, she took his chin and led it to her own. She gazed into his heart, hiding nothing.

"If they should catch us again, I am lost," said Rachel. "But if you take me for your own, ceremony or not, they may respect that."

"I doubt that."

"They may!"

His eyes flared as if he had realized some great revelation.

"Is that why you wish this?"

Her anger rose. "No! I love you! You, Simon!"

Surprised at her own fury, she took a deep, calming breath.

"I know this, what I want; it probably breaks everything you were ever taught," Rachel allowed. "I know my father would not approve. But I chose to come with you. I, me! I abandoned everything – willingly."

"Wait." Simon took a step from her, then another, as if by distancing himself, he could think clearer. "It was wrong what we did."

"What – a kiss?"

"It was more than that!"

I tensed at his outburst. A fire burned within his soul, or perhaps a myriad of flames, few of them in agreement. He had that look about him… that wild, unpredictable confusion that makes humans dangerous. Rachel also felt his conflicting passions, but within her eye I saw a firm determination he lacked. It gave her courage, kept her focused. It made her strong.

"You comforted me," she said. "We kissed. That was all."

"No," he mumbled. "It was more."

"All right – it was more. You gave me your kindness, and I offered my love. I am sorry… I didn't mean to scare you."

That last phrase startled him. He stretched his arms in the empty air, stunned as a bat in the midday sun.

"All that… that was unexpected," she continued, moving to soothe his mind. "Neither of us reacted well. But I have thought about it, as I suspect you did, and now I know what I want. You, Simon. You. And everything about you! I want to know your God. I want to be a part of your family. I want to be your wife."

Hearing her words, the shepherd turned his back to her, breathing deep as he pondered her meaning. When he circled back, something within him had won out, locking his brow and heart into action. Yet she did not give up.

"I don't mean to rush you," she said in clear tones, her eyes earnest, her heart devout. "My life lies before me, in your steps, and I embrace that. I do! I am not afraid. Whatever you wish is my wish. Whatever your God or family require, that I willingly accept. Here. Now! But I must know what you feel… what I can expect. Please, Simon – after these tortures, I need your strength. I love you. I want to be with you. Always."

I will ever wonder what it was that broke his defenses. Some phrase, some inflection… a tilt of her head, the Maker's breath in her hair, or the soft vulnerability of her eyes. The open love in her words. Whatever did the trick, once he gave in to its power, his heart drove him forward – though his mind still found grounds for resistance.

"And I would have you," Simon admitted. That said, his tongue loosened, pouring out his fears, his dreams. "I have never felt like this before! Desire burns within me… I want to hold you, to be with you, right now. But all my life, I have been taught restraint. Until now, I never considered – I mean, I never thought of myself that way…."

"Like what?" she interrupted.

"Well… a husband, I guess… a lover."

Her lips purred something pleasing. Then came laughter, a sound that lifted the glade and all around as might an invigorating rainbow. Even Simon smiled at its passing.

"Perhaps I was thinking of my father, and my mother," he whispered.

"Oh, no!" she giggled. "Never that!"

His eyes shared that, and yet he still looked embarrassed.

"But back there," he stammered, "after the fire, I was tempted… it was like nothing I have ever felt. It wrestles for me still! I look upon you and I remember the thrill of touching you, the scent of your hair… your eyes… your smile! And it hasn't changed! I see you now as I did then. And I still believe it is right. Yet it wasn't. Isn't."

With no hint of repentance, Simon removed his tunic and placed it about her shoulders. He stood before her in but his goatskin belt, pouch, and loincloth, his skin slick with sweat, his heart open to her.

"Before, when we kissed, I lost myself," Simon said. "Truly, it was as if I had drunk some old wine or a swift potion. I felt so overwhelmed! And that, that may be why our Lord tells us to wait. That feeling... it scared me. I felt naked, and out of control. That must be what our laws warn us about. That vulnerability."

A welcome warmth spread through him, like the sun's first light on a cool plain. At that point I think Simon understood what troubled him.

"I sinned, Rachel. I was ready to share with you my, my innermost self, that part of me only the Lord has seen. But such a sacred gift requires an even more sacred commitment."

"Which I have given," she declared with as firm a voice as I ever heard. Simon hesitated at that, then girded himself.

"It must be by His law," he decided. "By the laws of my people."

"Is all that necessary? Really?"

Simon offered a heartful smile, the kind only mates may share.

"I love you, yes, but I also love God, with all my heart," he said. "And my parents, almost as I do you right now. I will not dishonor my Lord or my family. I must not hurt them! And Reuben! I honor him, as you do, too, I know... I saw that when you spoke before. We must not impose on his faith in us. Let us wait, my love, in joy, not anger. In patience, not tension. For this is no small thing we would do. In marriage our lives will be forever joined. We must start it right. We must be prepared."

Tears welled about her emerald eyes. Simon pulled her into his embrace, kissing her forehead.

"You," she began, only to pause when she could not find the right words. I sensed fear, if not shame, in what she wished to say, and yet fear also drove her to know the truth. That desire won out.

"You're not scared of me," she said. "Are you?"

That seemed to puzzle him. "Scared?"

Her broken voice trailed in the dust. "Of what they did to me."

Simon stood there, looking into her eyes as if wondering what this meant. Then he held her close.

"No! Oh, no! Never! You are pure, Rachel; Nahum said so.

What happened before was nothing. Nothing!" He cradled her then, rocking the princess against his chest as one might a shaken cub. "We must observe His laws, my love.

"These things," he whispered, "they may not seem necessary to us now, these rules that guide us, but they were made by those who understand what we do not, who have experienced what we have only tasted. We must trust in their wisdom, have faith in His word, and make it ours."

The princess looked upon Simon, her wet eyes uncertain.

"You truly believe that?"

"With all my heart. For it is the will of my father, and my God."

"Then I will accept that. For you are my heart."

"No, the Lord is our center. And with His blessing, and yours, I choose you for my wife. This," he said of his tunic, "shall mark our promise. No one will remove it while I live!"

"I will die before someone takes this from me," she declared, her tone solemn and deadly. Yet I could tell his action pacified her. Content, she ran her fingers over his bare shoulders, bronzed by the sun, then over his stain-ridden wool sheltering her own skin.

"If you would have done this before," she thought aloud, "I could have washed it."

Together they laughed, and as with lovers, that joy united them. Never have I heard a sound so pleasing! With Reuben's return, they declared their love. He praised their embrace, their future together, and even their children. That very thought lifted Rachel's spirit as it embarrassed Simon. She beamed as might a star; he turned as pale as snow.

I shared their passions that day – and every day I dwell within those memories. Such moments may sustain one's life!

Whether due to their contentment or worn states, Reuben and Simon decided to move no further that day. Neither mentioned thought or fear of pursuit, though I guess it did not matter. They slept in peace through the heat of the day, the grove with its festive colors and scents serving as a true haven of tranquility. My bondmates shared a meal that night from the little they could scrounge from the wilderness – berries and roots, mostly – but their conversations bared their hearts. That sharing of minds quenched all their hungers. I rejoiced in their honesty and faith, knowing they built relationships to stand throughout their lives.

If all humans could give of themselves this way – learning to accommodate each other's needs rather than shut out their problems or create divisions – this would be a more peaceful world. Yet few people wish for such clarity, as we soon discovered.

Chapter 19

Broken

The next day ended our seclusion. That, of course, was not Simon's wish, and certainly not mine, but circumstances demanded it.

In their early morning travel, Rachel made them pause so that she could bathe at a babbling tributary of the Kanah River, or so they called it. Why, I do not know. This human urge to name things, as if they have any right to do so. One wonders why they waste their time and energy… or why I do, thinking about this or them. But that is my weariness taking root… forgive me. So, they rested while she bathed. I doubt either brother wanted this, but neither could resist her. And that makes sense… I would not even be here if Seth could have resisted his women or their complaints, but then… ah. I am more tired than I knew. Back to Rachel and her fondness for water. To everyone's benefit – yes, mine too, I guess – she did manage to clean some of the grime out of Simon's tunic, but that was the best that could be said of her efforts. Everything else dismayed the young shepherds.

Perhaps it should have been apparent before, but as Simon waited, trying to plot an escape route that avoided Shiloh or some other point fallen to the Assyrians, the closer my bondmate drew to despair. The stone ribs that make up Ephraim's western hills lined up with the sun in many cases. That meant their vales and cuts emptied into roads and trails heading towards Samaria, which promised Assyrian sentries mounted on fast, rested stallions. Avoiding those courses would force us to tackle meandering paths up and down ridges or around their sprawling shoulders, clinging to shadows to evade some spy's line of sight.

Their debate started when Simon saw no alternative.

"Is this what you planned all along?" he asked Reuben. "To risk pursuit down a merchant road?"

"Why not let our horses run? We must move faster, Simon! And father suggested we head for Tappuah."

That name meant nothing to me. From Reuben's pitch, I guessed he referred to some human community, probably one that lies along a road. But something in that word "Tappuah" alarmed Simon.

"Surely they are not waiting for us there!" he said in a tone close to worry.

"Not our sisters," agreed Reuben. "But who knows of father, or grandfather. You know father likes ending each trading season there."

"Yes," my bondmate muttered. "Every summer."

"He likes the wine," Reuben said with a shrug.

Simon chuckled. "You know what grandfather would say about that." He hung on that thought, as if it brought forward some memory he had not considered. "You think they are safe?"

"Probably. They are strong. You know that."

Sensing his brother's anxiety, Reuben asked the Maker to watch over their travels. Together they chanted a song of David – I no longer remember the words, but that they offered a message of surprising depth. At its end, someone said something that sent Reuben rolling in brash, joyous laughter. They soon shared this without care of nearby ears. I listened in heartfelt joy. Such love is oh-so intoxicating!

Not quite finished with her bath, Rachel said nothing. Her wet hair tumbled about her face, hiding her warm smile, though I felt her joy in her risen heartbeat, her confident breaths. Perhaps there's more value to this water bathing than I allowed, though it surely cannot compare to mud.

"They might be home by now," Reuben speculated, "wondering if *we* are savoring that wine!"

That brought a soft grin to Simon's lips, but his humor soon faded. For such thoughts hardened his mind. He had no intention of heading into the western plains; he feared such open passages. At least the Ephraim hills provided cover behind or within their rocky vales, overgrown brush, and leafy groves. He valued such seclusion… any seclusion.

"Did any pursuers take our bait?"

"Not that I saw," Reuben said, returning his thoughts to those Samaria escapades. "Not at first, anyway. Several focused on hunting down a lion that chewed up your highness's bloody cloak."

"Stop that!" she called from the stream. "I have a name!"

The brothers shared a soft chuckle, keeping their backs to the waters. I suspect this reflected something they called modesty. I also ignored her so that I could hear them better, for up to that point, I had not considered what role I had played in all this!

"That was my blood, I would bet," Simon said. Reuben grinned.

"They spent the morning darkness hunting for the beast," he went on. "Their riders poured all over those hills – looking for more than one, they said many times – but they found nothing I could see. I waited till daybreak, then followed after you, thinking we were clear. But as the sun rose, I saw at least a hundred riders start down the roads, going pretty much every way possible. I didn't wait to see more."

"Wise. Forgive me for questioning you."

His words suggested some sort of closure, and yet he stared into the hills as if his thoughts remained elsewhere.

"Listen," Simon urged.

His brother gave him a questioning glance, but Simon waved it off. So Reuben paused, as I did – and once I could block out the clutter of insects and birdsong, the human breaths, their heartbeats, I heard nothing but a hawk's distant call. Even the breeze brushed calmly against the earth. The sky above lay still.

From the stream came Rachel's delicate voice, bouncing in splendid harmonies to the flow of the waters.

"She is blessed," Reuben whispered.

"Wait!" Simon took his brother's shoulders. "Listen! There are eyes upon us, and the winds have ears."

Who could ignore such guidance? We listened, discerning nothing. We waited for Simon to explain his fear, but he never did. It was during all this that Rachel emerged from the pool, holding her wrap out to dry. The shepherds mounted their horses, anxious to depart – and avert their eyes, I suspect – so she slid into her clingy garb and climbed atop her ride. Simon directed them into the water, wading upstream a fair distance until they reached a barrier of stone slabs and barbed brush. At that point, our young leader struck south, resuming his cross-country assault on Ephraim's stone ridges. I welcomed this wilderness getaway, for these high trails slowed their movement enough that I could keep pace without tearing my paws anew. But escape was not our fortune, it seemed, for this southern path soon led us onto slopes claimed by man long before my birth – terraced farms of grapes, olives, grains, and grasses, all about a pair of tiny settlements with many sheepfolds. These rambling fields showed few signs of caring hands, and their isolated villages lay quiet, with not even a stray hound for company.

"Some good efforts here, not long ago," Reuben said of their planting, which worked around sandy crests, trickling creeks, and stubborn boulders. "But why leave their work untended?"

Simon did not wish to find out. Keeping watch over our horizons, we skirted around two more such homesteads and a third village, not encountering anyone until we rounded a low stone wall. Our approach awakened a dusty shepherd, who saw our stallions and ran.

"Wait!" Reuben called. He prepared to chase him, but Simon said they should let the man go.

"I fear the devils beat us here," he whispered. "It is time for speed."

"Which way then? Aphek? Arumah?"

That last name brought a smile to Simon, but he soon dismissed whatever lay behind that.

"I fear we must find a road and go wherever it leads."

Reuben halted. "You changed your mind?

"I was never that certain to begin with."

"You were hard against any open road when I brought it up. Are we that desperate now?"

"No."

"Then how…" Reuben's tongue stalled.

They brought their steeds to a halt. Rachel drew close but said nothing. Simon looked to her, then his brother, his eyes shifting from their faces to the horizons.

"I am not sure what to do," my bondmate admitted. "Let us pray for guidance."

Rachel stayed atop her horse, looking somewhat lost as Simon and Reuben stepped down to kneel. Folding first their legs, then trunks, chests, and arms, their skulls rolled downward to rest on the ground just before their knees. That left their spines pointed like arrows toward the sun.

Touched by this, I lay still to join them in prayer, asking the Maker to provide an answer. It did not take long, though the process took an unexpected form. With an abrupt shift of a knee, Simon rolled across his right shoulder. When his toes settled upon the earth, Simon stretched forth his legs, practically leaping to his feet.

Closing his prayer with warm thanks, Reuben lifted his head and said, "Well?"

"We join ranks with a merchant," my bondmate decided.

"What? Are you teasing me?"

Simon drew his arms about him. "Do you remember Shechem?"

"Yes," his brother answered. I could see he hated the thought.

"Why do you think it still stands?"

"Because its people paid tribute!"

"Because its leaders favor survival over a day's riches."

Rachel scowled at that, but Simon tried to talk around it.

"Shiloh resisted and was destroyed. But Shechem values trade over their freedom – as do the Assyrians." When Reuben's eyes betrayed his doubts, Simon took a deep breath and continued. "They are not that different from Hoshea's troops."

The princess spat something I did not understand, though her anger doing it struck home. Reuben held no such fury… just unspoken questions.

"Why did Hoshea's men have us return to Samaria? Why even let us return?" When Simon repeated it, the older sibling shrugged his shoulders and mumbled, "Because they liked us?"

"Hah!" exclaimed Rachel.

"Because we were trading them our sheep," Simon explained.

"Giving them," muttered Reuben.

"So it was," my bondmate agreed. "And that is why the Assyrians did not raze Shechem to the ground. It's why I saw their soldiers accompany merchant caravans from the city."

"Really."

"Yes!" Simon said. "The Assyrians need food, clothing, trade. Money. They still do! They will do anything to keep our commerce going – and get their share of the profits."

Rachel spat to Simon's feet, showing her exasperation with all this, but my bondmate paid it no mind.

"That's why we find a southbound merchant train," Simon stated. "At Lebonah, I would guess. That should give us cover those dogs will accept. A day or two's travel to Bethel – one, if our Lord smiles upon us – and we're home! A day from home, anyway."

The princess hesitated, uncertain of what to think. Reuben remained unconvinced.

"You think they would not notice the princess of Israel?"

"Would you?" Reuben moved to answer that, but Simon cut him off. "Look at her with new eyes, as if you had just met. The signs of her lineage – those fine clothes, her perfumes and oils – they're gone. All gone. She looks a waif, not a princess."

"Ah, but look at how she sits, with her back upright, her head held high." Reuben allowed a sly smile. "Look at her soft hands and fine skin. And the directness of her eyes! Our sisters would not act that way or show such signs. That reveals her heritage… her sovereign authority. I think I heard it called that. Sovereign… a kingship."

Noticing such things, I believe, marked a sign of genius. And Simon had to agree.

"But I can hide all that," Rachel interjected.

"I doubt it," Reuben snapped, his voice painting the breeze with sarcasm.

"I am my own master," she replied, a flash of anger sharpening her speech. Reaching within Simon's tunic to her undergarment, she tore off an oval strip and tied it about her nose and mouth. Then she slipped from her steed and slapped its side.

Reuben sighed as the spotted brown filly scampered away. "Why –"

"Would your sisters ride as you travel?" she snapped, cutting him off.

"If our father had enough mounts," Simon said in a soft reproach.

"Which is never," he added in a near whisper, "but such it is."

After a moment's hesitation, Rachel accepted that.

"Your family differs from most," she decided. "It's special, I suspect. But I have watched my share of caravans enter the city, and shepherds, and nearly all the women I saw – those not of wealth, I mean – they walked, upon their feet, as their men rode. Usually without sandals, too. I've seen this even when my father traveled. In truth, I took pride in this, for I had shoes and gowns and horses, even a stable of my own, when father granted me this. My attendants walked, but I rode, and I loved it, though now, now, well, it shames me, the way you make me think of this. But I loved my horses and my chances to ride. I loved my tower and servants and… but that is over, and I am so much better for it. I want this! If walking helps us, I will stride all the way to Egypt and back if need be. I will walk across my homeland with joy if I am by your side."

Her talk captivated everyone. It even made a little sense to me. Yet Reuben still held some concerns. He turned back to Simon with eyes full of doubt.

"This," he tried to reason through it all, "this is what the Lord told you to do?"

Simon shook his head.

"The Lord urged now only one thing of me – speed," he said. "That He insisted. Joining a caravan is what I had considered

before, but it seemed wrong then, putting us too close to the
enemy. But we're farther south now, not far from home. Speed
makes sense."

"More than staying out of sight?"

"I think so."

"I wonder why," Reuben pondered aloud.

"Does it matter?" Rachel cut in.

"Indeed," said Simon.

I waited, but he said nothing else. I wondered then just who he
agreed with, if anyone. Such simple human comments as
"Indeed" often made little sense to me... I wonder if they do
more harm than good. But in this case, that answer spurred a
smile upon Reuben's lips, which I think was a blessing.

"Well then," he decided, "to Bethel!"

From that point we moved straight south, crossing plenty of
cultivated fields, sheepfolds, and villages. The first communities
did offer some benefits, for the people of Israel left odd
assortments of supplies along their paths for travelers. In that
way, we – I mean, Simon, Rachel, and Reuben – enjoyed an
evening meal of olives, apricots, an assortment of vegetables, and
a few sides of dried fish. I grew frustrated nibbling on grass – a
feeling the humans soon shared, for the next town was a ghastly,
smoldering husk.

A warning came with the wind before we saw Lebonah – that
sick, sweet stench of decay. I prayed they would turn away, with
the sun already deep in the west, but Simon hardened, determined
to go on. We climbed the ridge in a circular pattern, our path
bathed in ebbing light, until a clearing opened in the trees.
Centered in the vast glen lay what was left of that wind-stroked
city.

I tried to look away – was not Shiloh enough destruction for
one lifetime? – yet I could not. Something within its
repulsiveness lured my darker self, binding me to this death as a
moth dives into flame. Oh, I warn you: never underestimate the
dark power of such horrors. Even the strongest hearts may fall
prey to its subtle corruption, as the Assyrians well know.

There was nothing subtle about this. The thick doors to the

eastern gate lay torn from their hinges and buried under a mound of decapitated bodies. Bloody spears staked the roadway, each one flying battle flags of human skins in the smoky breeze. About the crimson-stained walls lay scattered hands, feet, tongues, fingers, genitals, and bits of undecipherable oozing flesh.

I hung back in the shadows, not daring one step closer to this last resting place of uncounted distressed souls. Rachel cried out, skipping to Simon's horse for refuge. Reuben cursed, then prayed for forgiveness. Simon could but stare into the fuming husks that once provided a home to his kindred.

A hawk's shrill call broke our grieving. Finding it too mocking for my taste, I answered with a rolling roar of defiance. Only as my call echoed did I remember my need for stealth. I flung my stomach against the earth, but it was already too late. Their horses flinched and snorted at my call. With his love at his side, my bondmate held his mount firm, but Reuben had no such distraction. Turning his stallion about, he peered into the darkness above my head and drew a spear.

"No," Rachel urged him.

"Our pursuer will not feast tonight," Reuben stated. "That I vow."

The princess remained firm. "There has been enough killing," she insisted, her voice strained by past torment. But the older shepherd ignored her.

"Will you come with me?" he put to Simon.

This chilled me, listening to my bondmates as they considered slaying me. Simon looked to his brother and his beloved, then the gruesome specter of burning Lebonah. Darkness set about him, leaving his frame but a dark silhouette against the shifting light of a city ablaze. It cast a malevolent tone so unlike the soul I knew and loved.

"I would be a burden," Simon decided. "I cannot leave her alone, nor hunt with her at my back. But then, you should not go alone."

"You did," Reuben reminded him, "the night we left for Samaria."

"To protect the flock."

"This is much the same."

"No," Rachel countered. "We must not answer death with death."

"The birds have feasted tonight," Simon added in a soft voice I almost did not hear. "Should not lions?"

"That's a foul thought," Reuben grumbled.

From the hatred in his eyes, orbs accented by orange flames, I think Reuben still wanted to track me down. But he had no chance.

From the depths of his soul, Simon screamed. It was agony indescribable to hear or bear – far more than was Seth's death, when I could see him perform and understand his passing. The abrupt song of pain ripped the night as completely as those Assyrians had destroyed Lebonah. I surged to my feet at the sound, my heart thinking only to comfort Simon. It spurred me to race forward, oblivious to all other concerns. As I drew near the twilight shadows, Rachel joined his painful lyric, her anguish focused on her love. I saw then the black arrow piercing Simon's left shoulder and the blood streaming down his bare flesh. And I heard the horses. From their easy, loping strides, I knew these mounts carried Assyrian warriors. Only their fine stallions could outrace the wind with so little strain.

Reuben's horse reared, which probably saved his life. Displaying his mastery in the saddle – a trait surprising in a shepherd, I learned later – Reuben raised up to throw a captured Assyrian spear, his lips howling in anger. All these moves lifted Reuben and his mount from arrows that whistled through the smoky breeze. But a fourth bolt dove into the rump of Simon's steed. Kicking out, that brown horse charged into the night. Simon tumbled off, falling to Rachel's feet.

Battling against the pain, my bondmate tried to draw himself up. He made it halfway, his back leaning against Rachel's legs.

"How many?" he called out in a strained rasp.

That gave me pride; Simon's vigilance ever put other concerns above his own. But his wound worried me. I could hear his heart racing, his breath labored. I smelled his sweet flowing blood.

Reuben drew his horse about, placing himself between his

brother and their attackers. "Hard to say," he said, his voice grim. He leaned back, dodging a shiny shaft that glowed as it sailed through the smoky firelight. "At least twenty."

"Then go," Simon answered, pressing with his right leg to stand. I saw then he favored his left ankle… perhaps he had twisted it in his fall.

Rachel tightened her hold beneath his shoulders. "I won't leave you!"

"Go!" my bondmate hissed. "You must escape!"

"No!"

Simon hooked his left arm around her neck but could not rise. He tried again and again, crying out when the pain climbed too high. Rachel tightened her hold, only to be shoved away.

The approach of pounding hooves loomed ever louder. The wind shifted through beds of dust and ash. My nose caught a horde of foul Assyrian scents.

"Take her!" Simon shouted to his brother. "She must be safe!"

Rachel sought to bind herself to her love, but Reuben's strong right hand took the neck of Simon's tunic and yanked her away.

"No!" she screamed.

Throwing her to his back, Reuben kicked his horse into a full gallop. His voice chanted a prayer of David. Hers spat angry protests long after their stallion disappeared within the swirling smoke.

I crouched in the darkness. Faint shadows raced about me, their noses snorting, their hooves tossing ripped sod. I shivered, practicing patience as they passed, and guessed Reuben's estimate included less than half their number.

As the first nightmarish shape took form in the light of Lebonah's blazes, Simon somehow managed to gain his feet. The spear he leaned upon served him well as a staff, but when the intruder approached, that stout pole weapon showed its true value as a defense against the Assyrian sword. Still, it was not enough.

Drained by his wound, my bondmate could not evade the horse soldier's long blade. Down he fell, writhing from a single blow. The rider twisted his mount about and ran Simon down. At least two hooves struck the shepherd. His prone form bounced to a sick thud with each impact.

I felt those blows. As each landed, I feared I would die. I wanted to, to join my bondmate at his end.

A dark emptiness claimed my heart. What was I to do?

Satisfied with his actions, the rider pulled his steed to a stop and bent down to read the fire-lit earth. Three other horsemen drew near, staking Simon's resting place with their spears for good measure as they awaited their leader. After these men came many others… too many to count. Drawing into some sense of order, these horse soldiers started spiraling about their leader, shouting loud, boisterous curses as they waited for some decision from the one who cared to stop and interpret prints in the sod. That process did not take long. Rising before his men could complete a third circle, the leader shouted orders that brought their anxious parade to a halt. As their leader took to his saddle, his warriors found their places in a column behind him.

Strange it was, but in that flickering light, the first rider was beautiful to behold. A black silhouette as pure as the shiniest coal, his vest of iron scales shimmered at times as the vibrant firelight flickered upon his dark leather armor. It reminded me of a striking viper – not a welcome sight by any means, but impressive nonetheless. Pondering the truth in that reminded me of something I had learned long ago, of the Maker's ability to place beauty in all things, whether good or bad. That was as it should be, I was then told, since beauty had nothing to do with purpose or morality.

However truthful that may be, it relieved none of my guilt for finding something attractive in this killer.

Some Assyrian with a horn issued a deep bellow. Rearing his mount at that signal, the lead horseman charged back into the night, dead on Reuben's trail. The others soon followed, their hooves raising new dust to clog this bitter wind.

I clung to the earth, joining with the glen of Lebonah as it silently mourned the fallen. For I knew nothing else to do. Reuben was gone, fleeing with the princess. The damned Assyrians had picked up their chase. And Simon, my bondmate, lay dead.

That truth crippled me. Never had I felt so empty, so broken, and all from my wounded love for a human. That realization stunned me anew. After living most of my life without such direction, without genuine feeling for anything or anyone but the Maker, could I be so undone? And yet the truth lay before me. Simon was dead. Dead. And so was I.

I scrubbed my face in the dust and rocks, mindless of the pain. It was over. My life, my destiny, everything. All over.

Chapter 20

Flight

Most likely my misery kept me from hearing it. I lay with my head against the earth, my tears flowing into the Maker's plentiful dust, my heart collapsed in grief. Yet my instincts remained alert, monitoring the scents in the breeze and the sounds of the hills. In time I recognized one I had ignored – the deep, near-strangled billows of Simon's lungs.

It seemed impossible… incredible. I had seen him die! Yet the steady flow confirmed it. I listened, focusing every thought on Simon, and detected the stubborn rhythm of his heart. His legs flexed, stretched, straightened….

He was rising! All praise the Maker!

Even now that image thrills me, his darkened outline emerging from gray puffs of smoke illuminated by flashing flames. His form struggled first to his knees, then his feet. I watched in wonder as my bondmate swayed in the sooty fog, regaining his balance, his stamina. The shaft piercing his shoulder weighed heavy upon the man – or perhaps better said, its wound did. I could almost feel the pain as Simon fought to master it, even as my analytical side battled to maintain control over my love for this human. The kingship within me recognized Simon's injuries must have been less than I first imagined. Those Assyrian spears must have pierced the earth, not the shepherd, for I saw no blood on his skin but for the arrow. Such is the remarkable power of our Maker! In but a few moments, I knew Simon would be ready to move again. That's why it startled me when the human slipped back to his knees, his head drifting down to the broken sod. But I should have known better. His prayer soon filtered through the night's chaos.

"Blessed is the name of the Lord," Simon whispered. "Blessed are Your works. All praise Your glory! All proclaim You are God!"

Power rose within him, conquering his pains, his weakness, his fears. His head fell upon the earth, humble before the Maker, yet his faith was as the rock beneath his feet. That alone fueled his mending body.

"Heavenly Father," he declared, "grant me wisdom to know Your will for my life. I have followed Your steps as I could see them, but my eyes are clouded, my body drained. I fear… I fear missteps, Lord. Guide me! Open my heart to your directions!"

I think I heard water dripping from his eyes. It confused and amazed me.

"Oh, my Lord," he said as if admitting a sin, "I have given my love to one who does not know you. Protect her, if it is within Your will, until I can join her once more. You know her heart, her will to love. Give me wisdom to lead her to You, or better still, please reach out and guide her. Guard her under Your wings, that we might marry. For truly, Lord, I love her! I do not know how that happened, but I love her. With all my heart."

His tone turned cautious. "Is this wrong to ask? Since the lion hunt, I have felt Your eyes strong upon me, Your hand ever at my side. Until I suffered this wound, I knew for sure she lay in Your plans for me. But this," he touched the black wood shaft stuck in his left side, groaning at the contact, "this I know is not of you. Yet all things fall within Your plans. All things are Your tools.

"Even this," he allowed.

"If it is Your will, my Lord… please, guide me, that I may regain her hand. Strengthen me, that I may deliver her from the enemy. And grant me wisdom that I may be a reverent husband and father. In Your love and light do I pray. For You are God! There are no others before You. All praise Your name!"

With that, he took a deep, steadying breath and rose to his feet.

I stretched my limbs, expecting to move as he did, but Simon stood still, his head facing the earth.

"My fathers' words return to me," he whispered with some difficulty. "My Lord, if what I ask is not Your will – if I speak of my own wants and not Yours – I beg forgiveness. Please guide me to do what You need me to do. Your will, my Lord. Give me wisdom to see it and to understand. This I want most of all. Yes, this."

He breathed deep once more and opened his eyes. I heard his heartbeat strengthen. Pain obscured his plans but for a moment, and then he turned into the ruins of Lebonah.

That confused me, as you might guess, yet his steps were sure and steadfast. From a dead city guard Simon lifted a bloody bronze knife, and from the corpse of a large female he cut away a deep blue cloak. Stepping within the city's broken outer wall, my bondmate walked into a burned section of the village, his head shifting about as if he looked for something. His search ended at a circle of stones covered by wooden planks.

I considered drawing closer, then held my place, daring not to enter the ruins. But Simon showed no fear. Girding his strength, he pulled away the beaten timber to reveal a rope descending into a black hole. My bondmate drew up that damp hemp until he reached a wood bucket tied to its end, its mouth somewhat full of cold water. Simon sipped of this brew, swirled it about his mouth, then drank long and deep, sometimes spitting out the liquid to start anew. Once or twice he dropped the container back into the hole, only to yank up still more water to take in or pour over his bruised limbs. He then did some very curious things. When at last satiated, Simon tore that blue garb into long strips that he dropped into the wet vessel. He then turned his attention to the rope, extending it back and forth across the hole. To my eye, it resembled a spider's web. At some point my bondmate achieved some goal here, for he left the stretched rope alone and returned to the cloth slices. These he withdrew one by one, squeezed out their excess water, and laid the strips to dry across the web.

These efforts fascinated me. As Simon stood beside that well, surrounded somewhat by small lingering fires, I could see him quite well. With each delicate move, I watched pain flash through his eyes, his face. Crimson streams trickled from a scar across his brow, where the flat of a steel blade must have rolled to its biting edge. Blood also dripped down his neck; no doubt a spear must have nicked him. The worst stream flowed from that arrow piercing his shoulder. Protruding from the shepherd's back, its jagged iron head sparkled in the dancing flames.

Simon's determination allowed no rest. Taking a deep breath, my bondmate stutter-stepped from the well to lean against what remained of a nearby brick wall. He apparently used this to support his body for a task to come. Simon shifted a bit until he felt satisfied, then grasped the arrow's ash shaft in his left hand. His right hand held that knife. After edging around a bit more to leverage his strength, Simon began to work the blade's edge against that thin wood shaft extending from his side. I heard his heart rush and his lungs tighten, but only as the feathered tip fell free did Simon cry out.

I shared his anguish. Even at that distance, his pain burned my soul as if the wound were my own.

Perhaps that is not fair, for I have never carried an arrow in my flesh. But I learned here the terror such blows hold.

I sought refuge in prayer, only to hear my bondmate's muffled scream. I realized then he had not finished working on the wound. Twisting off the last fractured slivers from the shaft's sawed tip, Simon shoved what remained of that arrow deep into his flesh until I could not see its end from the flowing blood. He took a moment to master the pain, then reached back with his right hand to grasp the arrowhead in his fingers. Inch by inch, my bondmate pulled its shaft from his flesh. I wondered again and again how he kept from crying out. Then I spied the knife blade gripped between his teeth. I feared his jaws might break, so hard did he bite against that metal, but finally, the rest of that arrow fell to the earth, bringing that part of his marathon to its end.

At once, Simon spat the blade from his lips and cried out, only to gasp as he fought to silence that agony. I worried he would fall, so violent did he shudder, but while the young shepherd could not contain his whimpers, neither did he rest. Perhaps

Simon should have, but he refused.

Spewing forth his frustrations, my bondmate used the damp blue strips to bind his shoulder. It strained him, pressing those wraps about those throbbing wounds, but with patience and resolve, he managed it. Simon then secured his left arm as best he could down to his elbow, so that bandages protected almost half of his chest. I drew some reassurance from this, for his heartbeat steadied, as did his breathing, and the bleeding seemed to stop. I watched Simon take another long drink from a refilled bucket, plunging his head into what was left, and knew the Maker would see my bondmate through.

Or so I thought.

It was not long before new doubts billowed up. For after Simon emerged from the city, pacing himself to maintain his strength and mind, my bondmate turned north. Without hesitation he rambled down the path they had come by, crossing first one hill, then another. I followed at a fair distance, paying close attention to Simon's efforts. For despite his heartfelt prayer and determined will, as he continued north – extending his distance from Reuben and Rachel – I found myself wondering if his thoughts were indeed whole.

Only at the crest of the third ridge, the moon halfway to setting, did I realize his goal. For approaching us with a graceful cantor came a saddened filly, her blood-brown head held low as if from embarrassment. When Simon embraced the beast's shiny neck, I recognized it as Rachel's steed.

"Yes," Simon whispered, "we need you once again. Run with the eagles, my heart's love! We must race the wind!"

The thought of that made my pads sore, but our reality proved worse. For once Simon was ready, which despite his hurt did not take long, this spotted white mare broke into a sprint that made me dread the day I ever resolved to watch over this shepherd. Such speed! I looked upon her, at the lands we passed in a wink and nod, and wondered where this animal found such energy. But that praise, I soon realized, was simple blasphemy. Her heart and muscle spoke well of the mare, to be sure, but the power came from the Maker. And my efforts He also blessed, for as I mastered my anxieties, I found I could keep pace with little effort.

In mid-step I whispered my praises and rushed onward. For when the Maker moves within you, you should not question it.

I do not remember how or when we once more spied the gates of Lebonah. To be honest, I had no heart to return, so when Simon sprinted past the battle site, searching out Reuben's trail, I praised his vigilance. We launched our pursuit at last!

Our first surprise came in the woods outside the broken walls. As the sun rose, we found Simon's former mount lying on a pool of bloody sand, its head missing. My bondmate paused, whispering a curse – or a painful moan; I am not sure – then read the prints and charged off.

This trail proved easy to follow. With the Assyrians hot on their path, Reuben had little opportunity for a diversion. Indeed, with two humans on his horse, I feared the Assyrians had overtaken them. We needed only to discover where.

That became apparent at the crest of the next hill – though, in truth, I began to wonder if Simon already knew their destination. He rode hard and close to the filly's neck, his eyes focused ahead, never bothering to look for prints or other signs.

We came to a sandy ridge supporting little more than scavenger brush, which I could pass through unseen with little problem, though Rachel's horse could not. Before our separation, Simon would have traveled around this rocky knob, but as the trail crossed up and over, he followed. I crawled up the slope to observe from a distance. Peering over the rim, we found the Assyrian host, about 25 strong, dismounted before a massive cliff dotted with boulders, gravel slides, and dark, toothy caves. Ribbons of water sprayed down the edge to pool below the caverns, where it no doubt began a long run for the Sea.

About half of the Evil One's hounds probed the narrow straits leading to the top of our Maker's soaring monument. The other soldiers crept with caution into gaping cavern mouths. Each warrior bore a blazing torch to peer into the darkness.

The last fighter, he who wore the cone-shaped helmet of iron and bronze – the man who had struck down Simon, I realized –

that man paced in frustration in the fall's cool mist.

Oh, did my blood boil for him! Hungering for fresh meat, I felt a heartfelt yearning to stretch my claws into his neck.

That notion made me glance about, wondering what Simon would do here. The answer froze my swaying tail.

Waving his one free arm, Simon drove his mount into a hard sprint along the ledge.

"Fools!" he shouted at the enemy. "Dogs! You will die for this!"

The devil's leader barked commands into the crags. Half of his foot soldiers dropped their torches to draw stout bows. In the blink of an eye, these warriors sent arrows soaring after Simon before their flaming branches settled upon the earth. Most of their shafts fell short, for these men held smaller, less powerful weapons the men called close-quarter bows, but two soldiers fired longer arrows from lengthy tethers. One such shaft flew wide. The other passed just over Simon's head.

Turning his horse, my bondmate charged west, screaming insults at the Assyrians with every breath. Dust soon obscured him.

About half of the pursuers rushed to their steeds, eager to accept Simon's challenge. Their skill impressed me; before I primed my legs and claws for the run to come, these men settled their stallions into some sort of organized formation. At a hearty shout from their leader, this cavalry arm raced after my bondmate, leaving the other soldiers to probe deeper into those caves. I tracked the riders from high, rippled crests, charging first west, then south, then north, all the while wiping waves of their dust from my lips – and falling ever more behind. Soon too winded to continue, I slowed to catch my breath and ponder this chase. For the more I considered it, the more pointless this seemed. Simon would never ride away from the princess. If Reuben had abandoned his horse before this cliff, these hills, then Simon had to come back. His escape was but a diversion.

A diversion!

That realization awakened me. Reuben had to be somewhere about the cliff!

Spitting out what seemed a mouthful of sticky powder, I rambled to the top of the crest and looked west, then south. By luck or the Maker's fate, I saw Simon scrambling through a field of scrub brush just past the cliff's broken edge. It made no sense until I realized that filly must have abandoned him. Somewhere at the start of his escape, my bondmate had dismounted and hid, spurring Rachel's spotted mount to run free once more.

The Assyrians followed her.

Amazed at my bondmate's audacity, I turned to pursue him – only to find my path blocked by one of the most enormous lions I had ever imagined. This shocked me, for I had not sensed any sign of his presence – or the others he obviously led. His sweaty mane paled against my own, a fault shared by most males commanding these hot plains and hills, but his brash eyes showed no envy or remorse – only anger, most likely at a newcomer's encroachment.

I stumbled backward, for the wind changed, revealing more of my brethren. Extending my paws to stop my downward slide, I glanced around to map my maneuvering space. Only then did I realize how I stood at the bottom of a rocky ravine surrounded by lions of every size and manner. They held the high ground, cutting off my every escape.

Chapter 21

Revelations

I fell to the earth, gripping the soil with my claws but otherwise holding all but my heart still. Twisting to view the lions enclosing me, I bared my teeth to the great beast I assumed led this coalition of kings and queens. From the many vivid scents now choking each breeze, I knew more than one family faced me. Perhaps my wanderings had drawn them together, but I doubted it. Most likely the chaos of these invading Assyrians fueled unrest among more than humans.

Their leader flared his lips and showed his teeth, then bellowed one impressive roar. Others around him did the same, creating a clash of thunder that sent many loose stones tumbling my way.

I echoed their calls and flexed my muscles to show off all my healed wounds. I wanted my brethren to know I understood battle and birthright. I held no fear, though my heart did reel, having anticipated and dreaded this potential turn every step of my way. You cannot run rogue without bloody confrontations over territory.

The leader accented his screams with jolts, jerks, and jumps, moves copied by those around him. He lifted his aged lips with gusto, prideful of his impressive fangs, and roared all the more. His front paws clawed the earth and sky, each mark a symbol of what he held in store for me. The old and young did likewise, giving no ground.

Seeing little else to do, I stood and faced them all, proud and defiant. I spread my legs and cast my scent upon the earth, claiming this place. Having been led here by divine purpose, I let all know that I would not back down.

The leader screamed his outrage and sprayed forth his own hold over this soil. Then he charged, creating a small landslide in his wake. I prepared my limbs, crying out imposing shields while watching his rambling descent for signs of weakness and strength. While I longed to find some opportunity to exploit, I expected first to give ground and defend my flanks. I would observe his tactics: how he moved, what he favored, what he protected. I would seek to survive each of his attacks, striking only when my best advantage opened. For I could hear his heartbeat, see his flexing muscles, note the swings of his tail, and read the lessons of his scars. I knew his abilities outmatched mine. But my experience… that might hold the key.

And there lay my great mistake, for I forgot the Maker.

The king of this gathering grew ever larger in my sight. I braced myself, for I saw no clear signs of just what my adversary would do. On he came, charging down the ravine as only a lord of creation may, a master of fury framed in billowing sod – until he stopped. As the dust settled, so did he, choosing to stare me in the face. His teeth dripped bile, and his hot breath filled my nostrils with pestilence, but he did not attack. Rearing on his hind legs, this monarch sliced through the breeze with his claws and roars. I met him there, slapping my paws against his. He came down, snarled of bloodlust, and rose once more. I matched him. We descended together. He bared his teeth anew, looked me in the eye, and sat down. His tail, brow, nose, and mane… all stilled in messages of truce.

This I did not understand. Had we been alone, a turn like this could suggest my opponent had tested me… that he would shower me with his scent and take me into his pride. But other lions surrounded us, some balking at this peaceful change. I watched them all, wondering if open battle might still consume us. Tensions burned the air. I realized then that this king seated before me was not the gatherer or leader this day – simply the most defiant, the brash one who naturally took charge whenever given a chance. And yet even he gave way to whatever brought them together… a presence I now felt in the earth at my feet, the wind rustling my fur, and the air in my lungs.

Another king strode down, and one more. Soon all the leaders joined us, young and old, some with pride, others reluctance. Some decided to sit or lie within this fold in the soil. Others paced in their uncertainty. A few anxious ones scowled at those drawing too near, though most just bared their teeth and breathed hard. My first opposer looked on, sitting before me, his head rising upon massive shoulders to stare down into all our eyes.

With a frightening jolt, I realized this was not a coalition of lions. Most of my brethren did not wish to be here. Something held them together in this place. I wondered what this foretold until another bolt of enlightenment came forth. Even in the daunting presence of this giant lion, I stood alone in the center. All their eyes fell upon me, questioning me.

As I pondered this, ever more confused, I watched how, at odd times, their gaze shifted to my neck, then my eyes. They examined my back, paws, and tail, but ever their attention returned to my neck, or better put, my mane – that majestic spread of fiery hair that is my mane.

I often forget how so few of my brethren share this great wealth of hair. All males I have ever seen, they carry on each day with short, scraggly bristles amassed about their jaws and ears – curling carpets thicker, but otherwise little different, than those of their mates. My presence filled many with envy over the long, plentiful hairs that shade my neck and chest. This reminded me how others often assume my mane reflects my superior strength and vigor. Females also believe this, which I long ago accepted as a blessing but otherwise gave little concern.

Birds sometimes share tales of seeing others of my kind bearing my regal crown. Such sightings came from distant parts of the Maker's awe-inspiring creation, which explains how I have never met such kings. Indeed, of all males I have known, even among my sons, only Seth bore fur like my own. Perhaps that explains why I pay this gift little mind, for I face the daily task of cleaning these temperamental strands, untangling their snarls, and pulling free persistent barbs and nesters. My brethren know nothing of the burdens this crown presents.

But that little mattered. As these kings and princes drew their families around me, watching and waiting, I recognized that all these events stirring our lives somehow ground together. Apparently the Maker wanted me to know these things. Whatever purpose He intended would soon fall upon us… an insight that stopped me cold.

Us…

That idea snapped against my weary stubbornness. A mind may grasp only so many revelations at a time before it gets pressed too far. Then resistance plants its claws against further change. And when that happens, my heart always falls back on one simple truth: The Maker weaves His plans beyond my understanding. It was my calling to accept and abide within them, whether I grasped them or not.

From the northern hills rose a shrill human horn. The blast raised the ears of everyone around me. Soon answers echoed from distant hills, which drove my comrades to their feet. From the other side of this mountain came sounds of rustling horses and the thunder of hooves. From what I could tell, the assembling Assyrians at the caves turned their riders west, no doubt to join those trailing Rachel's steed.

That mattered little to our gathering. With that commotion, my brethren scattered, leaving me alone once more.

I drew a deep breath and waited, offering a prayer of gratitude as I listened to the world about me. But nothing stirred. No soldiers appeared on my horizon, and no lions returned. I was alone.

Thanking the Maker for His many gifts, I girded my heart, snorted the last dust from my nose, and headed south to find my bondmates.

Chapter 22

Resistance

Topping a crest in the earth, I soon spied Simon making his way down this peak's ragged southern slope. Its crumbling shoulders extended through patches of wild vegetation into an olive grove bounded by fig trees. The tenders of these fields were not about, so I crossed under their branches to reach untamed growth about the crag's southwestern rim. The vast expanse of Ephraim's hills offered a vista for my pleasure. The highlands of Judah blazed in the golden sun, shining far, far across the horizon.

Below me, in a sharp, dense slope of gnarled cedar, walked Reuben and Rachel, their steps weary, their clothes soaked and stained with dank earth. An exuberant Simon had scrambled halfway to their perch before Rachel heard his approach. My bondmate cautioned them to be silent, but they refused.

"I wondered if you would recall these cliffs!" Reuben exclaimed, embracing his brother.

"Almost forgot," Simon admitted. He welcomed his brother's greeting, but his eyes remained on Rachel. Her long, passionate stare told of her love.

Their reunion was a joy to behold.

"Not to worry," Reuben said with pride. "I have always remembered which cavern led all the way through. Though the underwater part ran longer than I recalled. A lot longer." He took a deep breath, then added, "She's a better swimmer than I am."

Rachel laughed. "I wasn't scared this time! Now that I knew what was going on."

The brothers spoke of earlier visits to these caves, their tales broken at times when Rachel voiced aggravations with the mud and clay, but I did not listen. Distant shouts grabbed my attention. I settled upon the earth to concentrate on the winds and soil, and I heard it all – hoof strikes, dislodged rocks, angry shouts. On the far side of this peak, the Assyrian host must have returned to the waterfall. They had discovered Simon's hoax but not his trail. That, at least, gave us some advantage.

Mixing among deep shadows, I drew near my bondmates to hear Rachel studying Simon's bandage. Reuben stared at the wound from a distance, wondering if he should get involved in what threatened to become a heated exchange.

"It grows tighter," Rachel guessed. "Does it not?" When Simon nodded, she tried to reason with him. "The more it dries, the worse it will get. I must redo this."

"Not now," Simon decided.

"How did you clean it?"

"I washed it with water."

"That's all?"

"What choice did I have? There was no time! Is no time."

"If we wait much longer," she stated with cold precision, "we may never have enough time."

"She's right," Reuben decided. "You cannot trust water from a well like that. The Assyrians probably poisoned it all."

"I would be dead now if they had," Simon reminded him.

"Oh, it wouldn't strike that fast," the princess said. "Not always."

"Or they sank wastes there," Reuben continued, not ready to give up. "They do that often, you know. A calf or a lamb. Or just their droppings."

My bondmate stiffened, then started walking south.

"Don't be stubborn!" Rachel snapped. "It must be checked!"

"When we are free," Simon grumbled.

"That might never happen," Reuben pointed out.

"Then it will not matter, will it?"

Through the morning we marched, hearing no signs of pursuit.
Simon urged us to run, and twice he broke into ragged, loping
sprints. But his strength and endurance drained with the light, his
wounds growing ever more painful. Rachel strode beside him,
knowing better than to press her beloved. Reuben proceeded on
to scout our path. To our good fortune, his trail eased our stress,
leading us south into a shallow valley between dust hills I had
haunted before. Though Simon feared exposure in the open
fields, I welcomed the respite, for this path ran somewhat straight
and clear, with few signs of prying eyes.

Reuben must have agreed with me. "The Lord has blessed us,"
he decided.

"How can this be a blessing?" the princess wondered aloud,
motioning towards Simon's wounds.

"It could be far worse," my bondmate replied.

In His light we traveled, making surprising speed. So well did
our journey pass that more than once Rachel contemplated
redressing Simon's wound, and though he refused, his resistance
weakened each time. But it hardened anew as the midday sun
warmed our backs, and with good reason – the loud echo of a
human horn. My bondmates turned to the sound.

"How close are they?" Reuben whispered.

Simon stood still, listening. "An hour's ride, at most."

He hobbled into a run, and the others joined him. To my
surprise, Simon led the trio up an eastern slope, a steep partition
of gravel broken by extended ribs of jagged rock and briar
patches. I drew near as they reached the top.

We stood at the edge of a long, narrow plateau, one bearing a
gentle grade flowing toward our southern homeland. A small
village lay in the center of tended fields, a shepherd's pasture,
and a thin line of vineyards. Far to our left ran a gravel road at the
foot of an almost vertical ridge of bare limestone.

"Hard to find cover here," Simon said. He glanced about once
more, then started towards the village.

"We could go back," Reuben suggested. But his brother would
not listen.

"There is no escape that way," he said. "And since they will end up here eventually, our only hope is to stay ahead of them."

Rachel muttered something unsettling, though I did not hear it. I had difficulty paying attention over the pain from my cracking pads and the spasms now wracking my spine. Simon chose that moment to break into an awkward run toward that settlement. Looking in that direction, I saw leaving the village a line of three carriages the humans called wagons, each one pulled by bored oxen. My lips soon dripped lust for those moving meals, but I brushed such thoughts aside – until my bondmates noticed.

"Merchants!" I heard Simon shout.

His interest stumped me until I looked anew at the burdens these oxen pulled. Those wagons held clay urns of different sizes, piles of cloth, wooden poles, and various pieces of hammered metal. Things only humans would need. I almost dismissed this observation, as was my habit, until I recalled that my bondmates were human and so might see something of value in that cargo. But to rush into the open raised all sorts of concerns. For Simon had correctly warned of crossing this plateau. If I stepped into those fields, I would surely be seen, and perhaps hunted. Yet I could not be sluggish, for my humans had already reached a slope of planted barley, putting them a fourth of the way to the brick huts.

To make matters worse – far worse – someone nearby chose that moment to blast another horn. It was not like those the Assyrians used. This instrument flowed through several tones, all lighter, smoother, and sweeter on my ears. But they came from a man's horn all the same, which meant trouble.

With great haste I drew my eyes across that plateau, finding no sign of the would-be musician. But my sight did fall upon points I initially ignored: piles of stones left at various places across my horizon. No doubt these represented rocks these farmers had unearthed in clearing this land, but to me, they offered hiding places in my need to cross this earth. Prizing these points of potential refuge, I hurried to reach the first one. When my passage drew no response, I stopped waiting and scampered to the second, then the third.

I made it halfway across the outer fields when the alarm rang again from what sounded like the village. I froze, wondering if I had been seen. But the few humans of the site, roused by the hollow ram's horn, looked instead at Reuben, who arrived first. Simon followed not long after, his hobbled walk aided by Rachel. I noticed with sadness how she made sure to adjust her veil. Since Shiloh, the princess had revealed her face to us, which was the kindest compliment she could offer. Now she hid her beauty once more.

The Maker smiled upon me then, sending the wind from the south. On its gentle breeze I heard the elder of the city look upon Reuben and shout, "Go away!"

"May the Lord bless you also," Reuben answered with light sarcasm.

"Take your lord and go! We want nothing to do with you."

"Your hospitality is appreciated," replied Reuben, welcoming the arrival of his brother. "We will move on. We are heading south, to Judah. Our homeland."

The elder, a white-haired man with a long beard flowing over his dusty brown cloak, looked upon my bondmates with utter contempt. The others behind him seemed to share this.

"No one here will help you," said the old one, holding his knob-riddled staff before him as a shield. "You think we want their swords at our necks?"

"Cowards!" To my delight, the princess strode forward. Some villagers backed away, but the elder met her with the tip of his staff. She thrust it aside, saying, "You would conspire with those devils?"

"Hold your place, woman!" the stubborn one demanded. But Rachel was not intimidated.

"Groveler!" she spat. "What were you promised for capturing us? Your lives? Your fields?"

"I care not for the promises of deceivers!" the man answered. "Assyrian vows are not worth the time it takes to hear them. But their threats are redeemed a thousand-fold if we fail!" He gazed into the horizons, lifting his hands to the heavens, and spoke of doom. "Our neighbors have burned. We have seen their homes razed to embers. And so it would fall upon us."

"We only seek passage south," Simon told him.

"Then go!" the man snapped. "We will give you nothing. We do not serve the devils, nor will we help you."

"May the Lord help you," Reuben offered. Those words he spoke from his heart.

"Your lord has abandoned us," the elder muttered. "We are punished. Let the devils do what they will! We'll not resist. Nor will we give in."

"You will die," warned Simon.

"We are already dead! Your passage here has assured that."

Throughout their talk, the other villagers stood in silence, as if mourning their fates. But as their elder acknowledged their doom, they turned away.

"Need it be so?" the princess shouted at them. "Must you give in?"

"Woman, you try my patience!" their leader snarled. "Who are you to attack us?"

Oh, did she carry herself proud then! Lowering her veil, she shouted to the world, "I am Rachel, daughter of Hoshea and Samantha. Princess of Israel!"

If he was impressed, the elder did not show it. Dropping his chin in acknowledgment, he said only, "So we were warned. Then our doom is truly upon us." He took a deep breath, then dropped his staff and opened his sorrowful beige eyes to their gaze. "Flee, my children. Go now. For before the night is out, the beasts will hear our horn and finish us."

"Why let them?" Simon said.

"Amos foretold this, lad, but we ignored him. Elijah warned us, but we didn't listen. Now it is over. Tonight we'll pay the debts of our fathers. Tomorrow we will be... who knows."

"With our Lord," came a voice from the pack.

Sometimes misplaced faith takes on great strength, for the human mind is strong, capable of great deeds and even greater despair. In this, these people deceived themselves. Not since the Passover has the Maker committed His subjects to dismay and death! Anyone who believes otherwise speaks falsehoods.

"You cannot just give in!" Rachel warned them. "Fight – or

flee! Do not the walls of Bethel yet stand?"

"Does it matter?" the man objected, defeated in spirit if not life. "This is our judgment. I will not defy my Lord by hiding from it."

I pitied my humans, having to endure that broken heart. But Simon did not allow my bondmates to dwell upon it. Taking Rachel's arm, for the elder's words had stunned her soul, Simon hurried my bondmates to the wheel ruts showing the eastern trail from the village. There, nearing the road, rolled the merchant carts.

My humans broke into a run. I sprinted towards another rockpile, ignoring the wandering eyes in hopes of keeping pace. As we reached our destinations, the earth at my feet throbbed with the deep pounding of hooves.

I did not need to hear the horn to know the Assyrians were nearly upon us. I crouched behind the rocks, then scampered to another pile, creeping south as I watched the northern horizon. Tension flooded my heart. With each step, my hair grew stiff, my lips dry. Bile burned my throat. I inched ever forward, and I watched. But when the devil's own came upon me, I was not ready.

With a roar as awesome as storms brewing upon the Sea of Chinneroth, twelve riders blazed past me. Their party split at the crossing, half circling the merchants, the others proceeding to the village. Only then did I notice my humans had disappeared.

A stiff gale broke upon us, drowning their voices. Yet as I watched the wagons, desperate to find my bondmates, I could see the Assyrian discussions did not go well. The three merchants tried speaking with the soldiers, then at them. Fingers waved. Hands rose in anguish to the skies.

Four of the riders turned their restless horses about. For a moment, it seemed all these humans talked at the same time, but few listened. One soldier drew his sword as the last craftsman rose to his feet atop his cart and dared point a finger into the Assyrian's face.

Irritated into action, the soldier began sorting through the weird and wonderful things within one wooden hold. The merchant, his anger almost beyond control, tried to shove the devil back. The Assyrians laughed at that until the black-haired tradesman drew a long Egyptian blade from beneath the bench at his seat and thrust its edge before the soldier's face.

Not knowing what would happen, I hurried forward – almost too quickly, as it turned out. At least one of the stallions sensed my presence and tensed, though his rider did not notice. Frustrated at standing still, an ox snorted and bellowed in the whistling breeze. The others stamped a bit but made no sounds, allowing me to again hear voices.

"Put it back – now!" the soldier demanded, more angry than fearful. "I don't care whose seal you carry. I'll cut your throat!"

If anything, the merchant grew more stubborn. Keeping his blade before him, he leaned back and said, "Have you known anyone who has slain a friend of the crown?"

He lifted his right hand, made a fist, and licked the worn bronze ring on his fourth finger.

"Here," he proclaimed, extending his arm to place his knuckles square before the Assyrian's nose, "here is the seal of Sargon. One of his personal seals, made just for me. For he likes to see when I come and where I go."

That interested me, so I crept closer, getting my first good look at this trader. Oh, he was slick! I could smell his fear and sense his rapid pulse, yet his brow signaled irritation usually claimed by a sovereign. His scarred cheeks witnessed of his ferocity and his hazel eyes told of nothing but hot fury.

To his credit, the soldier did not cower. But he did withdraw from the cart.

"Very well," he said, mounting his tan stallion. "Inform the king that his charges were kept."

"I will indeed," the merchant answered, brushing his curly black beard with his fingers. "Now get your men out of my way!"

I wondered if that would push this soldier too far. The Assyrian scowled but did withdraw his troops. At that, all three drivers snapped their reins, and the plodding oxen started forward. That's when I spied Simon's head emerging from under a pile of cleaned animal skins.

"Stay down!" the merchant barked. He leaned back to push my bondmate lower, all while snapping his reins to hasten the oxen. "They could still see you!"

"If those people talk, it will not matter," Simon muttered.

Curious, I turned to see what he feared.

At the edge of the village stood the elder, his head bent in anger as he confronted the mounted warriors. The second group of Assyrians joined them, reporting no doubt of the merchant's seal. Their leader seemed dismayed but did not order his riders back. Instead, this Assyrian officer turned against the villagers, who protested anew. This went on for several moments, giving the wagons time to disappear behind the plateau's southern ledge.

I lingered on to see what would happen.

When his aggravation could stretch no further, the Assyrian signaled his men to act. Riding among the small huts at sunset, the soldiers turned over water basins, scattered baskets of harvest, and threw down clothes hung to dry. One warrior trampled a townsman who moved to protect his goods. At the village's western edge, the Assyrians gathered timbers from a cooking fire and returned to the streets, igniting the dry sticks and grass of each roof they passed. Women and children charged in fear from the wreckage, sometimes to be run down without care. Soon every home burned under the winds that cursed this plateau.

Laughing, the soldiers spat upon the fleeing and dismayed villagers, then turned north. In their arrogance they passed into the settling darkness without torches, as if they were at home without light. I waited until their meandering line passed me by before striking down the last rider. His horse bolted, but I did not care; my heart pined for vengeance. Pinning the Assyrian in the center of the road, I snapped his feeble neck with one crushing bite. There I left him, discarded and broken, a sign to all the Lord's cowed believers that resistance was not futile – and that Assyrians were not worth eating.

Chapter 23

Escape

I regained my bondmate's company near midnight. They were not hard to find… no, far from it, for to my frustration, they had built a smoldering fire outside a cave northwest of Bethel. And that was not the only thing that set my hair on edge. Only one of the wagons had pulled off the road; the tracks indicated the others still headed south. Quickly I prayed the Maker would silence the tongues of their drivers, for I knew the Assyrians would find them. Most disquieting of all, I heard my weary travelers arguing amongst themselves.

"Don't be so stubborn!" the princess snapped at Simon. Then she turned her anger on Reuben. "Is he always this way?"

"I am fine," Simon moaned as I settled into nearby shadows. By the weakness of his tone, everyone knew he lied. Still, his heart beat strong – I heard it through the crackling fire, the snaps of several lonely crickets, a blissful multitude of bird songs, and our meandering breeze.

"Do not deceive yourself," the merchant warned, staring into my bondmate's eyes. "Take a good look."

They had cut away Simon's bandage to reveal a swelled puffiness about his neck and a mass of tortured purple flesh caked with black scabs.

"The Lord will mend this," Reuben held, though his voice lost some confidence as he gazed at that aberration of a shoulder. "We have endured worse."

"You," Simon reminded him with tired patience, "you are supposed to be on watch."

Smug as a hawk leaving an eagle's nest, Reuben slipped into the folds separating dark brush. I kept my limbs still as stone as he passed by; he did not see me.

"We should not have let them leave," Simon muttered, as if he stressed a point I would have made if I knew how. That caught me off-guard, for he was not one to remind people of disagreements.

"Enough of that," Rachel told her love. "Listen to Jarron."

The merchant – I guess his name was Jarron, for he turned at that word – stood pondering something in the fire, where a bronze kettle hung from a joining of knotted iron poles. Steam accented the breeze with hints of sour herbs and garlic.

"Madness," Simon grumbled, echoing my own thoughts.

"Many have said that," Jarron said with a laugh. But Simon did not appreciate his humor.

"Lighting a fire," he went on, "boiling such a stench. Anyone within a day's ride will know where we are!"

"Quiet!" the princess snapped.

"And you should be asleep," Simon countered.

That pushed her far. "Are you always this difficult?"

"Yes," Reuben called from the brush.

Jarron waved all that aside with a smile.

"My friends might agree with you," the trader told Simon while tearing apart a pale sheet of human cloth. He paused as if considering something, then started up again. "You know, once they did just that. 'You'll not remember much past that glass,' they told me. But I was determined to do it; five such pulls was the bet, you know. 'Down and straight to Aphek!' I said, and I swallowed the biggest mouthful of sour wine you ever saw. And I felt fine. Then I looked them straight-aways, and I said, 'Now to our wagons, my friends, and to Aphek I'll ride before you!' And I strode out, hitched my oxen, and made that journey in great haste, never once missing a rut."

Ripping apart the last band of cloth, he glanced at their confused faces and smiled. "Of course, we were supposed to be going the other way. And my friends, that's what they did. I just forgot that part."

With yet another chuckle he stood before us, so full of joy that Simon and Rachel soon joined in his laughter. Still, I wonder if they ever understood the tale. I did not.

"This," said Jarron, dipping the pale strips into the frothy kettle, "will draw out the sickness. It will help you heal."

That sudden return to reality stole my bondmate's humor. Simon looked with dubious eyes at the caldron, then squinted to study Jarron's face as the merchant stirred that repugnant broth. I could tell Simon fought a battle of his own, not wanting to offend his new friend, yet hesitant to submit to what this newcomer proposed. And then, there was Rachel.

"Healers are unnecessary," Simon muttered.

"It doesn't defy the Lord to use our minds," the trader argued, "to help wounds mend or to prevent illness. Medicines are tools, no different than plows or carts."

"It's not the same."

"Do you expect our Lord to always feed you? To clothe you? No, of course not. Indeed, was that not the point of Eden? That we had to care for ourselves? We had to learn this on our own?"

If that logic penetrated his reasoning, Simon did not show it.

"Sin," he whispered, "was our failure at Eden."

"That and pride," the merchant chimed in, cutting my bondmate off. "Our minds, my son, were made in our Lord's image. Our souls – not our bodies. The ability to create, to love and dream… in that, we are like our God.

"And so it is with our health, our nourishment. We eat foods that best strengthen our bodies, after all."

"Not always," interrupted Reuben's distant voice.

Simon appealed to the heavens in mock frustration. "Do you even know how to keep watch?"

"Sorry," his brother answered from the blackness.

Jarron could not limit his amusement to a smile. Laughing as might a bear after mastering a mighty ram, the merchant held his palms out to Simon, seeking forgiveness for his outburst. Rachel contained her mirth, though glee lit her eyes.

"When we pay attention, and we think of it," restarted Jarron, "we watch what we eat. We test the waters before drinking them. If we see or suspect bad things, we avoid them. If we feel pain, we figure out why. And if we can fix these things, like cleansing our water or digging a new well, we do it. If we can save a sheep or goat from a bog, we do it. Such it is with medicines. We use them. It is no different."

Simon stretched out his arm, then flexed his fingers. His face tightened at the cautious move. At times he turned his head to hide his pain.

I must say, I agree with Simon concerning medicines and healers. To some degree at least. To be honest, I might have agreed with Jarron as well if I could have heard him explain it again, but now was not the time. The merchant was filling the air with the most irritating odors as he pulled his drenched cloth strips from the broth to hang from somewhat straight sticks Rachel held.

"Where did you learn this?" the princess said while helping Jarron carry the cloths to Simon's side.

"This," explained the trader, relishing such talk, "this I was taught in Thebes."

"Egypt?" she exclaimed. He must have touched a dream within her. "Is this true?"

"Would I say otherwise? It is there I trade! Some of these herbs I can't get elsewhere… at least, that's how it was. Now, I do not know. Tyre merchants probably have them; maybe even Athens or Nineveh. Most likely, now that I think about it."

Giving Rachel a pair of patched leather gloves, Jarron told her to wring with care the simmering water from a torn cloth before using that to sponge clean Simon's wound. Drips splattered against her arm, but Rachel remained quiet, sometimes biting her lip to do so. My bondmate, who had retreated into his pain, cried out at his first contact with those steaming wipes.

"Patience," Rachel urged him. "It is already better. I can smell it."

"This will sting worse," the merchant warned. He then drew a ladle's fill of broth, let it cool somewhat, and poured it over

Simon's wound. My bondmate writhed, and water ran from his eyes, but Simon made no sounds.

Jarron examined the wound, then bathed that torn flesh a second time. My bondmate stiffened as that wave flowed down his side. Jarron grabbed an unused rag to blot that shoulder anew, then wrapped Simon's chest with torn strips drying above the cauldron. Jarron used the last wraps to bind Simon's arms above his elbows.

When his heart stopped racing, the young shepherd tested the mobility of his limbs. Rachel insisted he rest more, but Simon ignored her.

"I… I must be ready," my bondmate said. "Tomorrow. To fight."

"This arm will not bear a weapon for weeks," the tradesman said.

"Yes, it will."

The conviction in Simon's words demanded obedience… or forgiving patience. I have a hard time discerning between those moods. Jarron looked first to the princess, who hesitated to answer in her love for my bondmate. Reuben remained quiet in the shadows.

"A shield, perhaps," Jarron allowed. "I have a small one."

Simon gritted his teeth, clamped shut his eyes, and slowly managed to sit up.

"No, no, no!" the trader insisted. "Rest! You must rest."

"We must get to Judah," Simon replied. "Nothing else matters."

He focused his stern, pain-wrenched eyes on the princess, who met his gaze with a smile a whimsical imp would have trouble besting. But even if you could find such a lighthearted cub, I doubt his cheerful heart could have fazed Simon. Not content to relax or sleep, my bondmate climbed to his feet with all the grace of a wind-whipped willow. No one spoke, waiting instead to see what Simon could do. My shepherd paused, breathing deep while girding his mind and body for what lay ahead. Once he felt ready, Simon insisted we move on.

"That fire was a beacon," he reminded us, even as Reuben

stepped into the rippling light, his eyes broad with concern. Simon nodded to his brother, then said, "The farther we get from here, the better."

"We need rest," Jarron countered.

"Not here," Simon stressed.

Now, we were all too tired to move – at least I was, with my paws bleeding in the dust – but it was impossible to resist someone who withstood having hot stench poured over his bruised, battered flesh. Having no more protests to make, these humans drenched the flames with what the pot held, then reloaded those tools Jarron allowed them to use. Simon even helped, though Rachel told him several times to let things lie. Only when she threatened to hurt him did my bondmate relent.

Of course, she probably would never have carried out such a threat. Probably.

As they fit the last items into the crowded wagon, Jarron returned without his oxen. His worried eyes foretold his trouble.

"I doubt they will rise," he said, looking back to the bony beasts kneeling upon the earth. "Oh, are they weary! So weary. They refuse to move. And even more, I fear something spooked them. They resist my harness, my calls, even my food."

"Probably your cooking," Simon muttered, though I knew better. My scent soured their noses!

The four humans traded views. Then Reuben offered three words: "Let me try."

With Jarron's blessing, Reuben drew close to the sleepy bulls. He spoke warm, gentle things into their bent ears while rubbing his fingertips along the shallow crests overlooking their eyes. In a short while, the murmuring beasts nudged his forearms with their hair-shrouded horns. Once Reuben answered this with bright encouragement, the oxen rose, to the tradesman's delight.

At Simon's insistence, they added lard to the cart axle and cushioned its wheels with blankets and sheets. Reuben then hooked the oxen to that wagon and led the teamed beasts back to the rutted road, which circled two hills to a ledge of limestone deep within thorny brush. It was slow going but effective, taking us almost through the night. The cloths and lard silenced the craft well; I was close by and little heard its movement. Reaching a bastion of brush, Simon allowed their party to pull off the gravel passage for rest. I welcomed this. Finding a cave just large enough to curl up in, I whispered prayers to the Maker and retreated into precious sleep.

At first light I faced the sun and blessed the Maker for another day of life, then went off in search of a morning meal. Though loath to admit it, I was beginning to enjoy these little rabbit and squirrel chases. It was fun to stretch in the fresh sun and cool breeze, and as I got used to it, I doubted I could go back to being pampered by females.

I was wrong there, but that is another tale.

Of course, something more substantial to eat would have been better – a pig or sheep, for example, or better still, a nice, muscular oxen team – but there was no time for such a kill, and besides, without a family, I had little need for so much meat.

Before the sun cleared the horizon, I was crunching the bones of one fine hare. Then the deep bellow of a war horn shattered my contentment. Leaping to my paws, my claws stretched and ready, I bounded off for our camp.

Before I had even cleared my hill, there came a long-distance reply: a waffling tone from the southeast. Bethel, most likely.

Racing forward, I scrambled atop the rocky wall overlooking Simon's camp and nearly slid off a sandy ledge. Below me, Reuben glanced up to figure out what showered him with pebbles, then shrugged that off to help Jarron with their oxen. The princess and merchant rushed to reload the wagon.

"Leave it," Simon said, adjusting his loincloth.

Rachel did as my bondmate instructed, grateful to let their camping gear go, but Jarron persisted.

"You spend a lifetime gathering such things and see how you feel," he complained, drawing a handful of thick sheets into his arms. "This is my life you would abandon!"

"It could be your death," Reuben commented. With gentle words and caresses, he called the oxen to their feet.

"We must leave," Simon decided. He moved with all the grace of a tree, but at least he could move. When the time came, I knew he would do what was necessary.

Sorting a set of bowls by size into a goatskin wrap, Jarron tossed the tied bag into the back of the wagon and turned for more. That surprised me, for I considered he might just be a smart man. But Simon's hand on his wrist stopped him.

"Now," my bondmate said.

Even under Simon's powerful gaze, Jarron's resistance was so bitter, I thought the merchant might twist away for more camp gear. Yet with Reuben finished hitching the team and Rachel already in the wagon's hold, Jarron gave in.

"May the Lord help me gather more," he moaned.

Rounding two hills, then two more and others beyond that, we came within sight of the town they called Bethel. Reuben drew the wagon to a halt. Sorting through the brush atop a sandy knob, I looked long and hard at this southern temple city, not understanding just what I saw. But Reuben knew something of these things, as did Simon. Using soft, brittle words, they pondered what to make of that oily stench clinging to Bethel's blackened, empty parapets. They traded skepticism about thick beams and charred wooden platforms abandoned outside a broken gatehouse. No men remained to work these devices or the cracked fortress walls.

Just beyond that crossroads rose a wooden tower bound with plates of iron. It looked just like one I had seen in pieces outside Samaria. Greased axils readied its thick stone wheels to roll against the city walls, but no warriors stood by to manage it. Indeed, the scarred hills and trampled fields outside that citadel looked empty of life.

"I do not understand," Reuben whispered. Neither did I.

"Perhaps we should not question this further," Jarron wondered, though he remained still, protected and hidden somewhat in their wagon. "Perhaps we should move while our path remains clear. Take the road to the gates."

"No," Simon thought aloud. "We go around, then south."

"Why?" the merchant protested as Reuben's soft words called the oxen forward. "Bethel's streets offer the shortest path to your homeland."

"We must not go in there," my bondmate replied.

"The battle must be to the east," Rachel offered. She pointed to that horizon, where smoke tainted the winds.

"Pray it stays there," Simon urged.

The weed-pocked ruts they called a road curved along a line of small, rolling hills of grass and brush, the same gentle slopes I had seen leading to Judah's higher ranges. Sharper lines extended east and west. From both horizons echoed the horns of pursuit. They sounded oh so close! I took to running under cover of the crest, listening to my humans as their voices filled a warming breeze. Rachel twisted for some sight of what I heard.

"They draw close," she warned.

"They hope to drive us again," Reuben noted.

"And we cannot outrun them," Simon said with a frown, agreeing with his brother.

"Get out," Jarron ordered.

My bondmates turned to him in surprise, as did I. But his tight brow told of his concerns for them, and his love.

"Judah lies across these hills, my friends," the merchant said. "Run for it! I will continue down this path as swiftly as my oxen may plod. These Assyrians will follow me, I am sure… for a while at least. Perhaps you may escape!"

Reuben embraced the plan at once. Rachel kissed the tradesman's dusty cheek, embarrassing him with her gratitude. But Simon would not commit himself that fast.

"If they find you helped us," he began.

"What will it matter?" the princess said. "He has Sargon's seal!"

That brought a great laugh from the merchant.

"Nothing but a Philistia bobble!" said Jarron.

Enjoying her surprise, he licked the ring and held it before her.

"I keep it for luck," he explained. "Most people have no idea what Sargon's seal looks like, if he even has one. I just say this is it, with as much bluster as I can muster. I have fooled many people with this!"

"Philistia," Simon marveled. The cold hostility in his voice told what he thought of those people. And Jarron suffered from it.

Embarrassment flashed upon his eyes and brow, only to fade before his stubborn pride.

"I am a trader," he stated in his defense. "Who I deal with is not important."

"Sounds like Shechem," Reuben commented, nodding to his brother.

The trader stared at the two siblings with calculating eyes. "A hard thought, that is. If I had wanted the Assyrians to have you –"

"No one said that," Reuben cut in.

"Not with your lips," Jarron allowed, "but your eyes… they reveal all."

"Then we apologize," Simon said. "In our Lord's name, we ask your forgiveness."

They grabbed their staves and departed – not a fallen whisker too soon. For as they ran off, if Simon's wobbling may be called running, we heard horns erupt from the east. Jarron whipped the oxen forward. The beasts responded with a determined walk.

Oh, I hated to see them go! My stomach still grumbles, thinking of it!

With defiant patience, Simon turned his anxious hobble into a southeastern run. I watched his face as Reuben and Rachel followed, then outdistanced him. Simon's determined brow knotted in his battle with his shoulder pain. In his eyes burned a flame I knew would conquer, and indeed, it did not take long for his long gait to outreach Reuben's. But I wondered how long he could maintain this.

Taking whatever meandering paths they could find to avoid the hilltops – ravines, eroded gullies, sand traps, and the like – forced Reuben and Simon down a slow, winding passage towards Judah and home. To maintain my secrecy, I was forced to follow somewhat behind them. Yet I doubt they grumbled as I did. Indeed, except for occasional rests to check for pursuit, I heard little from my bondmates.

Such pauses did nothing but raise my tension. With every hill they climbed, horns bellowed to the sky, their cries ever nearer, their pitch ever higher. With every wind flowed the sour fragrance of hundreds of roaming stallions. That sweat enflamed my passionate hunger. Observing each windblown sign, as is my nature, I soon imagined Assyrian cavalry hiding behind every grassy knoll, ready to spring forth and pronounce my doom. Or provide my meal... how blessed that would prove! Yet when we rested and I edged up to the shallow heights around us, I saw nothing.

This breeze grew stronger as we rounded a mound of thorn-riddled earth. Then Simon stopped. From my position, I saw a long basin rolling south before my bondmates, its tall grass shifting about in circling winds.

"I am a fool," Simon whispered.

"You are not!" Rachel scolded him.

He pointed to the ledge at either side of the basin. "Do you see the tracks, the broken blades?"

"They are waiting for us," Reuben said, recognizing their danger.

I listened, not knowing what they meant. A shift in the breeze changed that. The air soured my nose with Assyrian sweat.

"We must leave!" Simon barked. "Now!"

"Which way?" Reuben wondered. But Simon was already gone, darting so close to me, I felt sure I would be discovered. At the last moment he twisted back for the road, crossing a ridge that curled south around a dark thicket.

"Wait!" Rachel called, her breath drained by their run. "Is... is it wise? To go there?"

Simon said nothing, sprinting up another hill at such a long, flowing pace that I doubted he felt his wounds or heard his love. Reuben paused to watch his brother, surprised Simon could make such an effort, then motioned for the princess to run.

"They knew," he explained, breaking his speech in full stride to take a satisfying breath. "They knew we would leave the road. They... they are waiting for us."

"So, we head back," she said, understanding at last. "But surely... that way's guarded as well!"

"Yes. We must pray for help."

Reuben urged her to push harder. She froze instead.

Emerging from the bushes came a squad of armored riders

upon snorting black steeds. Three mounts stopped as their warriors loosened long, black bows. The others lowered their iron-tipped spears and charged.

Chapter 24

Butchers

In that one swift segment of my life, probably little more than four breaths, I saw more wonders than most do in a lifetime.

The Assyrians made the gravest mistake of all, for to a man, they turned their backs on Simon.

Reuben gathered the princess behind him, his staff ready to parry any attack. I looked upon his determined yet hopeless stance and almost wept. But what choice did he have but folly? The shepherd could not abandon Rachel, even with five coal-black stallions stampeding toward him, their riders leveling shafts of barbed iron for his heart!

Onrushing hooves shook the earth. Reuben stood erect, his chin thrust forward in silent defiance. Rachel crouched fearfully at his back. The stallions came on, crushing the earth with each step.

In a blink of an eye, the center horse screamed, then leaped high and wide. The great black steed to his left shifted to avoid collision and stumbled, throwing his rider hard onto his back. The two warriors to the right desperately reared back, but their mounts could not keep from ramming into the flustered charger – which bled from an arrow plunged deep within his buttocks. Together the three corsairs tumbled to the earth, jostling or smashing atop their riders.

The hills wailed with the screams of the wounded. Now faced with just one attacker, Reuben took heart in his defense and thrust the princess back, seeking maneuvering room. I stretched forth my claws, ready to bound forward, but then I saw motion beyond Reuben's shoulder. There, atop an anxious horse jostling his rider, sat Simon, a black Assyrian bow pulled tight in his grasp.

Somehow he had dislodged the rider and captured his weapon! Incredible!

I watched my bondmate let fly an arrow point-blank into an Assyrian's chest, disabling him. But three others remained. As Simon scrambled to steady his frustrated stallion, an opponent's shaft whizzed past my bondmate's head. Another slipped just beneath his chin, somehow missing his flesh. The sight made me thank the Maker for that rebellious steed – perhaps he made my human too difficult a target! But just that quick my fears returned, for I saw a third archer take aim on Simon's mount, drawing back his string.

Things happen so fast when humans gang up on each other! It is so unsettling! They could benefit from our patience. But then, sometimes wonders come from this chaos.

Having unhorsed an opponent, Reuben let loose a spear taken from the fallen. It flew straight and true into the bowman, slicing his right arm as it lodged within his breast. The rider shuddered, then grasped for his throat. A black stake extended from his neck, thrown there by Simon's bow.

Gagging, the Assyrian slumped from his mount. His steed rambled away. The last of the devil's hounds followed the escaping beast, his heart gripped by fear.

With the attackers fallen or fleeing, Simon was able to calm his captured horse. But he lost none of his urgency.

"Hurry," Simon called to his brother. "Mount up!"

One saddled stallion waited beside his former owner as if he expected the warrior to rise and ride once more. The powerful charger snorted as Reuben drew near, but with soft words, this bondmate won the war horse's trust and climbed on.

The elevated view must have shaken him, for the shepherd issued a wail of sadness such as I had never heard before.

"Oh Lord, forgive us this," Reuben whispered.

Simon drew alongside his brother, extending a hand to grasp

Reuben's shoulder. My bondmate then slipped down to recover a quiver of arrows. Patting his stallion's neck, Reuben turned to the princess, who stood stiff as stone. He studied her, not understanding her paralysis, then looked to Simon, who knelt frozen on the ground, his eyes fixed on the hilltop.

There, within a ring of armored cavalry, rested three wood chariots, their hues white with golden trim. Beneath a red canopy on the center cart stood the Assyrian lieutenant we had seen outside Shiloh. His clothing was much improved – a sparkling suit of metal and leather armor stroked by a wind-blown cape of white and red, its surface decorated with golden swirls and stars – but his heart remained that of the calculating Ashur-jorath. With him rode two guards, one a leather-armored shield bearer, the other an archer – or so I was told later.

All three laughed in expected triumph.

Their arrogance so irritated me, I almost did not notice their prisoners. Then two warriors shoved a pair of bruised souls from the third chariot. The song of rattling chains pierced the wind. Sniffing the reek of old, weeping wounds, I closed my eyes and sank into woe. I could not bear to watch Elon and Gilead struggle to their feet, their hearts nearly broken.

I understood then the horror that could make Simon abandon his escape. For his fathers bore the scars of grievous torture.

They had little freedom to move, their arms shackled behind their backs at their wrists, those ties bound by thick chains to metal rings at their necks and ankles. From the filth clinging to their bruised and torn limbs, they must have been stripped of clothing for some time. But the dirt could not hide the evidence of lashings and burns. Elon bore a crimson scar carved across his left cheek, running from his ear to the folds of his neck. Perhaps it came when someone had shaved every stitch of hair from his head. Gilead, also clipped bare, carried gashes above each eye, and his slow-mending arrow wound oozed a crawling black stench.

Simon reached for his own wound. I bet he could not feel it, gazing as he did upon the agony his fathers had suffered.

"You were not supposed to be here," shouted Ashur-jorath as

he stepped from his chariot. "We felt sure you would press down into the valley."

"Let them go," Simon called. But the former lieutenant, now of the commander rank, gave my bondmate but a side glance. The carnage Simon had wrought was his main focus.

I saw two enemy soldiers crouched across the hilltop, their bows focused upon Simon. A third targeted Reuben.

"Most impressive," said Ashur-jorath, who gazed around the battlefield admiring the bloodshed. "Well done! What I would do to have you among my men!"

"Let them go," Simon repeated. Bitter hatred shrouded his voice. It chilled me, for in my heart, I felt sure the Evil One was at work in my human, turning his righteous anger into something foul.

The corruption of these Assyrians knows no bounds, but it is nothing before the pure evil that is Satan!

"No, my young warrior," said the commander, his fingers wringing through his beard. "Your run is finished. Return her to me."

The princess backed to Simon's side, but he acted as if he did not notice. Raising his stout body as a champion-born, Simon fit a long black shaft into his heavy bow, took aim, and shouted, "Never!"

Two more Assyrians targeted their bows on my human. Simon pointed his at their chief.

"Back off!" my bondmate shouted. "Do anything and I will kill him!

A slender smile formed on Ashur-jorath's lips. He lifted his left hand.

A sword tip burst through Gilead's chest, spilling dark blood across his filthy breast. That thin iron blade turned as the guard at Gilead's back gave his weapon a savage twist, splitting apart those aged ribs and churning their broken flesh. The Assyrian pressed his weight against the elder, wrestling with the hilt of his blade, but the shepherd's head had already fallen, lifeless.

I have witnessed death many times in my life, but never one as cold, as heartless as this. The earth itself seemed confounded by that malevolent act. My ears heard only the clanging of Elon straining against his chains. All else lay in silence.

From the depths of his heart came Reuben's prayer. "May the Lord give you peace," he whispered to his grandfather.

Rachel fell into a heap, sobbing. "It's my fault," she whimpered. "This… it is all my fault."

Two leather-armored soldiers dismounted as four others primed their bows, but Simon remained resolute.

"You have earned your fate," he told the commander, taking careful aim.

Ashur-jorath was undisturbed. As the chariot guards tossed aside Gilead's body, the commander turned towards Simon.

"Give her to me. Now."

"No!"

Thick black fingers yanked back Elon's hairless skull. At his exposed throat, in the grasp of a leather-wrapped hand, appeared a silver dagger lined with emeralds.

"This one will not be swift," warned the commander. "Each time you defy me, I will have them shave off a piece of skin, trim a finger, gouge an eye… or some other bit of flesh."

My claws shredded the soil beneath me. I watched that wretched Assyrian taunt my humans and half-wished Simon would strike him down. But then, he held but one arrow, and there was the princess to protect.

As Reuben looked about the trodden grass for a weapon, as Simon stood defiantly still, our princess drew herself up, resolution firm upon her brow.

"Enough," she told them all. She turned her gaze to the commander and declared, "Take me."

"No!" Simon spat. Two Assyrian butchers stepped forward, but the hatred in my bondmate's gaze stopped them.

Rachel turned her wet eyes to her love, then touched his bound shoulder. He did not loosen his ready bow.

"No more," she whispered. "No one else will die because of me."

"Nothing you do will stop them," Simon said. He retook his place before her, saying, "Their greed drives this. They seek a tool to destroy your father."

"A most effective one," Ashur-jorath agreed. His fiery stare focused on the princess. "Sargon, my king! King of Assyria, King of kings! He will take you before all Samaria. Oh yes! Right there, at the gates! And when he's finished, then I will take you. And you will be my slave. Mine! For life! And I assure you, I will enjoy that. Every day."

Reuben dove for a spear. Arrows flew, but none could touch his lithe form. Rolling to his feet, a finely crafted weapon in his right hand, he reared with grace, drew back his arm – and stumbled, screaming, as a black shaft lodged in his right breast.

"Finish him!" Ashur-jorath called.

I crept forward, detesting such needless slaughter. But my bondmate's actions stopped me. Simon aimed his notched arrow at the commander, then shouted, "Do anything and he dies!"

Their leader laughed, though none of his men acted.

"You want your father's fate?" called Ashur-jorath. "To be tortured day and night? Kept alive just to amuse me? Then go ahead! Release your arrow."

Elon cried out for his sons. An Assyrian guard struck his head with his fist, but their father still yelled, "Simon!"

A warrior plunged his dagger into Elon's side. Rachel screamed, as did Reuben, but his father said not a word. The Assyrian twisted the blade once, twice, then wiped the bloody shaft against their father's mud-caked arm.

Elon, contorting in his agony, remained silent.

Rachel wept, but my human did nothing, standing as solid as stone. I marveled at this, forgetting my bondmate had but one arrow.

The princess twisted him about.

"Kill me!" she implored.

He stared at her with empty eyes; his mind seemed lost.

"Kill me!" she repeated.

That awakened his soul. "Are you crazy?"

"I can take no more!" Tears rushed from her eyes. "Take my life, Simon! Then I'm no use to them. This will end!"

"No," Reuben stammered, struggling to his knees.

"Simon!" Elon cried.

His voice tumbled through the breeze. Laughing, the Assyrian guards had lifted his beaten form and thrown it onto the hillside.

Shouting his father's name, my bondmate ran forward. Rachel followed in his tracks, even as the enemy drew around Elon's still form. An arrow split the breeze cooling Simon's face, but he dodged the shaft, all the while keeping his own bow at the ready.

"Stop!" the commander shouted. I think he meant this for his own men, no doubt fearing wounds to Rachel.

An Assyrian foot soldier kicked Elon's head as the shepherd tumbled to a rest. In mid-step Simon let his arrow sail. That ruffian never hurt anyone again.

The mounted guards rambled down the hill, arming their bows. But the commander waved them to hold, for my bondmate had found another quiver among the dead. Oh, how quick he drew forth a black shaft! He was a marvel to watch!

Nervous, I edged to the lip of the crest. The earth told of rushing hooves.

Elon struggled to speak. His lungs had difficulty separating breath from blood, but some words came forth: "Remember... your God."

My bondmate stopped, shaken. Rachel took refuge in his shadow.

"Sad, such a death," remarked that Assyrian commander. "We shared some interesting talks... when he would speak with me. But all in all, he was wise for his kind."

Simon drew back one step, then another, his drawn bow never turning from Ashur-jorath. I could see the rage struggling to master him. Then Rachel surprised us all, darting out to grasp a hunting knife from a fallen warrior. Ashur-jorath laughed at that, then again when she scrambled to get behind her lover.

The Assyrian turned his eyes to Simon. "Enough! You cannot wish to die here, now. Like your fathers."

Everyone turned to a scream of desperation. Reuben stood there, desperate yet determined, having torn the arrow from his flesh. All our thoughts focused on him for that one shining moment, wondering just what this shepherd could accomplish.

But as he cast off that shaft, Reuben's strength dwindled away. Gazing at his running wound, he sagged to his knees, his energies spent.

I prayed for him. That such efforts should amount to nothing saddened me. But while the devil's hounds smiled, their hunger undiminished, Simon took courage in his brother's act. I looked upon him and saw his rage was once more under control. That gave him strength.

The commander swaggered in his confidence, content to play his games. It sickened me.

"Look around you," urged Ashur-jorath. "You cannot escape me. Not this time! Your fathers, they knew this. When you ran off with my prize, we tracked them down. Rather easily, too. We tortured them for a full day in that sorry place you call a temple. I thought they might know something of what you would do, but no. Neither one would give in. Proud men... strong in their own ways."

Reuben tried to show his contempt for the Assyrians but could muster little more than a whisper I little heard.

"Oh, I think they wanted to keep us there, hurting them," continued Ashur-jorath. "Just to help you. I came to admire them, your Elon especially. Oh, they both cherished honor – how they saw it, at least – but Elon, I could tell he wanted to kill me. I gave him a few chances, but he refused. His love for you restrained him. One must respect that, though it was foolish, thinking I might give you mercy. I offered him a swift death once. He refused me. Said that in life, there is hope. Silly, is it not?"

"No!" Rachel shouted. Then she paused, breathing deep to gather her wits about her. "No. There is hope. Always. In the Lord God."

That surprised me. Simon, too, I think. Here was this child of a heathen man, ignorant of the Maker for most of her life, now pledging her future to Him. It was inspiring!

"Deluded child," said Ashur-jorath. "I am your only hope. I am the servant of the great god Ashur, and of Sargon, King of kings. Under their authority, you live by my wish, you die by my command. There is nothing else."

"Fool!" Reuben spat from the bloody grass.

Simon knelt, his bow centered once more on the vile commander.

"You will not touch her while I live," Simon declared.

His target settled upon his heels. "You still choose death?"

"I live for my Lord."

The commander laughed.

"What confidence! You bested ten men here, true, but I have another ten at my disposal – no, nine; you slew one of those as well – plus six more riding my chariots. And these are but my flank sentries, the least skilled of my troops. A horn's blow away are legions of the best cavalry the world has ever known."

The Assyrian stood there, letting those words take root in Simon's heart, before coldly asserting, "Legions, my friend. More than you can count. And they are on their way."

The wind blew cold about us. I listened for all the things I loved – the chattering birds, crackling insects, waving grasses, whistling leaves – but all remained silent. Or so it seemed. Perhaps I was too bound up by my hatred and sorrow to hear them.

"You have lost," said that devil. "Resist me and your blood will mix with this dust, worthless and forgotten."

"So will yours," Simon warned.

The Assyrian smiled.

"So be it! We can trade our lives! But my men will still take her to Sargon. You cannot stop it."

I felt Simon's heart surge in rising confidence. His breathing slowed. Then my young shepherd laughed behind his bow.

The commander looked genuinely disappointed. "You would sacrifice yourself – for this?"

"I gave my life to my Lord long ago," Simon told him. Loosening his bow, he stood upright before his adversaries and folded his arms before him. "If I die, it is in His service."

The Assyrian stiffened. "So be it."

The nine Assyrian horsemen lifted their bows and primed the strings. As the breeze stilled, they took aim.

And I took off.

I knew not why. This was not my plan. But as I charged down the hill, blasting the valley with my courage-shattering roars, I felt only outrage… the need to strike down these evil spirits once and for all. It was all very uncharacteristic of me, I assure you – not even a true, conscious thought. But this feeling moved my heart as nothing has before or since.

One look at my onrushing form and the Assyrian commander scrambled for his chariot. The archers turned toward me, but their mounts lost their nerve as my voice shattered their ears and training. The chariot teams stamped the earth in their sudden fright, and when two found no drivers holding their reins – their crews having taken up their swords to approach the princess – the horses reared and fled.

These swordsmen prepared to greet me, their blades held ready. One fell victim to Reuben's spear, another to Simon's arrow. The others I disarmed, almost literally.

Without rest, I turned upon the cavalry and bellowed to the heavens. That alone spurred four stallions to flee across the ragged hillside. The other soldiers made a stand of it, keeping their mounts in line. One warrior hurled a shaft toward me – but that was his last act.

It was then, only then, that I realized I was not alone. Uncounted roars shattered these peaks from one horizon to the others. Up from the grasses swarmed lions without number, each one running down Assyrian footmen or pouncing upon riders.

I rested then, blood dripping from my maw and fur to pool under the flesh caking my claws. I felt great! Servants of the Evil One lay in tatters, their spirits removed from the earth. That was how it should be. The ways of the Maker revealed themselves! But my paws echoed from the pounding in the soil and the cries of avenging souls… an onrushing horde of Assyrian legions.

Though ashamed to admit it, I wavered under those ominous tremors. Doubts clouded eyes that had just witnessed the Maker's miracles. For my heart wondered, could all my assembled brethren stop these evil warriors? Was that even possible?

I glanced at Simon, pondering what to do. He stood there watching me, a serene stare accenting his weary face. The princess also waited, though for what I could not tell. I spied some amazement in her eyes – at my appearance, I guess, and perhaps at the carnage. Reuben, rising to his knees, had a more realistic fear about him but took hope from his brother. Not one of them understood their danger, though at the hilltop stood one who did.

"Sorcery, is it?" Ashur-jorath cried, his sword bloody from striking down two of my brethren. "Devilry of the worst kind!"

He shifted about as if looking for something. Suddenly leaping in satisfaction, he lifted high a gold-trimmed ram's horn from a steed trembling without his master.

"No matter!" shouted the Assyrian. "With one blast, I'll have enough arms here to slay all your world!"

In my heart, I feared he spoke the truth. Having spent his last shaft, Simon searched the grounds for more. Reuben sat too weakened to act, and I stood too far away.

The fire of the Maker lifted from my mind, and with it came sudden clarity. As if unaware of my actions, I found myself amid dead and dying humans who had hunted me throughout my life. Knowing what would descend upon us once that trumpet sounded, I ran for the hills.

The commander laughed, lifting the great horn to his lips. But no breath entered its chamber. To our surprise, the bloody head of a brown-quilled shaft pierced his chest. As Rachel cheered, I saw Ashur-jorath look in horror at the protruding bronze arrowhead. Awareness faded from his eyes as he fell to the earth and tumbled down the hillside.

"Who?" Reuben asked. But Simon did not know.

At that, the wind shifted, and I smelled oxen.

Chapter 25

Tales and tears

The reunion was unexpected and, I might say, irreverent. Looking down upon these rejoicing, wounded people, the brash merchant offered but two words: "Hurry up!" Rachel complied, helping Reuben into the back of the two-wheeled wagon, but Simon insisted on retrieving the bodies of his fathers.

"Leave them!" Jarron shouted, his black beard flowing in the breeze. "I hear others coming!"

Simon ignored that, focusing instead on dragging his father up the slope. Jarron watched my bondmate for a moment, stroking his beard and muttering things I doubt made sense to anyone but himself. Then he spun about, scanning the horizon.

"If they find out I did this," I heard Jarron say to the wind.

That's when he saw me.

"Another lion!" the merchant exclaimed in wonder and fear. "And a demon one at that!"

Rachel paused to question this, so Jarron pointed at me. I had stopped on the neighboring slope, standing in grasses I thought tall enough to hide me.

Reuben lifted his wounded body enough to reach the wagon.

"Magnificent beast," he said along the way, his aching voice still rich with harmonies and passion. "Look how freely his mane flows!"

Reuben's generous reply stunned the tradesman.

"It flows like fire!" Jarron shouted. "Never seen one like that!

And it's covered in blood!"

"The blood of our enemies," Rachel told their friend. "The hand of our Lord moved in its heart."

"He saved our lives today," Reuben added. And when Jarron scoffed at that, the lad told the story.

All that talk kind of stupefied me. I stood there, feeling the breeze against my skin, the sun warming my back, and an ever louder pounding in the earth. I stared at Simon dragging a second corpse to that creaky wagon atop Ashur-jorath's hill. Those tethered, weary oxen showed more sense, vexed as they were by overwhelming lion scents and blood stench. I listened to these humans spout words of praise about me, words that took time to say, hear, and understand, time that could have been spent fleeing our pursuers. And yet, for once in a long, long while, everything around me seemed at peace, as if this was how our Maker wished it to be.

In their words, in the truth of my deeds, I realized one side of my destiny had reached fulfillment. The Maker's hand had indeed been active in my heart, guiding my steps from Seth's first challenge to these shepherds. Perhaps even before that.

Here, in my unconscious sacrifice, it had gone full circle.

"But that's the sixth lion I've seen since getting here!" Jarron persisted. "Just what is going on?"

Were it not for the growing aura of dread I sensed in the soil, I might still have been there, overwhelmed by the Maker's work in my life. But the pounding, the scents in the shifting winds, the lingering warrior screams and shrieking lion strikes, the sound of spiraling vultures and hawks smelling fresh kill… all this swirled about me as a dark, looming truth. The Evil One had many minions in this world. Slay one, and the multitude will swarm, seeking revenge.

With that cold thought, I looked beyond the weary princess to Simon, who struggled to lay his fathers in Jarron's overcrowded wagon. With the Assyrians closing in, perhaps my destiny was not yet complete.

"Now," said Simon as he helped Rachel and Reuben into the wagon. "Now we go on. Down the road."

"To where?" Jarron wondered as my bondmate claimed a seat at his side. "The Assyrians own all these lands."

"South," Simon told him. "Go south."

"I tell you they are there! They will cut us off!"

"Not if you hurry!" Reuben interrupted, struggling to lie comfortably behind some cloth goods tossed above the bodies.

Grumbling orders to his oxen, the merchant turned his wagon south. I waited for them to get a fair distance ahead of me before starting on their trail, staying ever within the brush and tall grass.

Jarron urged his beasts to speed. His eyes rolled from left to right and back again.

"We're going the wrong way," the tradesman stated, drawing out his words. "There is no refuge here."

"Home," Simon replied. "We go home."

He might have said more, but I did not hear it. A deep Assyrian horn drowned his voice.

"There!" Jarron charged. "Did I not tell you?"

"You might have," Simon mumbled. Sagging under the weight of his wound, my bondmate cast his gaze forward as if searching the horizon. His weakness startled Jarron. I sensed panic rising in his breath, his heartbeat.

Simon lifted Jarron's discarded bow.

"You didn't tell us you had this," my bondmate muttered.

"I had forgotten," the trader snapped. Then his tone softened. "You think these Assyrians would have left me alone if they'd seen my bow? I kept it hidden. Well hidden. Like my sword, until I needed it. And then, well, I forgot about it. Till I saw that first lion."

With the Assyrians to my back, I pushed a bit west, crossing the road to get to Simon's other side. That forced me into one sprint over open ground, but the wagon's eyes were not turned my way, so I felt safe.

Dust soiled winds to the east. The merchant gave them but the briefest glance before proclaiming their onrushing doom. Simon noticed this but paid it little heed, for something else held his attention, something across the slope.

"The marker!" my bondmate exclaimed. He pointed to a

stained slab of rock sticking up as a finger beside the road.

"What of it?" Jarron wanted to know. Simon turned to his brother, asking if he recognized it.

"No," Reuben admitted, taking a deep breath. "Should I?"

"See King Ahaz's symbols? The stripes? The proclamation?"

Jarron called his oxen to speed, this time by name. The beasts snorted and churned on, as stubborn oxen will do when they decide to.

"It is the boundary of Judah!" Simon told his brother. "We are here!"

"We will be," the merchant stammered, "if we outrun them. Not that these Assyrians will care."

"They will," Simon said. "Look!"

From the slopes before us emerged a churning dust wave, one smaller than that to the east, but quicker and more turbulent.

Within both clouds I could see the shapes of riders. Many riders. And I heard pounding hooves through the breeze.

"Who will catch us first?" Rachel wondered aloud.

"It little matters, once we pass the marker," Simon stated.

I looked first to the east, then the south, and foresaw a grand convergence at that upraised chunk of carved, painted limestone. I ran forward, casting aside all discretion. With this many hounds of evil about, I would stand ready to strike.

Fresh squeals split the air. I could smell a hint of burning. From the wagon wheels came thin wisps of greasy smoke.

Jarron spied this. With a snarl, he pushed his oxen harder.

Horse soldiers thundered in from the east – tall, thick-limbed humans, their black and gray beards floating upon the wind. The sun sparkled upon countless iron plates accenting their leather shirts and leggings, those strange conical caps, and their damp lace-up boots. Those proud horses also bore sheets of dark scales to protect their necks and flanks. Hard they rode, shaking the hillside, and yet the stallions displayed no weariness, scorching the winds with their fiery eyes and scalding neighs.

Against this vanguard approached eight riders pushing their steeds at a hard gallop. These men bore less arrogance, their bodies firm but short, their soiled and torn cloaks more like those worn by farmers and shepherds I knew, of many different cuts and styles. Only one cloth brought them unity – black scarves worn about their heads to ward off the sun and sky. One among them stood out. This man of red hair and broad shoulders rode at their head, drawing all eyes with the glittering rings of silver atop his oiled leather vest and waistcoat. Upon his brow shone a shiny white disk. It lent a fire to his eyes, which focused with little kindness upon our wagon.

The air filled with hoof-thrown dust. I hid a few leaps behind the landmark, holding my breath as the oxen rambled past, almost dragging their whining wagon. With the southern riders drawing near, Simon had Jarron bring the cart to a halt. These horsemen did not rest at our side but went on to the limestone signpost. There the eight formed a line across the trail. At the command of the one, they lifted high their short swords of beaten bronze.

"Halt!" their leader shouted to the Assyrians.

That horde charged on. I felt the earth moan even more.

The scarlet-crested warrior stiffened atop his steed. I sensed confrontation within him, and it irritated me. Had my bondmate not sat beholden to this man, I might have stalked him myself.

"Halt in the name of King Ahaz!" their leader proclaimed.

A central figure among the Evil One's own held aloft his right hand. His troops came to rest a spear's length before the others, their stallions in perfect order, not one letting down his guard.

"Return our prisoners!" the dark-bearded chief shouted in shrill, slurring Hebrew.

A smile came from the blood-haired one.

"Greetings to you as well," he answered.

The Assyrian would have none of that. "Forget the pleasantries! I barely know your slippery tongue. Just return our prisoners at once!"

"I know not what you mean."

Simon moved to join the southern riders, his hobbled run revealing his wounds. The Assyrian bristled at his approach, but the southern leader did not seem to notice.

"I am Caleb," he announced, "commander of the royal host of King Ahaz of Judah. And you?"

"I am Ashur-memial," said that dark-haired one, his voice struggling to contain bitter anger.

"I greet you," said Caleb, "and welcome you to my homeland. Now tell me – by what right do you make demands of the king's right hand?"

That veiled threat meant nothing to this Assyrian. "The right of just revenge!" he snapped. "Those men slew our commander!"

Drawing a broadsword of shiny Damascus steel, the Assyrian aimed the point of his blade toward Simon, who now stood at the Judean's feet, his bandages red from renewed bleeding. Caleb turned with confidence to look upon my bondmate for the first time.

"This vagabond does not look capable of such a deed," remarked the commander. Turning to Simon, he said, "Is this true?"

Simon nodded.

"Then it is true?" Caleb asked again.

"Yes," said my bondmate with a sigh. "Their commander died at our hands. But only after he tortured and killed two of our party. My father and grandfather." His voice almost broke then. "They lie in our wagon."

This drew visible sorrow from the commander and grumbling from his men. Motioning to the Assyrians, Caleb asked, "And they inflicted your wound?"

"Yes," Simon answered, "and my brother's."

"They disobeyed the law of Sargon," Ashur-memial snarled.

"I thought Shalmaneser was king," said Caleb, his tone questioning both their answer and honor.

The Assyrians shared angry whispers before their leader ordered them quiet.

"Shalmaneser defiled Ashur and has been replaced," he said.

"In the west," Caleb agreed. "Your Sargon has not yet overcome the east, has he?"

His counterpart straightened in his saddle. His eyes flared.

"I would pay more attention to your own borders," he warned.

"Ah, but that is why I am here," Caleb countered. "My king had come to an understanding with Shalmaneser. Under his truce, we would not expect armed troops approaching our God-given lands."

"We demand our prisoners!"

The Judean commander turned hard as granite. "Make your demands in the royal court – not before me!"

A black flame heated Ashur-memial's gaze. "You would do well to hear me. You have but eight men. I have more than 200."

"And behind this hill," Caleb stated with cold precision, "gathers the royal host."

At that, his riders tore away their weathered cloaks to reveal leather armor much like their leader's.

"Why else do you think I am here, underling?" snapped Caleb. "Do you believe my king would allow Sargon's bloody fist to draw near his borders and not stand ready to bludgeon it? If you value your life, use your next breath in prayer, for I will allow no further insults against my crown."

The devil's hosts stiffened by that sharp response, but Ashur-memial was not one to cower.

"We will set aside the murderers for another time," he said with a slow, deliberate tongue. "All we want now is the girl."

"Why?"

"She was stolen from Sargon's slaves."

"She escaped his prison!" Simon snapped.

"Quiet!" Caleb ordered. That brunt command silenced not just my bondmate but the Assyrian. The Judean nodded for the mounted one to continue.

"I respectfully request she be returned to us," said Ashur-memial through pursed lips. "I assure you, Sargon's goodwill hinges on this."

"She is my bride," Simon stated.

"A northerner?" Caleb questioned.

"She is the daughter of Hoshea!" the Assyrian protested. "Our prisoner!"

"My bride," Simon repeated.

I saw those strong words take root in all the Hebrews. Caleb glanced at his men, then met Simon's gaze and nodded.

"Then she must remain here," the commander stated.

The Assyrian objected, but Caleb would hear none of it. At a simple raising of a finger, a Judean soldier lifted a horn to his lips. Before its first echo died, four other notes sounded from hilltops behind us.

"Tell Sargon that he can bring this up in King Ahaz's court," Caleb told the devil's own. "Now take him this word and get your troops from our border, or I will dispense with Sargon's guard and add his fine stallions to my king's stables. Go!"

Rarely have I seen more disgruntled looks than upon those bearded Assyrians! They muttered and pouted and cursed and spoke of foul deeds they would do to Judah, but in the end, they retreated. Only then did Caleb allow himself to relax.

It was much the same for me. As those devil hounds returned to their northern haunts, I felt my life was again my own.

Drawing their steeds to the wagon, the Judeans dismounted and offered aid. Caleb himself was most friendly. Looking first at Simon, then Reuben, this commander sent a rider to summon his personal physician from the nearby encampment. Then his eye settled on Jarron, and with it came a smile.

"The son of Eldari!" he crowed to the tradesman. "What are you doing here, mixed up in all this? I thought you never left the coasts!"

"Never meant to," Jarron said, embracing the commander. "But strange things have happened to me every step of this trip. A sudden wind made me turn into Ephraim, and a rockslide kept me from going back. Then these Assyrian dogs cut off the eastern route, so I had to come down this road – and found these people here."

"He hates high paths," Caleb told Simon.

"Yes, well, it was not my choice. It seems fate cast me here."

"I might say the same," the commander said. "My lieutenant was watching Bethel burn when a swarm of lions rampaged through the plains. I tell you, never had I seen so many gathered like that!"

Simon chuckled. I shared this. The Maker weaves his garments from ever-distant threads, it seems.

"We pursued several up this slope, but they slipped away –

and there you were, chased by Assyrians!"

"I am glad you did!" Jarron said. "Oh, blessed is the Lord! He stands ever at our side!"

They went on like that, praising each other and the Maker, but what was said little interested me. Indeed, I felt a warm confidence in my heart that my time here was done. I slipped deeper into the tall grass, my soul content, my destiny fulfilled. Or so I thought. Yet my heart felt one more need: to sneak a last look at my bondmate. Simon was easy to find, lying within the wagon, his head upon Rachel's lap. Wet from tears of joy, she wiped clean his face and lowered her lips to his. They kissed, once and again, and they shared whispers of love and thanksgiving. One of them laughed… I do not recall who. Then came tears of sadness. Simon leaned over to hug Reuben, who struggled to join in. Rachel embraced his left side, Simon the right. Together they gave in to their grief, lying alongside the bodies of their fathers.

I watched this, wiped dry my eyes, and knew my calling continued. But that, my friends, leads us to another tale, one for another day.

Book Two

By Kirby Lee Davis

Afterward
and Glossary

As you may recall, *The Prophet and the Dove* ended with Jonah's death and Nahum's plunge into slavery. These events happened because Adad-nirari, the governor of the Assyrian capital of Kalhu, overthrew his father Ashur-nirari to become king of all Assyria. Taking the name Tiglath-Pileser, which made him third monarch in his people's rich history to adopt that title, this nationalist would use his opposition to Jonah's ministry as a tool to unite his fractured people. His political and military reforms would lead Assyria into its most significant expansion period – one that would target both Hebrew kingdoms, as Jonah foresaw.

That underscores The Jonah Cycle's foundation. To understand how *The Prophet and the Dove* weaves its tale within known history, check out that novel's afterward, glossary, and study guide. I will include a smaller glossary here since this novel juggles fewer historical ties requiring explanation.

Lions of Judah carries The Jonah Cycle forward two decades to Assyria's final invasion of Israel. That prediction by the Dove took a few generations to realize because Tiglath-Pileser III focused on reorganizing his government, reuniting his kingdom, and reclaiming surrounding territories. He allowed the Israeli kings Menahem, Pekah, and Hoshea to escape conquest by paying annual tribute, although this did not come without bloodshed. Twice Assyria had to invade the northern kingdom before the Hebrew kings caved in. That second incursion ended when Hoshea assassinated King Pekah and agreed to Assyrian demands. Tiglath-Pileser rewarded him by giving Hoshea the crown

That tribute policy continued after the Assyrian titan died around 727 BC, leaving the kingship to his son Shalmaneser V. But when Hoshea rebelled, the Assyrians marshaled their troops to topple the Hebrew offenders once and for all.

That's as far as *Lions of Judah* goes into recorded history. Unlike Book One, which incorporates many actual or interpreted Hebrew and Assyrian timelines, Book Two presents a romantic, fast-paced adventure set in the shadow of Assyria's offensive. *Lions of Judah* ends well before the aggressors captured Hoshea or conquered Samaria, which required a three-year siege. But this novel offers many insights into how the invaders overran the northern kingdom, with hints of the rift that would see Sargon II take the Assyrian crown from his brother.

I wrote *Lions of Judah* roughly three decades ago, after I finished *The Prophet and the Dove*. The plots for these sequels flowed with rapid grace from dreams and prayer, and so, as my proofreaders tackled this novel, I went on to pen what would become Books Three and Four in The Jonah Cycle, plus a modern-day sequel. Because of that productive output, this book received far less editing at that time than the others – which proved quite an obstacle when I returned to these manuscripts in 2018. At one point I paused a year in my editing, finding many problems with this novel and no ideas on how to solve them. But with prayer and patience, the answers came to me.

Some may see *Lions of Judah* as a biblical follow-up of sorts to *God's Furry Angels*. While that guess makes some sense to outsiders, considering how I published *GFA* first and both novels employ a feline viewpoint, in truth, I wrote *Lions* almost a decade before my furry allegory. The only real connection between the two is my fascination with cats... which raises the question of why I would share this swashbuckling adventure from a lion's standpoint.

First, I thought this wartime love story offered the kind of escape and rescue tale everyone enjoys. Telling it from a lion's point of view gave me a different and unique perspective. This narrator provides a touch of fantasy. It allowed me to address human morality and theology from an outsider's line of sight without interrupting the action. It gave me some freedom to handle languages, cultures, and history a bit loosely, since our viewpoint character was no expert on such subjects. I also drew encouragement from how few people today understand the role lions played in the Promised Land – or that a surprising difference separated these predators from their better-known African brothers.

In researching The Jonah Cycle, my journalist/historian eyes ranged from translated Assyrian tablets and obelisks to recorded histories, academic and cultural papers, cookbooks, archival maps, military analyses, and many other sources. Unfortunately, I lost many of my personal records through some sloppy household moves over the last three decades, and from problems transitioning my manuscripts and notes through three different, relatively incompatible computer systems. I can point to some helpful general resource works, such as *The Assyrians* by H.W.F. Saggs, *The New Manners and Customs of Bible Times* by Ralph Gower, *Eerdmans Handbook to the Bible*, and the *Zondervan NIV Atlas of the Bible* by Carl G. Rasmussen. *The Prophet and the Dove* afterward, glossary and study guide provide still more resources.

Abraham – the starting point of the Hebrew people and heritage, as told in the Old Testament book of Genesis. Abraham became a spiritual patriarch in several world religions.

Ahab, King – the seventh king of Israel's northern kingdom following the division of Solomon's realm, and husband of Jezebel of Sidon. Both are reviled in the Old Testament for their disregard of the Hebrew faith.

Ahaz, King – an abbreviation of Jehoahaz II – the twelfth king of Judah, the Hebrew people's southern kingdom at the time of The Jonah Cycle. While historians split in defining Ahaz's

timeline, the Bible tells us that, upon taking the crown from his
father Jotham, Ahaz faced immediate pressure from the northern
kingdom's King Pekah and Aram's King Ansephanti Rezin to
join arms in resisting Assyrian aggression. Ahaz chose instead to
pay tribute to Assyria, first under Tiglath-Pileser III, then
Shalmaneser. Those events set the stage for Judah's limited
involvement in *Lions of Judah*.

Amos – one of the Old Testament's "minor" prophets. Active
during the time of Jonah and Hosea, his namesake book is
considered the Bible's first recorded prophesy.

Ansephanti Rezin – also known as Ansephanti or Rezin –
was the governor of Aram, a conquered providence of the
Assyrian Empire during the time of Jonah. From his palace in
Damascus, Ansephanti led a revolt as Assyrian power weakened.
Rezin then entered his territory into a defensive alliance with its
northern neighbor, the Urartu Federation. Ansephanti's kingdom
fell to Tiglath-Pileser's resurgent Assyria around 732 BC.

Aphek – this name refers to at least two ancient towns in the
Hebrew's northern kingdom, Israel. The Aphek that frequently
rises in the first two books of The Jonah Cycle lies along the
traveling route between the Israeli capital Samaria and the
Philistine port of Joppa.

Aram – an ancient kingdom east of Canaan, in lands now part
of Syria. Damascus was its primary capital. Its people were
known as Arameans.

Ark of the Covenant – a sacred artifact of the Hebrew faith
described in the Old Testament book of Exodus. Israeli craftsmen
made the ark to hold the stone tablets carved with the Ten
Commandments and other relics from the Exodus.

Arumah – a town mentioned in the Old Testament book of
Judges. While historians do not know where this community
stood, many suspect it sat roughly six miles southeast of Shechem
under the present-day ruins of El-Ormeh.

Ashur – the primary god worshipped in Assyria; one that also
went by the names of Assur and Asshur. The Old Testament book
of Genesis also names Ashur as the second son of Shem, the son
of Noah. Ashur and other sons of Noah settled the lands that

became Assyria. Note to book readers: for clarity, The Jonah Cycle uses "Assur" to refer to the Assyrian city by that name and "Ashur" to reference the deity. Asshur gets left out in the cold.

Ashur-jorath – an Assyrian soldier, lieutenant of the First Brigade of Aram, or so he states his title with his introduction in *Lions of Judah*. The first word in his name refers to his chosen god.

Assyria – an ancient culture that rose along the Tigris and Euphrates rivers in upper Mesopotamia, its lands ranging on today's map from northern Iraq to southeastern Turkey. Its people were known as Assyrians. That fertile area supported a cyclical empire-building culture that would reinforce or threaten regional stability (depending on your point of view) for two millennia. During Jonah's lifetime, Assyria's military influence experienced one of its lowest ebbs, but the tottering nation found new strength under King Tiglath-Pileser III. He reorganized its government and military, then led the nation into its most extensive expansion period. This phase underscores The Jonah Cycle.

Bethel – a city in the splintered kingdom of Israel where the northern kings established one of two temples intended to replace the sacred center in Jerusalem. These kings hoped this would stop Hebrew pilgrimages from Israel to Solomon's Temple in the southern kingdom.

Canaan – in ancient times, this was the general area where Moses and Joshua guided the Hebrew people to live after the Exodus. It owes that name in part to a grandson of Noah, also named Canaan, who settled that region long before the Hebrew people existed. These lands spread from the eastern coast of the Great Sea to the Jordan River, rising north from the Arabian Peninsula to the hills of western Aram. Today this area includes parts of Israel, Syria, and Lebanon. Some definitions of Canaan may feature lands east of the Jordan River. By the time of the Roman Empire, this general area was known as Palestine.

Chariot – a two-wheeled cart led by one to three horses. Its primary use ranged from a lightweight weapon/soldier platform to small cargo/personnel transportation needs and racing. Individually or in fleets, the chariot served as the tank of the ancient world when used on compatible terrain. Its carrying capacity and influence evolved with the user's ability to armor, stabilize, and empower this wheeled platform. Its value encouraged the development of road paving and maintenance.

Chinneroth, Sea of – one name used during Old Testament times for the great lake anchoring the northern edge of the Jordan River Valley. Hebrews settling the Promised Lands also knew this lake as the Sea of Chinnereth. From New Testament times, history has recorded this body of water as the Sea of Galilee.

Cubit – an ancient unit of measurement, its actual length depending on the user's culture. Various sources today have estimated a cubit extended about 18 inches or 44 centimeters. To present a biblical reference, in Genesis 6:14-15, God tells Noah to build an ark 300 cubits long, 50 cubits wide, and 30 high.

Curtain wall – in ancient times, this usually refers to a wall of stone or brick built for defensive purposes. It did not support a roof.

Damascus – one of the ancient world's great cities, capital of the land of Aram, now part of Syria.

Damascus steel – a forged metal renowned in ancient times for its unusual strength and resilience. It was usually found in swords, knives, and other weapons. Modern historians have little solid information about this legendary product. The methods used to forge this metal remain matters of debate. Even the term "Damascus steel" has multiple possible sources and meanings.

David – the third king of Israel's united monarchy; one of the great heroes of the Bible and our ancient world.

Elijah – one of the great Old Testament prophets, his ministry a thorn in the side of King Ahab of Israel's northern kingdom roughly a century before the works of Jonah.

Elohim – a Hebrew name for God at the time of Jonah. It gained greater use among later generations.

Ephraim – this name, which means "doubly fruitful" in Hebrew, holds great historical importance for ancient Israel. As the second son of Joseph, Ephraim fathered one of the twelve Hebrew tribes. His descendants settled in a hilly section of the Promised Lands, sharing their territory with the tribe of

Manasseh. By the time of The Jonah Cycle, this region was part of the northern kingdom of Israel. These lands offered a mix of agricultural opportunities. Rocky hills dominated the eastern areas, carved by numerous gorges along a steep descent past the mountains Gerizim and Ebal to the Jordan Valley. Ephraim's westward slopes boasted vibrant pastures with plentiful water.

Fertile Crescent – a unifying name for the watered basins of the Nile, Jordan, Euphrates, and Tigris rivers, along with their connecting Great Sea shores, where a large number of early human civilizations began. These lands stretch today from Egypt and Israel to southeastern Turkey, Syria, Iraq, and Iran.

Gentiles – anyone who is not a member of the Hebrew faith.

Gerizim – a mountain within the lands of Ephraim in the northern kingdom of Israel. Its peak rises almost 3,000 feet above the Great Sea (now known as the Mediterranean Sea). Gerizim's footprint connects with neighboring Mount Ebal to provide a narrow valley that extends toward the Jordan Valley. Their peaks stand about two miles apart.

God – in general terms, this word may refer to anyone or anything with perceived supernatural abilities or ambitions. When capitalized, this word refers to the God of the Hebrew and Christian faiths, the Creator of all that is, the Alpha and Omega, the Supreme Being, also known as I Am, the Lord, our Father in Heaven.

Golan – a plateau in northern Canaan, east of a body of water known in ancient times as the Sea of Chinnereth or Chinneroth (later the Sea of Galilee).

Great Sea, the – a large body of water today known as the Mediterranean Sea.

Hebrew – descendants by blood or faith of Abraham, Isaac, and Jacob, central figures of the Old Testament book of Genesis. All three patriarchs came from a family chosen by God to father the people of Israel. They are known as Hebrews, or Jews, an ancient slang word adapted from the name Judah.

Hosea – an Old Testament prophet whose marriage to the adulterous Gomer symbolized God's relationship with the Hebrew people. When Benjamin (in Book One of The Jonah

Cycle) first met Hosea, our narrator dismissed that prophet as a beggar. Later, Benjamin came to admire Hosea, loving him as a father.

Hoshea – the 19th and last monarch of ancient Israel's northern kingdom, who historians believe ruled from around 732 to possibly 721 BC. He gained the throne by assassinating King Pekah, who had sought to join arms with the border kingdom Aram to resist Assyria's encroachment. Hoshea then made amends with Assyria's King Tiglath-Pileser III, who gave his new vassal the northern kingdom's crown. But after his benefactor died around 727 BC, replaced by Shalmaneser V, Hoshea would break ties with the Assyrian empire and bring about the invasion depicted in *Lions of Judah*.

Isaac – father of Jacob, son of Abraham. A historic father figure and patriarch of the Old Testament and Hebrew people.

Israel – a name with many meanings. It refers to the Old Testament patriarch Jacob, who God renamed Israel, his sons fathering the twelve tribes of Israel. This name also applies to the northern kingdom formed after the death of Solomon. In modern times, this noun is the name of the Hebrew nation.

Jacob – the son of Isaac whose children formed the branches of the Hebrew people. To complete this transition, God would give this Old Testament patriarch a new name: Israel.

Jeroboam II, King – often referred to simply as Jeroboam, the thirteenth king of the northern kingdom of Israel. He held that throne for 41 years, according to Old Testament texts. His reign carried into The Jonah Cycle.

Jew – an ancient slang name for the Hebrew people, drawn from the root name Judah. Over time, this word gained widespread acceptance and usage.

Jonah – also known as the Dove – an Old Testament prophet who sought to escape God's mission for his life, but through a series of miracle feats, he gave in to deliver God's warnings to Nineveh. Jonah also led the military forces under Jeroboam II, the thirteenth king of the northern kingdom of Israel.

Judah – a name with many applications. Judah was the fourth son of the Old Testament patriarch Jacob. Judah's descendants became one of the twelve tribes of Israel. After the death of Solomon, the southern kingdom took the name of Judah. As the land of Jerusalem and the Temple, the Hebrew faith became known as Judaism. A shortened form of that – Jew – became a slang name for the Hebrew people.

Kanah River – a muddy stream that meanders west from the Mount Gerizim floodplain to the Great Sea (now known as the Mediterranean Sea). This brook served as the boundary between the tribal lands of Ephraim and Manasseh in the Promised Lands.

Lebonah – a community in the northern kingdom of Israel located just north of Bethel, near Shiloh. Nahum mentioned the "massacre of Lebonah" while narrating *The Prophet and the Dove*. Readers encounter this tragedy in *Lions of Judah*.

Lord, The – a term that, over time, became accepted as a primary name for God.

Maker, the – the name of God as used by the lions of Judah.

Manasseh – a name with many applications. Manasseh was the first son of Joseph and Asenath. The descendants of Manasseh became one of the twelve tribes of Israel, settling after the Exodus in a hilly section of the Promised Lands. This region they shared with the tribe of Ephraim, descendants of Joseph's first son. Manasseh also was the name of the kingdom of Judah's fourteenth king, the oldest son of King Hezekiah. Hezekiah was the son of King Ahaz (or Jehoahaz II), leader of the southern kingdom at the time of *Lions of Judah*.

Mazzebah – the Hebrew word for a standing stone, a marker set in place to honor a covenant with God. Using such stones to mark agreements or events was common among many ancient cultures in the Mesopotamian area.

Moses – one of the great figures not just of the ancient world, but all human existence. If you don't already know this, read the Old Testament book of Genesis (to prime the well) and Exodus (to grasp the significance of it all). Wrap it all up with Leviticus, Deuteronomy, and Numbers. Ideally, you may read these through Dennis Prager's *The Rational Bible* series, though that will take time, as he's only published three books to date. But they're important ones.

Nahum – a biblical prophet who enters this novel series as Benjamin, a young slave and comrade to Jonah in Book One of The Jonah Cycle. Historians suspect this prophet was active in the southern kingdom of Judah during the reigns of Hezekiah and Manasseh. Nahum's self-titled Old Testament book captures prophecies against Nineveh, the great capital of Assyria, and Thebes (or No-amon, as that Egyptian capital also was known).

Nineveh – the legendary capital of Assyria that, from Israel's perspective, anchored one end of the known world with one of its most dangerous societies.

Pirathon – a settlement in the Promised Land that predated the Hebrew occupation. Historians believe Pirathon lay south-southwest of Shechem in the northern kingdom of Israel.

Philistia – a culture created as groups of the Sea Peoples settled on the southwestern coast of Canaan. These settlers became known as the Philistines. As the Israelites attempted to possess the Promised Land under the leadership of Joshua and his successors, they failed to oust the Philistine coastal settlers who could escape to the seas when threatened, a skill and defense the Hebrews never mastered.

Ram's horn – a literal term that refers to the use of a hollowed horn of a ram as a signal device or musical instrument. Horns from other animals might also see use, depending on their ability to turn channeled air into amplified sound. Modifiers came in the shape and length of the horn, its composition, holes cut into its passage, or the way air was forced through it. Their frequent use helps explain why the cornet, trumpet, and other manmade devices are known today as horns.

People also used hollowed animal horns for holding and transporting water, grains, berries, and other consumables.

Samaria – the capital of the northern kingdom of Israel at the time of Jonah, Benjamin, and Simon. The city fell to Assyrian troops around 722 BC.

Sargon – known in history as Sargon II – was an Assyrian king who retains a fair measure of mystery, with some researchers debating his background and how he rose to power. Historians generally accept ancient claims that Sargon, like

Shalmaneser V, was a son of King Tiglath-Pileser III. Shalmaneser took the crown when his father died and continued his father's aggressive policies while Sargon led the Assyrian armies. Many historians suspect dissension between the brothers led Sargon to depose Shalmaneser and claim the throne around 722 BC. This parallels the fall of Samaria, the capital of the northern Hebrew kingdom. Sargon, an aggressive military leader who often led his troops in conquest, would retain the kingship until he died in battle two decades later.

Satan – the reviled name of the Lord's chief opposer, said by some to be a fallen angel. While not all Israelis in Jonah's time accepted the existence of Satan, speaking his title was frowned upon.

Sea of Chinneroth – one name used in Old Testament times for the great lake at the northern edge of the Jordan River Valley. Hebrews settling the Promised Lands also knew this lake as the Sea of Chinnereth. We have known it since New Testament times as the Sea of Galilee.

Shalmaneser – known in history as Shalmaneser V – took the crown of Assyria after the death of his father, Tiglath-Pileser III, around 727 BC. Shalmaneser continued his father's policies but not his successes. His clash with the Israeli King Hoshea causes the conflict in *Lions of Judah*. Shalmaneser was deposed by his brother Sargon around 722 BC.

Shechem – a Canaanite city that fell to the Hebrew tribes settling in the Promised Land, as told in the Old Testament book of Joshua. Claimed by the tribe of Manasseh, Shechem served for a time as the northern kingdom's first capital. That seat of government would then move to the town of Tirzah before ending up in the city of Samaria.

Shiloh – a Canaanite town that fell to the Hebrew tribes settling the Promised Land. This hilltop community became an assembling point and spiritual hub for the people, with the tabernacle and Ark of the Covenant residing there for many years. After the Philistines captured the Ark, as recorded in 1 Samuel, many historians believe Shiloh was destroyed. Archeologists have uncovered a layer of debris on its suspected site dating back to around 1060 BC – roughly 340 years before the *Lions of Judah* timeline. But 1 Kings notes the resettlement of Shiloh during the reign of Solomon – just over two centuries before the events in this novel.

Solomon – the last king of the united Hebrew kingdoms, as told in the Bible. This son of King David and Bathsheba made his mark as a legendary dispenser of wisdom, an accumulator of inestimable wealth, the builder of the first Hebrew Temple in Jerusalem, and the author of the Old Testament book Ecclesiastes, among other highlights.

Tappuah – a town along the tribal lands of Ephraim and Manasseh in the *Lions of Judah* timeline. It also was the name for one of the four sons of Hebron, as mentioned in 1 Chronicles.

Thebes – an ancient Egyptian city, also known as No-amon or P-armen, that rose on both sides of the Nile River. Thebes often served as the capital and spiritual center of that historic nation, rising and falling with the culture's fortunes. During the time of Jonah, Thebes lay in a rebuilding stage under the growing influence of the Kushites, also known as the Nubians.

Tiglath-Pileser III – one of the most noted kings in Assyrian history, launcher of this ancient nation's last significant expansion period. In Book One of The Jonah Cycle, he took his crown at the end of Jonah's ministry. At that time he was known as Adad-nirari, the governor of the ancient city of Kalhu and son of the Assyrian king Ashur-nirari. As king, Tiglath-Pileser III successfully focused on reorganizing his government, reuniting his kingdom, and reclaiming surrounding territories. This led to his involvement in biblical lands; Old Testament authors referred to him as Pulu or Pul. Tiglath-Pileser III reigned from about 746 to 727 BC. He died just before the events of *Lions of Judah*.

Tunic – a human body garment, usually austere, extending from the shoulders to the hips or knees.

Yahweh – one of many Hebrew titles referring to God. Centuries after Jonah, the word would become too sacred for Hebrews to speak aloud.

Book Two

By Kirby Lee Davis

Could you help us out?

This is an independent production. As a small business, we have limited distribution and marketing resources. So if you like one or more of these books, please:

- Consider giving copies to your friends and loved ones.
- Tell others what you appreciated about these tales, what moved you, the lasting impressions.
- Post reviews on reader and retailer websites, from Facebook and Instagram to GoodReads.com and the most valuable of all, Amazon.com. Such reviews are **extremely helpful** to our marketing efforts!
- Ask for these novels at your favorite bookstore, and encourage them to stock them on their shelves.

Please help us spread the message, so that we may continue our efforts. Thank you so much! We appreciate it!

www.kirbyleedavis.com

Printed in Great Britain
by Amazon

18748333R00139